Author, Author

a Midcentury Gay Romance

Will Forrest

HARDCASTLE BOOKS

A Note For Readers

This book is for mature audiences. It depicts explicit sexual activity between consenting adult partners, including shibari bondage and dominance/submission.

Characters experience or make reference to the following:

- alcohol abuse and recovery

- binge drinking

- eating disorders

- in-patient psychiatric care (not shown on page)

Please Read Responsibly

AUTHOR, AUTHOR

The freedom to read is essential to our democracy. It is continuously under attack.

from The Freedom to Read Statement (1953) by the American Library Association

Jazz

1957

I PRESSED MY EYE to the knot hole and waited. Dan arrived a minute later. Holding my breath, expecting every moment to be found out, I watched as the strapping captain stripped off his uniform, revealing his body thick with muscle, his skin tanned so perfectly I knew he must sunbathe nude. All this with his back to me, and as he turned to face me I–

"Shit. Ow. Shit. Goddammit, I'm done for. I'm ruined. I'm…talking to myself too much. Ow."

The cold water wasn't working anymore. Nor ice nor heat nor anything else Ben had tried to numb the burning ache in his wrists. He had to find a solution. Maybe Joan had something in her arsenal of pills. If not pain-killers then a tranquilizer or two. Then he'd at least not mind so much that he was on the brink of losing everything.

Not that there was much to lose. Baron Press had been running on fumes for months. If Ben didn't get this book written, and the next, he'd soon have nothing new on the rack, and there went his buyers, on to the next pulp press. And then there were the mail orders to fill. Letting his aching hands dangle, he closed his burning eyes.

He woke with a start in his chair. Someone was banging on his apartment door. Ben stayed seated, stiff with pain and barely breathing as he ran down the list of his creditors and whether any of them knew where he lived.

"Benny, open the door for Chrissakes. I know you're home."

Only for Joan, and not just for her arsenal. He scraped himself out of his chair, stumbled to the door, threw the deadbolts and let her in. Her busty figure done to the nines in poison green shantung, her fox-fur stole reeking of Pall Malls and *Vol du Nuit*, she sailed past him into his cold water flat and flopped down on the unmade bed.

"Benny, what the hell?"

"Why, what's happened?"

"You! You went and happened. Why do you do this to yourself?"

"Do you mean work? See, there's this thing called money. You have lots and I have none and the only way to fix that is—"

"You know what I mean." She pointed her cigarette at the typewriter on his desk in its pool of lamplight, a miserable stack of finished pages to one side, an unscalable mountain of blank pages to the other. "You're gonna crack up, trying to hold it all together by yourself."

"I'm always looking for writers."

"I can't write 'em like you. You know that."

"You mean blue?"

"I mean fast."

Joan was a fabulous poet, with an acid sensitivity he

hadn't expected from the scion of a family on first names with the Rockefellers. She had started working on a novel some years ago, and now and then showed Ben a page or two. Beautiful stuff with absolutely no commercial appeal. He was quite sure she'd be famous soon.

"If you can't write," he said, "find me someone who can."

"I'm trying, baby." She crushed out the lipstick-stained butt of the half-smoked cigarette in the coffee can he kept for her by the bed. "In fact, I got a hot lead."

"You do not. Or you'd have brought him with."

"What makes you think it's a he?"

"Because no sane woman wants to associate herself with a publisher of stroke books?"

"Present company excepted?"

"I said no *sane* woman."

"My mistake."

She was lying, of course, but Joan's lies were so charming, so typically benign, that he let her bully him into shaving (badly with cold water) and getting dressed (passably, for he didn't have anything good and what he had was dirty) and going out to paint the town if not red then at least a little pink.

They started with dinner at the Rainbow Room, Ben counting on Joan's connections, looks, and ferociousness to make up for his tragic brown flannel and bristly chin, as he'd missed that little patch beneath his dimple again.

After fawning over Joan, the maître d' led them to a table on the west side of the room, where the soaring windows looked towards the New Jersey shore across the glitter of Manhattan and the black velvet ribbon of the Hudson. All around them sat the city's cognoscenti: actors and models and singers, their agents and hangers on, city councilmen and mobsters and their respective cliques of lawyers, murmuring to each other across the heavily draped tables, their secrets being kept by the soft tinkle of piano drifting across the Rainbow's famous rotating dancefloor, which at this early hour was dark and still.

"The usual, Frank," Joan said, waving off the menu being offered by the waiter who had materialized at her elbow. "And he'll have the prime rib."

"Joan," Ben hissed, his heart seizing as he measured the cost against his total inability to pay it.

"Ignore him," she said to the unblinking Frank. "Prime rib, medium. Shrimp toast. And two martinis. No, make it three. He'll want one too."

"Joan, please–"

"Shh. It's on me," she said as Frank departed. "Well, Daddy, but he won't bat an eye. Last month, I took Candy and Prue out to the Cotton Club, and you should have seen the pile of oysters. Dom Perignon by the bucketful."

"I hate oysters."

"I know, that's why I ordered you a steak."

First came the drinks, which kept appearing as quickly as they drank them. By the time the meal arrived, he was loose and feeling something close to happy. Drunk enough not to care that even picking up his knife and fork sent pain stabbing up his forearms.

He doggedly worked through the square foot of beef while Joan nibbled at the corners of her shrimp toast. Despite her curves, the girl seemed to live on nothing but nicotine, gin, and moxy, and she was likely to outlive him. At least he would die with a full stomach, as long as she let him sponge off Daddy.

By the end of the meal he could have happily laid his head down on the table and slept. No such luck as Joan bustled him out to the elevator then into a cab. She was as high as him, leaning against his shoulder, her speech slowed from its rat-a-tat to that languid drawl picked up from her Carolina cousins.

He didn't even know what she was talking about. Maybe the cousins, for her story seemed to involve a car trip and getting lost and wasn't it a riot? He kept nodding and smiling, trying not to think about the half-written page, the half-finished book waiting at home. The worst thing he could do was start writing it in his mind, as he'd never remember a word of it.

The cab let them out on the edge of the Village. At least he fit in here, with the poets and novelists and dope fiends, the sloe-eyed boys in shady alleys, the muck. Joan fit in nowhere, which is how she got away with everything. Like breezing past the club's queue and the doorman with no more than a wink and a dizzying smile, Ben treading on her heels in fear of being separated from her.

They were shown to a pair of chairs, the teetering table between them just big enough to hold a couple of glasses. Joan ordered scotch neat for them both, the fumes making his head spin. The club was hot, packed, loud, and smoky. All the tables faced the same direction. As the hubbub of voices began to die down, Ben's fearful premonition was confirmed by the sibilant tick of a foot settling on the pedal of a hi-hat.

"Joan..."

"Relax, Benny. You're gonna like these guys."

"I'm not."

"Not if you go in with that attitude."

"You know I can't stand—" His next words were swamped by the bleat of a tenor sax, and he knew he was done for.

"Remind me why I put up with you," he hissed in Joan's ear as the rest of the band settled at their various implements of torture.

"Because otherwise you'd starve."

She was right. She was his best friend and his last resort and a complete bitch for putting him through this again and again, as if exposure was all it would take to change his mind. He'd been exposed to more than enough jazz, thank you very much, and he had yet to budge. Joan was a convert, her desire to win him to the bebop flock bordering on proselytizing. It made no difference. Joan could sing its praises night and day and the music would sound exactly the same.

As the drummer started in on a shuffling seasick rhythm, Ben picked up his glass, which was empty. He set it down too hard on the rickety table, which nearly fell into his lap.

"God, do I ever hate jazz."

A dark-haired man at the next table snorted into his glass. "What's your beef?" he said, his smooth voice carrying under the band's high-pitched twittering.

"It drives me mad, that pecking away. It's like they never stop tuning up. Get to the song already, will you?"

"That's quite the point of view to hold in a place like this."

"I'm not here because I want to be. I'm here because—holy moly, you're Harlan Avens."

The man—the legend—smiled behind his highball, his dark eyes unreadable in the multicolored shadows. "That's what the label says in my underwear."

Harlan Avens, author of the book that had changed Ben's life. Sitting there like a normal person. Making terrible jokes about his... "Mr. Avens, it is an honor to meet you. Though I'm sure you hear that all the time."

"Actually, I don't."

"That's ridiculous! You should have got a Pulitzer for *No Man's Land*."

Avens laughed, a loud, easy laugh that made people at the next table look his way. He was even more handsome in the flesh than in that photo in *Life*, with a hawkish profile and a stern jaw and very nice clothes in a quiet way, a gemstone glinting in his tie clip. Ben had read that article almost as many times as he'd read Avens' novel, so often that he might have redrawn the accompanying photo if he was any good at drawing.

Harlan Avens. In the flesh. Laughing at him? Who damn cared? "Mr. Avens, perhaps you've never heard anyone say this, but you're the reason I'm a writer."

"Is that a good thing?"

"Of course! Why wouldn't it be?"

"There's plenty that goes along with writing I wouldn't wish on my worst enemy."

"That goes without saying, sir, but–"

"Woah," he said, his hand up to halt him. "None of that *sir* crap with me. What's your name?"

"Me? Ben. Quirke. That's my last name. Of course, whoever is named Quirke? I'm sorry, my friend got me drunk and you really are the reason I started writing and...a bunch of other things, and...I'm annoying you, aren't I? I'm sorry, I'll leave you to it."

No Man's Land: an atom bomb would have had less impact on a teenaged Benjamin Quirke. The decisive prose.

The gutsy plot. The story hidden within that plot, of a young man abandoning his every innocence. Ben's first clumsy efforts at writing had been nothing more or less than an attempt to bring that secret story to the fore. Every page of which he had burned in the boiler in the basement of his building when he realized he'd written a confession.

The author of *No Man's Land* was laughing at him again. He was holding out his hand. With the care he'd use with a live grenade, Ben shook, his bony fingers crumpling in the man's firm grip.

"A pleasure to meet you, Mr. Quirke."

"Oh no, sir, I mean, Mr. Avens. The pleasure is all mine."

"That's a bit greedy."

"What? Oh. Right. You can have some pleasure. Have all you like. Oh God, why did I let Joan do this to me?"

"So, Mr. Quirke–"

"Ben is fine."

"Sure thing, Ben. So do you write just for yourself or do you let other people read it?"

"Not everything. But I've published a bit. Here and there. I run a small press, actually. Nothing you'd know, of course."

"You don't know what I know. Maybe I've heard of it."

"It's really a very small press."

"What do you do, chapbooks?"

Shit. "Ah. Well. A bit more commercially oriented than that."

"You're not one of those pulp presses, are you?"

As his hero grinned at him, strangely eager, the club exploded in applause, though how one knew a jazz number had ended was beyond Ben's understanding. All of this was just about beyond him as Avens shifted his chair nearer and leaned closer. He wasn't laughing anymore.

"Which one?" he asked. "Not Grove, I know those guys."

"Baron Press," Ben gasped, nearly spitting, half hoping Avens misheard.

"You don't say? Your covers are great."

"Oh. Thank you?"

"And some of the stories are better than I expected."

"You've read them?"

"I'll read anything. I pick up a lot of cheap books in truck stops, diners."

"And you remember them?"

"If they're any good. Are you just the publisher or do you write them too?"

"I have to, to keep up with the orders."

"So which ones are yours?"

"Do you really want to know?"

"No, I'm stringing you along because I got nothing better to do."

Ben flinched at another startling blast of brass. Avens wasn't letting up either, his hand on the back of Ben's chair, effectively trapping him.

"So? Dish."

"Um. Let's see. *The Bride Wore Blood, Co-ed Confessional, Starmaster Five, She Lies, His Secret Sin*... There's loads more, but I sort of forget them once they're written."

"*She Lies* was pretty good," Avens said. By God, was he ever handsome when he smiled, his eyes alight. "That scene with the chandelier?"

"True story. Happened to my friend, Joan...who isn't here anymore." Classic Joan, to drag him to some club or party then disappear with her better friends. All of whom treated Ben like either a servant or a joke. "Well, you saw her."

"The doll in the fur? Yeah, I can imagine that happening to her."

More applause, which swamped Avens' next words. Biting his lip at the hot scent of the other man, Ben leaned closer to hear him: "I said, do you want to get out of here?"

"Why?"

"So we can hear ourselves think. Plus the booze in this joint is..." Avens rolled his eyes.

"A piece with the rest of it?"

"You said it. Come on, I know a place."

Lola

THE BASTARD KEPT GETTING more handsome. The effect was nearly unbearable. Bear it he would, because the moment so closely resembled Ben's adolescent fantasies that to change a thing was to ruin everything. Burst the bubble and wake Avens up to the ridiculousness of taking a man like him out for drinks.

"I gotta level with you," Avens said after they'd walked a few blocks. "I don't have a place. It just seemed like the thing to say. But the restaurant in my hotel is pretty good."

"Your hotel?"

"Not *my* hotel. Just where I'm staying."

"Oh, I didn't think...I don't know what I thought."

Avens chuckled, a soft huffing of air through his nose. "I'm thinking you don't meet a lot of writers."

"I do, but not like...you. I'll confess, *No Man's Land* spoke to me like no book ever had. So after all these years, to meet the man who wrote it is...well, it's a dream come true. You really did change my life."

"And for that you have my sincere apology."

"Oh no, Mr. Avens, please don't. Apologize, I mean.

You—" How to say it? How to say it in the middle of a city street to a man he'd just met, who he felt like he'd known for years? "You might have saved my life."

Avens' smile had faded, his eyes wide and filled with something like alarm. Under the streetlights he looked younger, his face barely lined, his hair jet black.

"I was just a kid," he said, a catch in his creamy voice. "I could never write that book now."

"No. No, you couldn't."

"Too much has happened to me since."

"Of course. And it wouldn't mean the same if I read it now. Things happened to me too."

They walked for a few minutes without speaking. When they reached Sixth Ave, Avens hailed a cab, holding the door open for Ben, who nearly cracked his forehead as he hurried to get in.

"Hey, I know who you are," the cabbie said to Avens in the rearview mirror as they pulled away from the curb.

"Oh, yeah?"

"Yeah, you're that guy. You were in, you know, whatchamacallit? *Oklahoma.*"

Avens shot Ben a look. "If you mean the show and not the state then no, I'm not who you're thinking of," he said to the cabbie, who was spending more time than Ben liked with his head craned to look at them.

"Sure, you are," the cabbie said. "You was one of the cowboys, weren't you?"

"Sorry to disappoint, but you're barking up the wrong tree."

"Well, you look just like him. Boy, could he dance. The wife thought so too. She's gonna get a kick outta this."

"Out of you meeting the wrong guy?"

"Hey, I'll take what I can get. Though there was this one time I got a real celeb. What's his face, from *Sunset Boulevard*?"

"William Holden," Ben heard himself say. God, how many Saturday afternoons had he spent in dark cinemas lost in that film? Too many for his own good, and none of them for the plot, all of them for Holden's jawline and the bend of his eyebrow.

Avens and the cabbie swapped celebrity near misses for the rest of the ride uptown. Climbing out of the cab, Ben's heart stalled. He had less than two bucks on him. Maybe fifty in that envelope under the breadbox. He could no more afford a meal at the restaurant at the Gramercy Park Hotel than he could have afforded that steak Joan had bought him earlier. Perhaps he could lie to Avens, leave the table before the waiter got to them, slip out the back door and...lose this chance to get to know the most important influence of his masculine life.

"Don't worry, this one's on me," Avens said as he joined him on the sidewalk. "Actually, it's on Knopf, so go to town, order whatever you like."

The doorman was already holding the door for them, and acknowledged him with a *good evening, Mr. Avens*, granting Ben a perfunctory but not hostile nod. Coming into the glitter and glitz of the restaurant and its enormously wealthy clientele, Ben's eyes glazed over, his hands beginning to shake as he realized how drunk he was. And sweaty, and very badly dressed, his fawn flannel showing every speck of dirt, every stain, every wrinkle, as well as being six years out of style. Even the waiters had nicer clothes. Avens meanwhile...

Damn it, how did he keep getting more handsome?

Their table was off to the side of the room, Avens' profile reflected by the mirrored wall, so that Ben faced a pair of him. Hadn't he once tried writing a space-age story just like this? People duplicating themselves, no one knowing who was real? Right at the bit where the scientist was going to kiss his cloned twin, Ben had lost his nerve, tearing the pages into confetti before incinerating them. As if that was enough to erase the rest of the story from his mind.

Avens ordered steak. Ben nearly did as well, for he hadn't even opened the menu, but his first charity dinner smoldered in his guts like a lump of charcoal. Not eating a free meal was a sure-fire way to insult a man at Avens' level, who clearly knew how broke Ben was. He ought to show his gratitude. "Shrimp toast."

"Very good, sir," the waiter said without a hint of judgment. What a pro.

"What was that?" Avens said with a frown once the waiter had gone.

"My order."

"You don't have to cheap out. I said you could get anything you like."

"Someone's already fed me." He wasn't a man, he was a stray cat.

"Joan?"

"Oh. Yes. She's too good to me."

"As long as someone's being good to you."

The waiter was back, or a different waiter. Sommelier, that's what you called the one who brought the wine. He did the whole bit too, showing the label, wafting the cork under Avens' nose, offering him a mouthful, which he waved away before ordering a scotch and water.

"I know," Avens said once the man had filled Ben's glass

and left them to it. "Red meat, red wine, but I thought the Moselle would suit your meal better."

"Suit me?"

"Your shrimp toast."

"Oh. I don't even like shrimp toast."

"Then why did you order it? It seemed like your, you know, thing, seeing as you didn't even look at the menu."

"I panicked."

"Do you do that often," Avens asked with what may or may not have been a smirk. "Blindly order seafood? Sorry, I'm probably not helping," he went on with what was most definitely a smirk as a shameful heat began to creep up Ben's neck. "We could go somewhere else."

"I don't care. I mean, take me anywhere. I mean...you understand you're not meant to be doing this, right?"

"Making friends?"

"But I'm not a friend, I'm a fan. And a really, really big one. I've had dreams like this." *And so many fantasies.* "So I don't know what to do. How to act, what to say. And I shouldn't even be telling you this because you're going to think I'm nuts and this will be the only chance I ever get to meet you and I've already blown it. I'm sorry."

"Don't be. You haven't blown anything. I just..." Avens took a breath, let it go, then went on more quietly. "I don't get a lot of chances these days to do whatever I like. You seemed like an interesting person. You're a writer, you're smart, you have opinions. I don't care that you're a fan. I'd rather that than have you picking me apart."

"I would never. You're a genius."

He winced like Ben had stomped on his foot. "Don't ever say that again. I don't need anyone kissing my ass. I have an agent for that, dig?"

"I'm not, though. It's true."

"Genius is relative. And I sure wasn't a genius when I wrote *Land*. But no one's a genius when they're twenty."

"I know I wasn't."

"Yeah? What were you doing?"

"Watching Italians starve in a field hospital outside Cisterna."

"Shit." Avens' smile faded, his eyes darting over Ben's face. "So you're older than you look, huh?"

"Why, how old do I look?"

"Not nearly that much over twenty."

"You neither. I mean you're very handsome. I mean...I've put my foot in my mouth again, haven't I?" For Avens was staring at him with that same look of mild alarm as in the street. No, he was looking past Ben to the lush blonde in tight white satin approaching their table with murder in her sky blue eyes.

"Lola, what a surprise," Avens said with a pasted-on smile as he stood to greet her.

"Don't you *Lola* me, you...chump," the woman shot back, shaking her head so the strands of her diamond earrings shimmied.

"I'm sorry," Avens replied with a lift that made it sound like a question.

"Yeah, well you ought to be," Lola replied with another shake of her head. "You've been in town three days and haven't called me once. Not a note, not a bouquet, not nothing. Now I find you having dinner with some *man*?"

"Sorry for not introducing you. Lola, this is Ben Quirke—"

"I don't care if he's Ben Franklin! You know what, next time don't bother to call. Enjoy your meal." With that she scooped the wine bottle from its ice bath, looked Harlan in the eye, then upended the bottle over Ben's lap.

Avens wrangled the bottle from her as a squadron of waitstaff descended on them, shielding them from the other diners who were turning to watch the drama. Ben did nothing at all, too shocked, too shamed to know what to do, until a waiter tried mopping his lap. He snatched the napkin from him to make his own attempt, but the wine had already soaked through his clothes.

"I'm sorry," he said to Avens as the blond stormed off, her stilettos rapping on the marble floor.

"For what? You didn't do a thing. In fact you probably did me a favor. Come upstairs, you can clean up in my room."

"Your...oh God."

Harlan's Room

He was going up to Harlan Avens' hotel room. Lonesome, humiliated, more than a little drunk, and delirious from the effects of Avens' outsized influence on his tiny life, Ben briefly considered begging the nearest waiter to smuggle him out the back door, to spare Avens any more of his pathetic company and himself any further anxiety.

Avens wasn't paying attention, talking to the maître d'. And then he turned and gave Ben a funny smile, and Ben stood up and followed him as if hypnotized, out of the restaurant and through the brightly lit lobby to the elevators. A couple in eveningwear were exiting the one on the left and they ducked in as the doors were closing.

"I really am sorry about all that," Avens said, looking him up and down. "Lola's a...well, a piece of work. Got this messed up idea of me as a trophy husband."

"Good God!"

"You don't know the half of it. I've been playing dodge 'ems for years."

Avens' room was on the second to last floor from the top, and was a masterpiece of subdued luxury with its low furniture of Swedish teak. A startling view of Manhattan in all its electric glory spread below the uncurtained windows. The bathroom alone was nearly bigger than Ben's whole apartment, every flat surface mirrored like the restaurant had been, so that Ben undressed with his eyes half closed.

And then what? He could hardly wash his clothes in the sink. He dithered, pants in one hand and underwear in the other, until Avens knocked at the door.

"You doing okay?" he asked.

"I'm fine."

"You've been in there a while. Why don't you hand out your wet things and I'll call Housekeeping, see if they can't launder them for you."

A thick terrycloth dressing gown with the hotel's crest embroidered on the pockets hung from the back of the door. Trying and failing to ignore the fact that the last person inside the dressing gown had probably been Avens, Ben put it on over his shirt, belted it, knotted it twice, then cracked the door open and passed out his clothes, underpants and all.

He stayed in the bathroom as Avens spoke to the maid. Avens' shaving kit lay open on the vanity, the scent of his aftershave catching in Ben's nose as he glared at himself in the mirror, pushing his sandy hair into various shapes to see if it made him look less like an unwashed street urchin. Nothing to be done about the freckles, or the thin, permanently arching brows, as if his worries had frozen on his face.

He'd be lying if he claimed that he hadn't pictured this moment. Not so much the nightclub and the wine as the naked vulnerability. The chance of being caught. Of being taken advantage of, because if he succumbed to someone else's seduction that meant he hadn't sought it out himself. Hadn't risked his neck for a lay, had let it come to him, let the other man bear the blame.

And Harlan, by God... Of all the men to whom he might succumb, for it to be his idol, his hero, his unwitting muse, the reason he wrote books, the reason he'd survived his youth... His harsh breath ringing off the tiles, his cock stiff with want, Ben locked eyes with his reflection, willing himself to quit this dangerous game, give up his sickening obsession with the man who was presently knocking on the bathroom door.

"You okay in there?" Avens asked as Ben yelped.

"Nothing! I mean, what? I mean, I'm fine."

"You sure?"

"Never better."

"Then will you quit lurking in here like a peeper?"

"I didn't want to be a bother."

"You're not a bother. I'll even get them to send up the shrimp toast."

"I don't like shrimp toast," Ben said automatically. "Wait, are you making fun of me?"

"Of course not," Avens replied cheerfully. "Well, maybe a little. Come on, if you can face down a fascist you can deal with talking to me for an hour."

He was right. It was awful but he was right and so Ben unlocked the door then cracked it open. "To be fair, I never faced down anyone," he said to the sliver of Avens, who frowned.

"Not even in Cisterna?"

"I was a medic."

Avens' eyes flew open. "Shit. You guys..." Sighing, he

shook his head.

"Hardly the hero, am I?" Ben said as he emerged from the bathroom.

"Don't ever think that," Avens said, clapping an alarming hand on Ben's shoulder. "You saved lives."

"Not many."

"But you tried. I was only in it for the killing." Again that odd little smile flashed across his lips before he turned away. "Something to drink?" he said with force, marching for the liquor cabinet standing open by the window.

"God, yes."

"Scotch?"

"Anything."

"Are you always this easy? To please, I mean," Avens added quickly.

"I take what I can get." Ben cringed inwardly as Avens' back stiffened. Installing himself on the couch, he stretched the housecoat over his bony knees, his mismatched socks sliding down his shins.

"Trying to get me tight?" he asked as Avens passed him a highball half full of pungent liquor. The sort of question he'd ask Joan, who would have said *of course, otherwise you're no fun*. Not the sort of question he should be asking a man. Certainly not one he just met, as Avens startled then stepped back sharply.

"No! Not at all. You aren't, are you?" he asked with a worried pinch of his brows.

"A bit, but that's never stopped me before." Ben sipped the scotch, watching Avens over the rim as the man poured his own.

Something had changed, some shift in the balance of power, Avens' shoulders rising and falling with his harsh breath. Once armed with his drink, he lingered behind the other chair, stroking a fingertip over the nap of the upholstery, looking near but not at Ben.

"Mr. Avens–"

"Call me Harlan. Please."

"Harlan. There's something I've always wondered about *No Man's Land*."

"You wouldn't be the first to wonder. I sure didn't write it to be understood. So don't expect a straight answer."

"I don't. In fact you don't need to answer at all."

"Ask your question."

One chance. He had one chance, because the odds of meeting Harlan Avens again were next to none. Clearing his throat, Ben relaxed his choking grip on his glass. "It's about Bull, when he's in hospital. That scene late at night, when he and Sterling are alone and–"

"It's true."

"So I'm right, and they do..." Even now, in private, in front of the man who had written the story, he couldn't say aloud what he'd always suspected, that under cover of night and the author's silence, the characters had made love.

His face half hidden by his glass, Harlan nodded with a single jerk of his head, and something in Ben's chest came loose. As if he'd let go of a breath he'd been holding since birth.

"Thank God," he sighed. "Otherwise I'd have been wrong about everything."

"What do you mean, everything?" Harlan croaked.

"It's like I told you. You saved my life. Not on purpose," he added as Harlan shook his head. "But still, you did. Because if it was only me who felt that way, who couldn't help how he felt about men, then…well, I would have been crazy, right? But if there were other boys like me, other men, that meant I wasn't always going to be alone. You're not just a writer, Harlan. You're the reason I'm alive."

If he never spoke another word to this man, at least he'd said what mattered. Not that words could ever match what Harlan's writing had done for Ben. His book had been a beacon in the dark, a life preserver, something to cling to in the storm of adolescence and the lonely days and nights since. A message from another world where his desires weren't a curse but a joy. Bull's defiance–his pride, his unwillingness to compromise in the face of total defeat–was stronger than any law.

Harlan had told that story. Harlan had saved Ben's life. At the moment he looked in need of saving himself, clinging to the back of the chair, his other hand shaking so hard his teeth struck the rim of the glass as he swallowed most of the scotch in one mouthful.

"That's a new one," he said, his voice coarsened by the burn of liquor. "I've been told I'm a pervert, a criminal, a Zionist, a lunatic. Never that I…" Shaking his head, he covered his mouth.

"I don't mean to burden you," Ben said. "But every time I've imagined meeting you, it was to say this to you."

"You imagined? How old were you? When you first read Land?"

"Fifteen."

"Shit! I ruined you. Me and that damn book of mine." He raised his empty glass to his lips absently then lowered it again, his eyes bright with feeling.

"You know, I thought about burning it," he said half to himself. "Every page I wrote, I fought with myself not to tear it to pieces and flush it down the drain. And then you'd have died. Oy…" He shoved his fingers through his hair, leaving it a black snarl.

"You didn't ruin me. I'd known all along I wasn't ordinary. I just never knew that I wasn't the only one."

"And now?"

"Now it's something I can live with."

"Oh, and that's an improvement, is it?"

"To not being alive? I'd say so."

Leaning heavily on the back of the chair, Harlan dropped his head. "I should never have brought you up here. I must seem like a real…I don't even know what. A creep."

"You didn't coerce me. No worse than Joan does, at any rate."

"But she doesn't…she would never take advantage of you."

"Are you saying you would?"

"No! Never."

"Then there's no problem."

Except that being taken advantage of was exactly what Ben wanted. He'd written countless books about it: the eager young naïf, the studious older man with a streak of danger. Falling in the neighbour's pool, losing a term paper, the threat of a speeding fine: any situation that gave the older man the edge, put the younger man in his debt.

A censor-dodging lie, that men never met as equals. A truth, because he was not Harlan's equal. He was the youth, the student, the fall guy, though not half so naive as his made-up boys. Christ, no one was that stupid. As stupid as he'd been to think this meeting by chance meant anything, that it could lead to the land of his dreams.

Someone knocked at the door and Harlan leapt to answer it. Ben took what was likely the last sip of his drink, the smoky tang of the top-shelf liquor stinging his lips and tickling his throat. A sensation he wanted to remember for the rest of his days.

This too: the sight of Harlan's funny little smile, the one that made his eyes crinkle, as he approached with an armful of Ben's clothing. His hero, his savior. A meeting that wouldn't have happened if Ben had been braver, stronger, if he hadn't let Joan push him around. A meeting that shouldn't have happened, because wasn't it better to have your dreams stay dreams? Instead of an infinite world of potentials, he was about to be left with a handful of memories.

He dressed in the bathroom, again with his eyes lowered, not needing to be reminded of his deficiencies. Better that Harlan never knew how frail he was, how soft. How unlike a man another man might want. Lately no one wanted Ben. A constant, sometimes a comfort, to have no one demanding his attention, doubting his sincerity. No fights, no heartbreak, no problems. Nothing at all.

"Is everything alright?" Harlan asked as Ben returned to the sitting room.

"Don't think these pants have been so clean since I bought them." The wrong joke to make, as Harlan's false smile stalled, died. "But thank you. For giving me so much of your time. I'll remember this always."

"I will too."

"I hope Lola doesn't stay mad at you."

"She can die mad for all I care. Thanks for not taking it personally."

And then there was nothing left but goodbye. Harlan

walked him to the door where they shook, Harlan clasping Ben's hand with both of his, his eyes bright with untold feeling. They didn't speak, for there was nothing left to say.

The closing of the door echoed down the hotel hallway like the dropping of a coffin lid. Ben made it all the way to the elevator before he started to cry.

The Backer

He should have asked for an autograph. No, he should have tried harder to get Harlan into bed. Then at least Joan would have believed him, as she knew how frequently he scored, that is to say almost never. She'd have seen it in his eyes, or smelled it, or whatever way she could always tell when he'd gotten any action. As it was, anyone he told about meeting Harlan Avens either didn't know the name or didn't believe a writer of his importance had spent four hours entertaining a nameless no one like Ben.

As the weeks passed Ben started to wonder if he still believed it. Not that he expected Harlan would look him up. Though he could have, if he wanted. Baron Press wasn't in the city phone book but it did have a post office box which he checked weekly as it was usually full of manuscripts. All sorts of manuscripts, and a writer had to have turned in a real stinker not to get an offer from him. He'd still never catch up. While other presses flourished, he was barely getting by, late for every printing deadline, rushing every edit, working eighteen-hour days and hating all of it.

And his wrists. Now they hurt whether he was typing

or not, his diet of coffee and automat hamburgers underpinned by Joan and her arsenal of uppers, downers, pain killers, mood changers, appetite suppressants, and whatever else young socialites traded under the tables at the Cotton Club. She left his weekly doses in jars with color-coded lids: red for mornings, blue for evenings, orange for the ones that knocked him out completely.

It was a muggy afternoon sometime in July when he roused from a hazy half-slumber to the sound of someone knocking at the door. Then kicking, which meant it was probably Joan.

"It's open," he called. Or croaked, his tongue laying in his mouth like a block of wood, his head spinning when he tried sitting up.

"Jeez Louise," Joan said, fanning her nose as she walked in. "Please tell me that's not you I can smell. It's like a skunk had a baby with the men's room in Penn Station."

"How do you know what the men's room in Penn Station smells like?"

"Never you mind. Here, take this."

"What is it?" he asked as she gave him a large white tablet.

"A breath mint. So don't swallow it, dig?"

She sat on the end of the bed, perfectly turned out in royal blue with a white bolero, her auburn hair freshly re-auburned, the whole ensemble putting him in mind of the French flag. "Benny, why are you doing this?"

"Because this is what I do."

"What, kill yourself for that stupid company?"

"It's not stupid. Baron's my life."

"It's gonna end your life if you're not careful. When'd you eat last?"

"I don't know. When did I see you last?"

"Jesus jumping Christ, Benny, that was four days ago!"

"I'm sure I've eaten since then. Glen stopped by. I think. He brought Chinese. Or was that last week?"

"That was last *month* because I was here. Ben, you gotta quit."

"Impossible."

"Then at least take a break from writing."

"That's even more impossible."

"What's the point if it kills you?"

"Then I died doing what I love."

"You don't love this. You can barely survive it."

"Sure, things are tough, but I've been getting some really good submissions lately and they've barely needed editing and I'm on a roll with this new book and think I'm losing my mind and God, Joan, what the hell am I going to do?"

He was trembling. Nuts to that, he was vibrating, his body threatening to shake apart. If he could breathe he might have screamed. She was right and he was dying and it was his own fault for trying to be a hero, trying to do more than was possible. And not even for anything meaningful. Who wanted to be remembered for spewing filth across the discount book-racks of America?

"Does this mean you're ready to let me help you?" she asked kindly.

"Yes. How? You do enough. I don't need more pills."

"That's for sure. I mean real help." From her skinny purse she took out a skinny book and a pen. "Is a thousand enough?"

"A thousand what?"

"Dollars. Heck, I'll just make it two."

"Joan! You can't do this."

"Says you." She tore the check from the book and handed it to him. "This isn't a gift, though. It's an investment. And it comes with conditions."

It was made out to *cash*. "Joan, no bank will honor this. They'll assume it's a con. I'll end up in Riker's."

"Not if I go with you to the bank. Trust me, I write a lot of checks. Now, about those conditions..."

It wasn't a gift. She expected it back and with a profit, and typed up the contract herself. "And if I find out you didn't get yourself a secretary," she said as he signed, "I'm going to stop being a silent partner and become one of those really loud ones."

"Where am I going to find a secretary?"

"They got this thing called a classified ad."

"I mean, what kind of woman is going to be willing to work for me?"

"The kind who's too broke or too stupid to care."

"I'd rather have the first than the second."

"That's on you, buddy. Come on, we'll grab something to eat on the way to the bank. And brush your teeth or they really will huck you in Riker's, for attempted murder."

WITH JOAN'S FLOAT HE paid the back rent on the office and six months going forward, plus his outstanding debt to the printers. He bought a second typewriter, a well-kept ten year old Underwood, from a retired dentist, then placed a carefully worded ad for a secretary in the back of the Post. To his surprise, he started getting replies. He was much less surprised by the applicants' disgust, at times fury, when they found out what they were being hired to type.

After a few weeks of this he wanted to pull the ad. Joan refused, threatening to re-run it herself if he did. The applicant he'd just interviewed reminded him of that woman Lola from the restaurant. Same brassy blond hair, same pushy tits, same benighted attitude, like he ought to be grateful she was giving him her time. Same level of disgust when he didn't knuckle under.

"Spare yourself the embarrassment, sister," she said to the next applicant waiting in the other room. "You don't want what he's selling." She slammed the door on her way out, making the windows rattle.

Ben counted to ten. "Next, please."

Like chalk and cheese, night and day, she was the last woman's polar opposite: petite and lumpy, her dark hair cropped short, wearing a misshapen gray suit that might have come from a WAC demob charity kit. She settled in the hard chair facing the desk and was about to set down her square handbag when Ben cleared his throat.

"I don't recommend putting anything on that floor."

Her eyes widened briefly as she took a better look. Then she put the bag on her lap. "Thank you for this opportunity, Mr. Quirke," she said in a firm voice that didn't quite hide its southern origins.

"Don't thank me yet."

She blinked, again firmly. "Mr. Quirke, I'll cut to the chase. I know what you do here. I know the kind of books you sell. And I want you to know that I have no problem whatsoever with lewd content."

"You don't?"

"Not a bit."

"In that case you're hired."

Her brows lowered briefly. "Don't you care about my typing speed?"

"The average typing speed in this office is currently zero words a minute. Anything is an improvement."

"But–"

"Miss–"

"Ms."

"Ms. Masterson…" The name rang a bell, but he shook it off. "Ms. Masterson, you are the first applicant who hasn't screamed, spat, or tried to slap me. I assume you're competent or you wouldn't have applied. And if I can cut to the chase as well, I'd rather not have to hire anyone at all. If I can get it over with today, you'll be doing me a favor."

"Mr. Quirke?"

"Please, call me Ben. And welcome to Baron Press." He stood and offered his hand and they shook, her decisive grip sending little spears of pain up his arm.

"Are you okay, Mr. Quirke?" she asked as he winced.

"No, which is why you're here. Any chance you could start immediately?"

Melody started the next day, citing other interviews

she needed to bow out of. What a professional, and too good for Baron. He was sure she'd quit by the end of the week. He therefore got her to start with the most important job: retyping his massacre of a first draft of that book he'd had in the works for a while. Hot stuff, with a military theme that appealed to men who liked more action with their sleaze, set in the futuristic dream world of the year 2031 so he didn't have to worry about realism. Or libel charges.

That Ms. Masterson could read the draft at all was a testament to her skill, for he'd typed a lot of it with a pair of pencils clutched in his aching hands, pecking at the keys like a swearing, frustrated bird. The handwritten parts were even worse, and after the fiftieth time she'd asked him to come out to the front room to translate, he moved the Underwood into his office and surrendered a corner of his desk.

"I have to ask how it is you're not offended by...everything," he said, returning to the filing cabinet after helping her through a particularly sticky section that he must have written in the middle of the night.

"It's nothing I haven't seen before. Or written."

"You write?"

"Sure do. Got a couple things printed, even."

"That's amazing! By who?"

"By you."

"Wait, are you M.M. Masterson?" Author of *Passion's Price, Genoa Girls, The Sins of Barbara*. Books he struggled to keep on the rack, so quickly did they get snapped up. Written by this stick of a woman with a boy's haircut and a run in her stocking and a suit even uglier than his unkillable brown flannel.

"One and the same," she replied, not looking up from her typing.

"I'll confess I expected you to say *Ladies' Home Journal*."

"You wouldn't be the first."

"You haven't written any others, have you?"

"I got a few kicking around the drawer."

"Bring them in. I get so few decently written books in that category. Your description of the female anatomy is..."

"Excessive? Grotesque?"

"Wonderfully detailed and very appealing to a portion of our readership."

"Oh yeah?"

"The more detailed, the better. Brings that touch of vérité they demand."

"Oh, I got vérité," she said as she slapped the carriage return.

"Yes. I noticed."

Blue Books

Finding Melody Masterson—or being found by her—was a stroke of pure luck. Like most authors, her typing was merely adequate, and she had applied for the job at Baron on a whim when she couldn't land one at a better office. They got on well, though sometimes she reminded him of Joan. Or Joan reminded him of Melody. Either way, God help him if he introduced them to each other. He'd never get a minute to himself.

She was a much better editor than typist, good enough to do most of it on a first read-through, delivering clean copy in half the time he took, mainly due to his habit of forgetting to edit. He loved to read, and had an endless supply of new books. Books that no one else had ever read, even if some of them were hardly worth the paper they'd been submitted on. Anyone who provided a return envelope (postage paid, of course) could have that paper back. Otherwise he'd drown, or have to start using it for wallpaper, for overnight everyone in America had decided to become a writer, and half of them were for some god-forsaken reason submitting to him.

He'd had to rent a larger post office box. One sticky Tuesday in the middle of August he and Melody were reviewing the week's crop of no-hopers. Among her more important duties was vetting the manuscripts by reading the first page or two, to decide if it was worth either of their time to read any further.

"These are all junk," she said as she pointed to the tallest stack of manuscripts on his desk. "These ones are the maybes, this is a you-gotta-be-kidding-me, this one has too much nookie–"

"Hang on, what's wrong with that?"

"Trust me, Mr. Quirke, it's too much nookie."

"We could trim the blue words."

"Then the only words left would be *he*, *she*, *in*, *out*, and *again*."

"Never mind."

There were blue books and then there were the utterly unprintable. None of those ever seemed to have return envelopes. A humiliating number of them had therefore found their way into the bottom drawer of Ben's desk for a guilty revisit after business hours, and he made a mental note to set aside *Truck Stop on the Road to Hell* for personal review. You never knew when you might find a diamond in the rough.

Unsurprisingly, given what he paid in rent, the main door to the office let in every sound from the corridor. Every cough, every fart, every footfall. At the sound of footsteps on the stairs, he and Melody froze, counting the seconds as the steps grew nearer, then stopped at the office door.

At the first knock, Ben yanked open the bottom drawer of his desk, kept unlocked during the day for this very purpose. As Melody scampered off to answer the door, he shoveled the manuscripts into the drawer, locked it, and slapped the key onto the auto-shop magnet he'd glued to the underside of his chair.

"Do you have an appointment with Mr. Quirke?" Melody was saying to the caller.

"No," the man replied in a deep, creamy voice. A voice made for night clubs, hotel rooms. "But I think he'll see me."

That voice. Harlan Avens. In his office. Here.

Hat in hand, Avens came into Ben's office and shut the door. He looked thinner, a little older, a tension around his eyes that hadn't been there before. As if Ben had anything to compare to except that one evening, every second of which he'd replayed in his mind until it felt like a movie. Same smile though, with a lift on one side that made his eyes sparkle as they shook hands.

"Am I ever glad to see you," he said, and if he didn't mean it he was a hell of an actor.

"Why?"

Harlan laughed, that same easy laugh (laughing at him! In his office!) as he fetched the spare chair from the corner and sat down. "You haven't changed, have you?"

"I'm much better now."

"You get over your allergy to bebop?"

"God, no. That's incurable."

"Too bad, I was hoping we could get together later."

"I'll go anywhere you like," Ben said, feeling behind himself for his chair, not wanting to look at anything but Harlan, coolly handsome in a sage green linen sport-coat while Ben sweated in his old brown flannel. "That sounded desperate, didn't it? I'm not desperate, I'm...confused.

Why are you here?"

"Because I didn't know where else to turn."

"What's wrong?"

"Nothing." A lie, Harlan's eyes flashing coldly, like when he'd spoken to Lola. "But I've got this book I want published and I thought you'd be just the man for the job."

"But I'm nobody. Why would you want to publish with Baron?"

"Honest answer? Because you're a nobody."

"I see. Wait, that doesn't make sense."

"It will once I explain it." He looked over his shoulder, the clacking of the Underwood's keys audible through the even thinner inner door. "Can we go somewhere more private?"

"Don't worry about Ms. Masterson. She's incorruptible. Or already corrupt. She's a writer, I mean. For Baron."

"That's generous of you, letting a writer use your office."

"It's not like that. She types for me. And proof-reads. And sorts the mail and–"

"A secretary, I think you call that."

'Right. She's that." He wasn't making sense. Had he eaten today? How much coffee had he drank? He'd given Joan back most of her pills, hadn't popped a benny (oh God) in a week, maybe two. It was this man making him tremble.

"Harlan..." And it was such a joy to say his name, see his face. Here, in front of him. Here. "What sort of book did you write?"

"I didn't write it," he replied with that funny, perfect, crooked smile. "Alver Guest did."

A titan of inter-war literature, a writer whose legacy

made Avens look like a second comer. Published by Baron?

"Then why bring it to me?" Ben gaped. "Why not a proper publisher?"

"If you have the know-how to get a book printed, bound, and sold, you're publisher enough for me. And second, because this is not the Alver Guest you know."

"I don't understand."

Harlan exhaled deeply, settling into the chair. "About a week before we met last spring, I got this letter from the State Department. They're still going through wills and deed and art collections, trying to get property to the family members of, you know, victims of the war." Running a hand over his hair, he cleared his throat. "Long story short, I got a letter. Turns out someone's been trying to return some of my grandfather's property.

"Your grandfather?"

"Alfred Geist. Better known to the gentile world as Alver Guest."

"You're kidding me," Ben gasped. No wonder Harlan wrote the way he did.

"I kid you not."

"That explains a lot. I mean, that you ended up being a writer too."

"Not really, seeing as I never knew him. He left my grandmother while she was still pregnant with my mother. Though it sounds like she was better off without him."

"I've heard he wasn't easy to get along with."

"A nice way of saying he was an asshole, which apparently he was. All that aside, I went over to collect, and to see what else I could learn."

"And?"

"And what? The whole of Europe is a mess. Everyone's

still broke except the Americans, and most of us are as big assholes as Geist was. Point is, Geist had this property outside Koblenz. Which was a real nice place before the SS started using it as a...a comfort station."

"Oh. Oh God..." Ben had been on duty when they'd freed a house of Italian girls, and the memory of their gaunt, abused bodies were among the most haunting of his service.

"Don't worry, it's being demolished."

"But I should think a part of Guest–that is, Geist's history would be worth preserving."

"The house didn't make him famous," Harlan said sharply. "And now it's a wreck. I just want it gone."

Rather than press him, Ben let it go. "So is that where you found the book?" he asked instead.

"Not exactly. I'd been in Rhineland about a week dealing with it when I got a letter from someone who'd known him indirectly. The son of a woman who'd had a fling with Geist, right about when he'd left my grandmother."

"Wow! So does that make him your half-brother or something?"

"He's not Geist's kid. Says he was four or five years old at the time. But his mom must have been a real knockout, because he gave me a book Geist had written about their affair."

"Are you telling me you found an unpublished Alver Guest manuscript? You can't be serious."

"I am completely serious."

"But...for the love of God, Harlan, why would you want that published by *me*?"

"Like I said, it's not your average manuscript."

"You don't mean it's blue. Oh God, is it?"

"So to speak," Harlan said with a smirk as Ben's mouth fell open. "I told you, he wrote it for his mistress."

"You can't be serious."

"Do I not look serious?"

"Not entirely. You've got that gleam in your eye, like you're making fun of me."

"I swear, I am not making fun."

"It still doesn't explain why you want my pathetic little press to have anything to do with it."

"Because, and my lawyer agrees, this has to be a secret. Even if I found a publisher for it, I'd want to keep it quiet as long as I could. And I've been a writer long enough that I don't trust any of the majors with this."

"You don't trust your own publisher?"

"I haven't even told my agent. Big firms have too many eyes, too many ears. Too many middlemen who hate the firm and hate the editor-in-chief and want nothing more than a chance to snatch a plum out of his hands. Or worse, ruin him. I've had some real ugly letters from distant relations, not to mention the Alver Guest Historical Society, since I started poking about. But the book, that's my property. His writing, but my right to publish it."

"Wow." A stupid thing to say, but Harlan's tale was stupefying. "Wow, okay. I understand. I think."

"So is this something that interests you?"

"God, yes. I mean, it's a lot to even think about but...Alver Guest? Sorry. I'm just worried that..." Ben looked around at the fiberboard walls, the cracked window, the bare light bulb dangling overhead, the general shabbiness of his life "Well, that I won't do it justice."

"There's nothing wrong with your books."

"There's not much right with them."

"Look, Baron's books aren't the point. What matters is your connections. A printer who won't call the vice squad. Distributors who handle blue books, shops where they don't care what's between the covers as long as it sells. And I'm willing to put in whatever money it takes to make this all happen."

"I don't need any more silent partners."

"That's not what I'm offering. Think of this as more like a bribe."

"Did you say *bribe*?"

"I'm buying your silence. And your time."

"But–"

"You can't tell me you've got money to lose. To pay off the cops. To cover bail."

"But...Alver Guest would never have wanted to be published by a press like Baron."

"Alfred Geist is dead," Harlan said firmly. "He doesn't give a damn. I want this published, and I can't do it by myself. I need you, Ben. Someone who can get a book to market without going through a big house. So what do you say?"

He'd dreamed of landing a deal like this. Prayed, in his darker hours. Now it was being handed to him with a blank check attached. The sort of deal that would either make him famous, or see him jailed for gross indecency.

"Okay," he heard himself say. "I'm in."

"That's great," Harlan said, springing to his feet to pump Ben's hand. "That's such good news."

"Is it?"

"It sure is. I didn't know who else to ask."

"Wait, you aren't leaving, are you?" Ben asked as Harlan started for the door.

"What, you think I'm walking around with it on me?" he said with a laugh. "I'll come back tomorrow, bright and early. Unless you're busy, that is."

"I'll make time for you. For this, I mean."

"Good. Not to mince words, but I expect to be your number one priority from now on."

And then he was gone, and it might have been a dream, if not for the scent of his skin clinging to Ben's hand. Now and then throughout the afternoon he sniffed at it, to reassure himself that yes, Harlan Avens had been here and yes, he wanted Ben's help, and yes, he had in fact said that he would come back tomorrow and that wasn't just Ben's wishful thinking. He startled, banging his knees on the underside of the desk, as Melody knocked on his door.

"You doing okay, Mr. Q?" she asked through the crack as he rubbed his kneecaps.

"You can come in. I'm decent." A bundle of nerves bound up in a cheap brown suit but decent, though something made him clasp his hands over his lap as Melody opened the door.

She stopped, her eyes wide as she looked him over. She was dressed to leave, her stolid purse under her arm, and as he quested about for something to say she came into the room, tutting and shaking her head.

"You ought to get out of here, Mr. Q. Grab yourself something to eat on the way home."

"Was he really here?" Ben blurted as she unclasped her purse. "Avens, I mean. That really happened, didn't it?"

"Of course, Mr. Q," she said, cooing like a night-nurse as she took out a cracked blue billfold. "Didn't he say he'd be back tomorrow?"

"Yes, but...you do know who he is, don't you?"

"Yes, Mr. Q. And he's a real nice guy to have looked you up like this."

"You can't tell anyone," he said as she came around to his side of the desk.

"Who would I tell?" she said with a smile. In her hand was a five dollar bill. "Take this and get yourself a hot meal, will you? I'll bill it to petty cash."

"We have a petty cash?" he murmured as she tucked the bill into his shirt pocket.

"Don't all businesses have petty cash? Come on, I'm locking up."

Though he fully intended to return the bill unspent tomorrow, he got within ten paces of the nearest hot dog cart before his desperate stomach overcame his poverty. The first dog tasted so good he had another, then he pocketed the rest of the change for next week's lunches.

His feet were leaden by the time he got home and dragged himself upstairs, yet he lay awake for a good hour or more, the bedsprings sawing every time he rolled over, his head buzzing with contradictory fears. Avens would never come back, or he would, and would want all Ben's time, would bankrupt him by making him neglect the necessary work to keep Baron running. He'd be an argumentative so-and-so, throwing his weight around, making demands Ben couldn't meet. Or he'd be too soft, not a self-made hero but a craven, cowardly man, a betrayal of Ben's ideals.

He'd damn near set his watch by Avens' word for years, seeing himself reflected in the pages of *No Man's Land*. Not entire, for the characters Bull and Sterling were men in their prime, gifted all of life's advantages, so that it was that much more destructive when they threw it all away.

What was Ben beside such towering personalities? A shadow, a sliver, a shaky reflection in cheap glass. A real person, but barely a man. So why on God's green earth did one of the greats of modern American literature want him to publish a book by an even greater legend?

He groaned as the hot dogs churned in his stomach. He couldn't afford to lose them. Quite literally couldn't spare the money to buy a second dinner if this one ended up on the rug. He sat up, then stood up, then snatched his hat from the table, yanked on his jacket, and staggered into the night to the nearest phone booth to call Joan.

Door to Door

He grabbed a few hours of sleep around dawn, then lollygagged down to the YMCA baths to wait for them to open at six. The water woke him up, to the morning and to the stale smell rising from his cruddy suit, though the steam in the change room did draw out some of the wrinkles. His hand no longer smelled like Avens' and after a few overly eager sniffs he shoved it in his pocket as he made his way to the office.

A sooty delivery truck was parked in front of his building, and he slipped inside behind a man in dirty coveralls wheeling a dolly laden with boxes. A heavyset older man dressed in the same stained serge stood in the foyer with a clipboard, counting the boxes standing in piles at the foot of the stairs.

"Hey, are you Mr. Press?" he asked as Ben sidled around the boxes.

"There's no one here by that name," Ben replied curtly.

"You sure?" he said, squinting at the clipboard. "I'm supposed to leave these with a Mr. Baron Press."

"Oh! That is me. That's not my name, but—oof!" He

took the clipboard in the chest as the delivery man shoved it at him.

"Whatever, mac. Sign here." He pointed with a grubby finger at the bottom of the mimeographed form.

"And what is it I'm signing?" Ben asked, for the blurry purple print was barely big enough to read.

"Receipt of goods."

Ben blinked at the name on the top of the form: Langley Libations, a dime store operator from Jersey who had been one of his more reliable customers. "What happened?"

"Beats me," the deliveryman said with a shrug. "Mr. Langley said get rid of 'em."

"I can't store all these books. I barely have room for myself."

The man shifted his toothpick to the other corner of his mouth. "Look, mac," he drawled, "I've been driving around with this muck in the back of my van since four in the AM. Langley don't want 'em, the printer don't want 'em. If you don't want 'em, the next stop is the East River."

"I'll take them. It's fine. I'll manage."

He signed the manifest with the delivery man's inky pen. The slimmer man, who looked to maybe be the son, was leaning on the handles of the dolly, having finished unloading the truck. At a nod from the older man he trundled out the door.

"Pleasure doing business with you," the man said, shoving the pen into his pocket.

"Wait, you're not going to take them upstairs?"

"They told me door-to-door."

"But my door is up—"

"Look, buddy," the man said sharply, his burly chest swelling. "*You're* gonna be in the East River in a minute.

Langley said door-to-door."

"Fine. Here is fine."

He was still sorting the piles when Melody arrived. She stood guard while he started porting the books. Two brutal hours later, Ben fell into his chair, his head thumping, his arms liquefied. Boxes of books stood everywhere, lining the walls two deep and waist high in both rooms, crowding around the desks and reeking of damp cardboard and the oily scent of ink. As Melody resumed typing, he laid his head on the desk…

…and woke up with her shaking his shoulder. "Hsssnn…ghr…"

She whistled low, fanning her nose as she stepped back. "Do you even own a toothbrush?"

"Altoids in the drawer," he managed through his numb lips.

She slapped the tin of mints and a comb on the desk. "Get it together, Mr. Q. You got company."

"Who?"

"Avens."

"Shit!" He sprang to his feet, bashing his thighs hard against his desk. "Ow. Shit. Why?"

"You mean why is he here or why are you out to lunch?"

"Either. Or both."

"Don't worry, Mr. Q. He's not looking so hot himself."

A lie, because there he was and he was still goddamn perfect. Harlan Avens, staring about at the fortress of boxes, a canvas bag under his arm, a look of disbelief on his handsome face, though maybe he didn't always have such dark shadows under his eyes. As Ben gaped at him, Avens set the bag on the desk and maneuvered the other chair out of the corner.

"What's that?" Ben asked as Avens extracted a cardboard box from the dingy canvas.

"Our book."

CALLING IT A BOOK was a stretch. Hell, it was barely a manuscript. The only thing uglier was the crumpled, oil-stained shoe-box it had been hidden in, which might have been a valuable artefact but which looked like a murder lurking on top of the filing cabinet as Ben picked through the pile of letters, notepaper, and other odds and ends Harlan had dumped on his desk. Who knew why that poor woman's son had kept the evidence of his mother's fling? A sensible person would have sent it to the dump.

"I swear there's a plot," Harlan said as Ben unfolded another crackling page. "At least, I managed to find one."

"And what am I meant to do with all this? It's an artefact as much as it is a manuscript. I can't mark it up."

"How about if you transcribe it? Edit from the copy?"

Ben unclenched his hand, the ghost of remembered pain poking at his forearms. Thanks to Melody, he hadn't typed or even held a pen for any length of time in weeks. He might trust her but Harlan didn't even know her, and this book was a much bigger secret than Ben usually needed to keep. "That would work."

"I'll leave it with you while I see to a few things," Harlan said, putting on his hat. "I'll come back at dinnertime and see how you're doing."

"Sounds good."

Once Harlan had gone, Ben gave Melody the rest of the day off, sat down at her desk with the manuscript, and typed until he was grinding his teeth against the pain. He lasted half an hour. He kept going because he had to, and when Harlan returned just after five he had resorted to his pair of pencils and was doggedly stabbing at the Underwood like it was a block of ice.

"Sorry I'm not further along," he said as Harlan flipped through the handful of completed pages.

"Does your typewriter stick?"

"I don't think so. Why do you ask?"

"You didn't capitalize anything," he said, dropping the pages on the desk. "By the third page you gave up on the space bar, too."

"I didn't give up. It's just that the space bar is...slippery."

Harlan wasn't buying it, frowning at him like Ben had started speaking Greek. "Does that girl of yours find she has the same problems?"

"Not at all. She's a godsend. I–" There was nothing to gain from lying to Harlan. "I've hurt my wrists so I can't type very well right now. Which is more or less why I hired her."

"Huh. Alright. I suppose I should have seen this coming."

Nothing to gain; everything to lose. He had failed his hero, like he'd feared, though he'd hoped it would take longer than twenty-four hours. As Harlan began tidying the papers away, Ben got up and went to the window. Nothing to see from his dismal angle but the grating of the fire escape and the dirty wall across the alley where the light never fell.

"May I?" Harlan said. When Ben turned he was sitting at the Underwood. "Or will she need this again today?"

"I sent her home. What are you doing?" he asked as Harlan cranked a blank page into the machine.

"What I should have done the minute I opened that shoebox. No offense but your copy is..."

"Abysmal?"

"Pretty much. Don't suppose you could run out and pick me up a coffee, maybe something to eat. We're gonna be here a while."

Insistent that he didn't need money, Ben sprinted to the nearest diner, where he bought four hot dogs and two coffees. Passing a bodega, he was tempted to buy a few bottles of beer, but he had a decent bottle of scotch in the filing cabinet they could lean on if they had to pull an all-nighter. If *they* had to. He was about to go all night with Harlan Avens.

Crushing this thought and burying it deep inside where it wouldn't pop up and ruin everything, he hurried back to the office. Harlan had finished several pages.

"Wow, you're really flying—"

"Shush," Harlan said, his eyes not leaving the machine. Ben shushed, if that was a word, setting Harlan's coffee within arm's reach then retreating to his office to eat. After ten minutes or so Harlan joined him, his neck cracking audibly as he bent it side to side.

"I need a shower after that last scene," he said with a grimace.

"How about lunch? Help yourself. They're all the same."

Half-sitting on the edge of the desk, Harlan peeled back

the foil. "Are those pork wieners?"

Ben sniffed at his hot dog, wondering if he should spit out his bite. "Why? Is yours off?"

"No, I just don't eat pork."

Ben had heard plenty of rumors that 'Harlan Avens' was an assumed name. There were rumors these days about everyone: who was hiding an affair, an indecent act, a queer uncle; who was a Red, a pinko, a Jew. "I swear, that wasn't a test," he stammered. "I don't care what you are. Or who. Or...I'm an idiot."

"Don't worry about it."

"I can get you something else to eat."

"Forget it, will you?" Harlan said with an edge of annoyance as Ben sprang to his feet and started for the door.

"I promise not to tell anyone. Well, you must have your reasons for not wanting it known you're Jewish," he said as Harlan groaned and covered his face. "It's not my place to question you."

"I owe you an explanation, though."

"You don't."

"I do. Because I want you to hear it from me and not some crackpot trying to claim I'm un-American just because I was born Hermann Metzger of Koblenz."

A sort of silence fell. No such thing as silence here, between the traffic and the sirens and the voices down the hall and the ringing in Ben's ears that had never wholly gone away from that week of non-stop artillery bombardment.

Harlan hadn't moved, his eyes fixed on the wreck of papers atop the desk, the freshly inked pages atop the grime-flecked remnants of the past. A shared past that tied them even closer together. Ben had seen what fascism did to its victims. Harlan might have been one of them. Had risked his life to keep others from the same horrific ends.

"I knew a Metzger, overseas," Ben said, his voice dragging in his throat. "Brave kid. Lost part of his leg. It could have been worse," he said as Harlan grimaced. "He took it well. It was the boredom that was getting to him, waiting to be healed enough to travel. I was on night duty and we got to talking. His father was a tailor, and after a little he asked if we didn't have needle and thread so he could stitch up his pant leg.

"I had a shirt that wanted mending, and we sat up talking for most of the night. The next night someone else asked about darning a sock. We ended up having a good little sewing circle for a few weeks. Of course they all went home in the end. So did I, eventually."

"I'm glad you made it back in one piece," Harlan said. His grin faltered as Ben made the same sour face. "What did I say?"

"It's nothing."

"Bullshit. I'm a big boy, I can take it."

"I wouldn't know where to begin."

It was one thing to admire a man. Another to reveal yourself to him, let him know the worst of you, the holes that life had punched in you, the ratty snarl within.

"Does it ever feel like you left a part of yourself behind?" Harlan asked softly. So soft, yet Ben felt it detonate deep in his lonesome soul.

"At least I'm not the only one," he gulped, sniffing as he shoved away his tears.

"That was against nature," Harlan replied, shaking his head. "They say it's a jungle out there, that human nature is kill or be killed but I don't believe that. I think we need each other. I think...I think we were made to love one another."

"You believe that after what we went through? You're a better man than I am."

"Without love, there can be no peace. What else is worth dying to protect? What's a family for, what are friendships for, if not to love each other? Shit, now you got me going." Sniffling, Harlan blotted at his welling tears with his handkerchief.

"Sorry to be a wet blanket."

"Forget it. I'm sorry for sermonizing at you," he replied.

"I guess we're even."

"I guess so."

Another silence, broken by the thump of Ben's heart, as Harlan gazed at him with a look of tenderness. More like sympathy, or outright pity, for the half a man he'd been since demob, living hand to mouth in a business that was bound to break him, sooner or later. Until then he'd soak up every bit of joy, every chance this chance was giving him to repay Harlan for all the ways he'd saved Ben's life.

He cleared his throat, the sound ricocheting off the bare walls. "They say to never meet your heroes, because they'll always let you down. I'm glad to find out that's not always true."

Harlan laughed dryly, blushing as he ran his hand over his hair. "Believe me, there's still plenty of time for me to disappoint you."

Impossible, but Ben let it go as they sorted the mass of papers. He locked the lot in the bottom drawer of the desk and they called it a night, Harlan holding on a second too long as they shook hands in the street, staring at Ben like he was trying to read his mind. Then his gaze softened and he let him go, whistling as he walked away, leaving the scent of his skin once again clinging to Ben's hand.

Saint Joan

BEN WANDERED HOME IN a funk, the air stale with the promise of rain, the sunset dripping red through the torn clouds. Speaking of the war, even a relatively pleasant part, had stirred up his old fear, memories rising from the gloom and merging with the city sounds into a terrible cacophony: a tank's rumbling tread in the thunder of a passing truck, the airborne violence of thunder as the clouds thickened overhead. Half blind to his surroundings, he was thrown back into awareness by the blare of a horn as a taxi swerved to miss him when he stepped off the curb.

Heart in his mouth, he leaned against a lamppost to catch his breath. He was perfectly safe. He was home. He was in New York, not a dusty canvas tent halfway round the world under a fascist bombardment. He didn't need to be dragging up the terrors of over a decade ago when there was more than enough danger in the here and now.

Hadn't Sam Roth just got three months? For selling a book, in a case that Roth had managed to carry all the way to the Supreme Court, and then lose. The same sort of book that Baron thrived on. Ben's business, his future, his whole life was devoted to a cause that could ruin him.

He reached his building as the first fat drops of rain burst on the sidewalk. Instead of a refuge, his apartment felt provisional, the walls hollow like a stage set, his life exposed to all the world. Poised between exhaustion and the first signs of nervous panic, he fumbled open the jar of downers with shaking hands, washed down a sleeping tablet with a few gulps of water straight from the faucet, then dropped into bed and gave up trying to fight the darkness.

THE NEXT DAY MELODY started working through the list of Ben's distributors, looking for someone to take on more stock. She hit on the notion to offer a two cent discount, and by the end of the third day had cleared out a good half of the boxes in the office. In the meanwhile, Ben and Harlan worked their way through Geist's manuscript, Harlan typing while Ben proofed.

Alone, Ben might have tossed the whole thing in the nearest trash can and gotten on with his life. But Harlan both wanted it done and made the work tolerable: his jibes and his sympathy for Ben's disgust, his diligence and the way Ben kept catching him looking at him. Not staring, just looking, then turning away with that lift at the corner of his mouth.

Rather than cobbling together a narrative, they had

agreed to transcribe it verbatim, a presentation of the document as written, meaning some 'chapters' were as short as single sentence. If there was a date, they included it, but many of the papers told nothing of their history. Poems, some stopping in the middle of a line, others carrying on for pages. Descriptive passages of Geist's daily life—his breakfasts, his work, his lover and her young son who had grown into the man who had given Harlan the manuscript. Other scenes of his lover, some plainly erotic, some grotesque, full of blood and disaster.

Guest's mature novels were lessons in brevity, sparely ornamented, conveying their meaning through action. His unpublished work was a fever dream, swarming with metaphor and deviant allegory. As a pure work of fiction it was barely readable. Without the name Alver Guest on the cover, it was likely unsellable, having more merit as an artistic statement by a renowned master of his craft than as a book you might want to sit down and read. Even his blue scenes were off-kilter, a phantasmagoria of insects and nectar and melting flesh. Sex as murder, sex as suicide, suffocating himself in her vulva then being reborn from her mouth, leaving Ben with a sense that the man had written them while high as a kite on opium.

Why couldn't Harlan have shown up with a nice little kitchen sink drama, or a second *No Man's Land*? Anything other than a book so blue it turned Ben's stomach, by a writer so famous that there'd be no chance of his book getting published without someone noticing. But Harlan wanted it done, and that was reason enough. If he was willing to pay, Ben would see it published. He'd come too far to refuse.

On Friday morning Harlan had errands to run. Without

him, Ben took a break from the poetic smarm to work on a few tasks for Baron. Mel was competent and diligent but there was only so much he could lean on her. Partway through proofreading the translation of a book smuggled in from Europe (what Hamburg thought you could do with a horsewhip...) he was thinking of breaking for a late lunch when he heard the rat-tat-tatting of Joan's lethal heels up the hollow staircase and along the uncarpeted hallway. Only a few lines from the end of his page, he didn't get up to let her in. Joan knew how to open a door. He'd forgotten he'd hired a watchdog.

"Hey!" Melody cried, springing up from the desk as Joan advanced across the outer room. "You can't just walk in there like that. You need an appointment to see Mr. Quirke."

"Oh, it's Mr. Quirke now, is it?" She paused in his open doorway, perfectly Joan: tailored like a blade, dripping fur and sapphires, a gloved hand on her jutting hip. "Benny, I gotta talk to you."

Behind her, Melody bristled with indignation. "It's fine, Melody," he said as Joan strode into his office. "Joan's my back–"

"His best friend in the world," Joan said brightly, slapping him on the shoulder. "Ain't that right, Benny?"

"Sure thing, Joanie. So, what's up?"

"Gee, I don't know," she said, rolling her eyes at Melody, plain and brown and fierce as she glared at Joan from the doorway. "Sounds like I need an appointment to talk to you anymore."

"You, Joan, never need an appointment. You know that. In fact why don't I introduce you properly? Melody Masterson, this is Joan–"

She slapped his shoulder again and harder, her smile unflinching. "Just Joan will do."

"Okay. Melody, this is Joan."

Joan swayed towards her, extending a gloved hand. "A pleasure, Miss–"

"Ms."

"*Ms.* Masterson. Truly a pleasure." Pursing her velvety lips, she caught Melody's fingertips in a coy grip that Ben had seen bring stars of sports and screen alike to their knees. No one outdid Joan when she really poured it on, and she was dumping it all over poor Melody, who stood blinking under the assault.

Into this massacre walked Harlan Avens. The women sprang apart, Joan wobbling on her stilettos while Melody felt her way to the safety of her desk.

"Am I interrupting?" he asked. Joan came to attention, her shoulders back, gaze locked on Harlan.

"I do believe we've met before," she said to him in her best mid-Atlantic a la Audrey Hepburn. Holding out her hand, she advanced on him. "You sure do look like a man I'd remember meeting. Wasn't it at Peggy's, last autumn?"

"Guggenheim?" Harlan said with a pinch of his brows as he briefly clasped her fingertips. "Right, I remember you."

"Wait, you know him?" Ben asked her, his stomach dropping. Some best friend she was, to never mention she'd met his idol.

"More like seen you around. Remind me of your name, would you?"

"Joan," Ben hissed, "this is Harlan Avens!"

"No shit!" she cried, her uptown poise thrown aside for the tomboy she was at heart. "Benny, I'm such a bitch. I didn't really believe you. I mean I did but...you have my sincere apologies. You too, Mr. Avens," she said, taking his hand again and pumping his arm like he'd just signed a bank loan. "I didn't give you enough credit."

"Joan," Ben warned as Harlan stared first at Joan then his hand, but there was no stopping her once she was warmed up.

"I mean, I didn't think a guy like you'd be smart enough to figure out what a gem our Benny is," she said. Her smile tightened as she jerked Harlan's arm towards her, bending his wrist back sharply.

"So you listen to me, bub," she purred with deadly intent. "I don't give a damn who you are. If you mess with him, you mess with me. And believe me, brother, you don't want to mess with me." Smiling sweetly, she released him.

"I'll take it under advisement," Harlan replied, rubbing his wrist.

"You do that. And as for you," she said, rounding on Ben, "I see you've got your hands full. I'll leave you to entertain your handsome friend here. Enjoy your day, all." With a last wink at Melody, she swung her satin hips out of the office, leaving behind the fading sound of stilettos and a cloud of *Vol du Nuit*.

Ben woke first. "Sorry, Melody. I should have told you about Joan. Nice, er, interception, by the way."

"Yeah," she replied vaguely, still gazing at the door. "Real nice."

"Anyway, you can knock off for the rest of the day."

"Knock off. Yeah. Yeah, ok." She started for the outer door, then checked herself and returned to her desk for her purse.

"Do you have much left to do?" Harlan asked him as the door clicked shut behind her.

"I really ought to get this out of the way," Ben confessed with a guilty glance at the marked-up manuscript. "Though one more day won't matter."

"Go ahead and finish. I can entertain myself."

"I can get the Geist—"

"Please, no," Harlan said, rubbing his stomach. "I just ate."

"Do you want to read an even worse book while you wait?"

Ben gave him a few of the unprintable submissions from his bottom drawer and went back to his own barely publishable book. Harlan banished himself to the outer room when he couldn't stop laughing.

Ben's work went much faster without that presence chortling to himself on the other side of the desk. The proofreading done, he locked up the manuscripts. "What about Geist?" Ben said as Harlan handed him his jacket. "Shouldn't we be working on it?"

"We are. We're going to a business meeting. Where do you want to go?"

"For a meeting?"

"For a meal. My treat."

"You can't buy me dinner."

"Says you. And I hate to eat alone."

"You choose. I don't mind where we go."

"As long as they have shrimp toast?"

"I told you, I...You're teasing me again."

Harlan snorted a laugh. "Am I?"

"You know what, screw you."

"Not with that attitude."

Startled into silence by the implications, Ben let Harlan steer him out of the office and downstairs to the street. Though they hadn't settled on a destination, Harlan set off walking, Ben falling into step beside him.

A New York summer's evening, the buttery glow of late sunlight as glorious as the wafts of sewer gas were humbling, the ceaseless hum of the city an echo of the thrumming of Ben's nerves. Everything at once, and Harlan by his side, the fact of his friendship as improbable as plucking a star from the sky. Without the solid presence of the desk between them, Harlan was closer than ever, and Ben walked with his hands in his pockets to hide their shaking.

"So tell me a bit more about yourself," Harlan said as they stopped at the curb to wait for the traffic to clear. "Were your parents doctors?"

"My mother, definitely not. As for my father, he could have been. I never knew him." Wonderful, to open with a bum note as Harlan's eager smile fell.

"Then how did you end up a medic?" he asked more quietly.

"I knew how to thread a needle. And blood doesn't bother me."

"Really, Ben?"

"Yes. Turns out there's only so much a stitch can do."

The light changed and they walked on a few blocks without speaking, Ben working up the nerve to apologize for wrecking the mood. Harlan beat him to it: "Sorry if that's a sore spot."

"It is and it isn't. I don't think about it much."

"Still, I'm sorry. That had to be rough. So then where did you learn to thread a needle?"

"From my mother."

"Was she a nurse?"

"A seamstress. And yes, she taught her son to sew. Hoped I'd become a tailor. They make more money than seamstresses, for a start. But when you're around something all your childhood, sometimes all you want to do is get away from it. Fat lot of good it did me."

"How so?"

"Because instead of doing something sensible, I enlisted. Her only child. I don't know what would have happened to her if I hadn't come home. That's why I volunteered for the medical unit. Thought I wouldn't be getting shot at as often as everyone else." Only to find that being shot *over* was nearly as horrific, and that surviving an air strike was sometimes worse than being killed. He shook off the queasy memories of blood and pain. "When I got back I couldn't work, couldn't be around people, so I laid low in her apartment. Her arthritis was catching up by then, and...I started doing her piecework."

"You what?" This seemed to shock him the most and he slowed to a stop. "Are you kidding me?"

"Not all of it. I'd just finish the last few units when her hands hurt too much. But then it was a few more, then half. Her vision was starting to go. I don't think she sat down at the machine once that last year. After she died, I kept at it."

"At what? Her job?"

"It was easier than moving on. I'd been the one picking up the bundles and dropping them off. The factory manager knew me. Got away with it for nearly two years."

"Benny, you poor schmuck."

"There's nothing wrong with garment-making as a profession."

"There is when you make piecework wages. No wonder your wrists are shot."

"Shit. I never thought of that."

Sighing like he had in the office, Harlan laid his hand on Ben's shoulder. "I believe this calls for a change of plans," he said with something like his usual grin. "Let's go do something fun."

"Dinner's fun."

"The hell it is. Last time I took you to dinner, you ordered a meal you don't even like and got a bottle of wine dumped in your lap. That place was making you uncomfortable, anyway. I should have known better. So I want you to choose. Anything you want to do, we'll do."

"We will?"

"We can go to a movie. A nightclub. No jazz, honest. Whatever you like."

"You won't like what I like."

"Don't sell yourself short. Me, I like all kinds of things."

"We're probably too late to get tickets."

"It's not even six. And now *you're* avoiding answering *me*. Tell me where you want to go and we'll go."

"You really mean it?"

"Hundred percent."

Ben wanted to believe him. Wanted this not to be when it all fell apart, when someone saw him for who he was and decided they didn't like him after all. Do or die, and he'd find out what Harlan thought of him.

"I'd like to see *West Side Story*."

"Where's that playing? The Winter Garden?" Harlan asked, not missing a beat. When Ben nodded, he stepped into the street and whistled for a taxi. There were plenty around at this hour and one pulled up in seconds.

"Go ahead," Harlan said, opening the door for Ben, dithering on the curb. "What is it?" he said as Ben didn't move.

"I...nothing."

"Tell me."

"I thought you'd try and talk your way out of it."

"Are you kidding me? What kind of friend would I be if I did that?"

Grinning, he got in the cab. Ben followed, his senses reeling. Harlan was his friend. He was friends with Harlan Avens. He, Ben Quirke, was a close and personal friend of the renowned American writer Harlan Avens. With whom he was acutely and painfully in love.

That was what this was, right? This giddy sense of hurtling through space at ever accelerating speeds, soaring high above himself, the city, the world. This constant awareness of the other man's every aspect, from the sound of his breath to the heat of him in the air.

Harlan was oblivious to Ben's crisis, humming to himself as he tapped his fingers on his knees, his face revealed, hidden, revealed by the sulfurous light of the streetlamps. Ben wanted to sing along, or throw himself across the seat and into Harlan's lap. Biting his lip, he turned away, terrified by the strength of his feelings, and the so, so terrible fallout if all his instincts were proven wrong.

Harlan was not Bull. Bull was not Harlan. Bull was a character, a figment of Harlan's imagination. A stand-in for every young man's frustrated need for significance in an uncaring universe. A fiction, not a confession, and confusing the two was the worst mistake Ben could make.

Risky Business

Though Harlan was ready to pay for box-seats, they had to settle for first mezzanine. Settle being a pair of seats dead center with a sweeping view of the stage and a minimum of heads to look past. Ben still missed half of the first act, one eye on Harlan to be sure he wasn't having a bad time. He seemed glad enough, laughing at the right parts, applauding with enthusiasm at the end of every number, and by the second act Ben had stopped watching Harlan and given himself to the spectacle on stage.

"How many times have you seen this?" Harlan asked as they filtered back into the auditorium after the intermission.

"This is my first."

"It seemed like you knew all the words."

"Was I humming along? Oh God, Joan hates that."

"Nuts to her. I think it's cute."

They settled in their seat as the overture began, but Ben couldn't see the stage. Harlan's knee was resting against his. Harlan Avens thought he was cute. Was taking him out for a night on the town. Had made a joke about screwing him, back at the office when he had teased him about shrimp toast. The kind of joke you made when you were just a little bit serious.

So Ben decided to go home. He needed time to think. He thought. Wasn't that the sensible choice, the responsible choice of a grown man, to remove himself from the path of temptation? Then Harlan glanced his way and Ben's sensible, responsible choice didn't mean a damn thing as Harlan winked, bumping his knee against Ben's. Again, daring him again to move away or to stay, invite the touch or shy from it.

He thought. He hoped. He didn't know, and so he did nothing, let Harlan's leg press against his, unseen in the dark of the theatre, the tiny sensations—the seam of his trousers pressing into his skin, the heat radiating from that sole point of contact—so captivating that he half leapt from his seat at the explosion of sound as the audience burst into applause.

The rest of the show passed in a brightly colored haze. Time and again, he thought of asking Harlan his plans for after, but the last thing he needed was to sound, well, needy. Harlan had already given him so much: his time, his attention, this ludicrous chance, a night out. Things Ben hadn't even known he craved but that he could certainly live without. Surely the great Harlan Avens had better things to do than slum around Manhattan with a dirty little creep like him.

His head buzzing, he followed Harlan as the audience filed out of the theatre. Outside, Harlan darted across the street away from the chattering crowd to hail another cab.

"Where are we going?" Ben asked as Harlan settled beside him in the purring quiet of the back seat.

"Where do you want to go?" Harlan asked, his face unreadable in the flickering dark.

"I should go home."

"Is that what you want to do?"

And he couldn't say yes, because he couldn't lie to Harlan. He couldn't say a word, couldn't ask for what he really wanted with a witness in the front seat and his heart in his mouth, and so, coward that he was, he turned away.

"You can drop me off at the next subway station," he murmured to the cabbie, who touched the brim of his hat. Ben sat back, willing himself not to look Harlan's way, not to let himself be tempted by what he couldn't have. Harlan's breath seemed loud in the muted calm of the taxi. His hand on the seat was clenched to a fist, held tightly against his thigh. Like he wanted to reach out, close the gap, touch him...

"You getting out or what, pal?"

Ben's head jerked up. The cabbie was watching him blearily in the rear view mirror. Ahead of them yawned the entrance to the subway.

"Thanks for the ticket," Ben said, at last meeting Harlan's gaze. "I guess I'll see you tomorrow."

"I won't be around. I have to go out of town for a few days."

Yes, Ben was definitely in love, otherwise how could such easy words lodge themselves so painfully in his heart?

"I should have told you sooner," Harlan murmured.

"It's fine," Ben gasped. "No problem. I'll see you around." Regretting his every word, not merely now but since his birth, he shoved the door open and made himself get out of the cab. Which then drove away, taking Harlan with it.

Harlan was leaving town. Ben was staying behind. He'd found his reason for living, and he was already saying goodbye.

JOAN HAD LEFT A letter under his door, as she often did. Not her usual sort of letter, written in violet ink on pricey onionskin at some godawful hour of the morning after she'd slunk home, blitzed on champagne and miserable. This was a blank greeting card from a dime store, on the front a badly printed watercolor of two gamboling puppies, inside the words *CALL ME NOW* scrawled with either a broken pencil or a kohl eyeliner. Whatever it was, it had snapped off the third time she'd underlined *now*, leaving a ragged blotch.

The nearest phone was half a block away, in a booth on the corner. He stood staring at the card for a full minute, weighing his deep and sincere wish to crawl into bed and possibly never leave it again against the agony he'd endure if he ignored Joan's note. Thankfully her housekeeper answered the phone, which meant Joan was out, so rather than spend the next two hours feeding dimes into the phone while his feet went numb, he left a message and hurried home.

Reeling from the whirlwind his life had become, he slept like the dead. Brushing his teeth the next morning, Ben caught sight of his flat over his shoulder in the spotted mirror. Crumpled papers were strewn across the floor, mixed with dropped items of clothing. Paper cups littered the desk and the floor near his bed, half full of coffee, some gone gray. The home of a dying man.

Holding his breath, he emptied the cups down the sink. His trash cans were both overflowing and he made several trips to the basement incinerator before the room looked decent. By now it was nearly noon, and after dropping off his clothes at the Chinese laundry at the end of the block, he went for a walk. Not to go anywhere, just to go. To move, to live, to do anything besides sit in a dirty room and think about words. Words said so little, and some things defied description. In the end, they were just air, frail and temporary.

The thing with Manhattan was you really couldn't get lost. Go far enough in any direction and you either found a famous building or a river. Eventually he fetched up at the monumental pilings of the 59th Street Bridge, where he loitered at the railing for uncounted hours, watching the boats on the water as the setting sun dropped behind him and the sky paled from blue to gold. A solitary, secret joy, to be so perfectly alone in the middle of Manhattan, a tranquility he never could explain.

All afternoon the cloud-flown derricks turn.../Thy cables breathe the North Atlantic still, Hart Crane had written of the Brooklyn Bridge, and what a change these bridges must have brought about when they were first constructed: a new future rising from the tidal mud. On the stone wall beside him some punk had sketched a unimpressive cock and balls in dribbling red spray paint: the real future, happening now, as grimy and prosaic as the past.

Strolling home, he stopped at a pizzeria where he spent

the last dimes in his pocket on a slice. As much as taking Joan's investment had felt like failure, without her he'd have no chance of survival, let alone success. Without Melody, he wouldn't have time for Harlan and his book. Without Joan, he'd have never met Harlan at all. So many people were working on his behalf. For no reason but pity, he could only assume, as what could he possibly offer in return?

On Sunday, he surprised himself by going to church. He'd not gone since Ma had passed, and he avoided their usual aisle seat six pews from the front in favor of a place near the rear. The elderly woman beside him could have been one of Ma's friends from the sweatshop, with her dowager's hump and her delicate fingering of her rosary. Following the motion, lulled by the priest's mumbling voice, he was startled awake by the blast of the pipe organ as they began the recessional.

He drifted home in a fog of nostalgia, getting caught now and then in surges of pedestrian traffic as the city's churchgoers filled the streets. As the crowd on the sidewalk dissipated, he caught sight of a man in a camel-hair coat with dark hair and a fedora walking towards him. His heart soaring, Ben was about to call out when the man glanced up. Ben managed to turn his wave into scratching his neck as the stranger passed.

Of course. Harlan wasn't here. Harlan was gone and Ben was in love with him and he didn't know what to do about either fact.

When Ben didn't know what to do, he read. A refuge, a restorer, a blessed distraction. A light in the dark, and he'd barely shut the door before he was stumbling for the shelf, his threadbare copy of *No Man's Land* falling open in his hand on that scene. The one he'd read again and again, teasing out the truth that was too raw for words:

He had closed the curtains around my bed when he arrived and the nurse hadn't lit my lamp, and the quiet pressed on us. I hated the noise in the ward in the day and now hated the quiet, the way it amplified each movement and the sleeping breath of the other patients.

"They'll miss you at base," I said to Sterling.

"It's over now. I don't care what Jeffers does to me, it's over."

"Why did you come? You knew you couldn't get back tonight."

"You know why. You know me, Bull. Don't you?"

"I thought I did."

"You will."

"But be quiet."

The Contract

Monday morning Ben woke with a jolt to yelling and clanging of pots from the neighbors' apartment. The Erwins had the same argument every week on wash day when Mrs. Erwin went through Mr. Erwin's pockets and found his stubs from the racetrack. Ben's mother had once dated a gambler. An effortless, sentimental man with a mean streak a mile wide once he'd decided you weren't worth his time. They'd had to move apartments to get away from him.

Rather than drag himself to the Y, he boiled some water on the hotplate and had a decent wash. He then put on his second best, that is to say his only other pair of clean trousers, a gray tweed whose matching jacket had worn out long ago, and went to the office, picking up a fresh coffee on the way. He was in the middle of dialing Joan's number when he heard her—or a stampede of wild horses—start up the stairs. Racking his brain for what he'd done to make her so mad, he half jumped out of his skin when she suddenly slung open the door.

"Hiya, Mel," she said to a wordless Melody as she strode

past into Ben's office. "And you," she said, stabbing her finger at Ben as she advanced on him. "Who are you calling?"

"You."

"Good." She ripped the receiver from his hand and slammed it down. Plunked her rump on the front of his desk. "Benny, you crazy kid!" she crowed, leaning over to pinch his cheek. Hard, but it was better than the slap he expected. "Tell me everything."

"About what?"

"About your new boyfriend Harlan Evans, you dingbat."

"Joan!"

"Oh, Mel knows all about you," she said, dismissing him with a wave as he leapt up to shut the door.

"How?"

"I told her."

"For Chrissakes, Joan! You're going to get me arrested! And he's not my boyfriend."

"Then whose is he?"

"No one that I know of."

"Then ipso facto, I say he's yours. How'd you reconnect?"

"He came to me."

"You temptress!" She smacked his shoulder coyly, though it hit like a punch.

"I told you, it has nothing to do with...that," he said, rubbing the bruise. "It's all him. He walked in like, well, the way you do. Sat himself down like he owned the place and pitched me a book deal."

"Oh really?"

"Very hush-hush. I can't say much more."

"Don't worry about it, Benny," she said. "I know how contracts work."

"Contract?"

Her cheery smile hardened. "Don't tell me you haven't signed a contract," she said through her bared teeth. "Don't you get all your writers to sign a deal?"

"He's not the writer, though. We're editing it together, and really Joan, don't you think I can trust a man like him?"

"Benny, what the hell!" she shouted, slamming her fist on his desk and making the phone jump in its cradle. "You can't trust *me* without a contract between us. I didn't just give you that money, did I?"

"No."

"I made you sign off on conditions, didn't I?"

"Yes."

"Then what the hell?"

"I keep forgetting. Because he keeps...because he's...and I—"

"I don't care if you and him are on the way to the altar. In fact, if you were, you'd be signing a damn contract! Jeez, Ben, it's no fun looking out for a guy who keeps jumping into traffic."

"What do you mean?"

"I mean you get that boyfriend of yours in here pronto. We gotta get this hashed out."

"Right now? And I told you, he's not my—"

"Of course right now! I don't got all day."

"I can't just call him up and make demands like that."

"Yeah, but *I* can."

"Joan, darling, be reasonable."

"Don't you *darling* me," she shot back. "Either you get

Avens in here and get this shit in writing or I'm taking out my money."

"You can't!"

"Like hell I can't. Know why? Because unlike you and him, you and me got a freaking *contract*! Now get him on the blower." She stabbed her finger at the phone.

"I can't."

"Why not?"

"I don't have his number."

She snorted, sticking out her hip to give her somewhere to put her fist. "What are you, new? Which hotel is he staying at?"

"He had to leave town."

"When's he coming back?"

"I don't know." Meaning all he knew about Harlan Avens was his name. "Oh God, I don't know a thing about him. Joan, I'm an idiot! What was I thinking?"

"Did he not give you any way to get in touch with him?" As he shook his head frantically, she groaned. "Jeez Louise, maybe you are an idiot."

"He has to be coming back, though. He left the book with me. He wouldn't leave it behind."

"You sure about that?"

"Positive."

He explained the situation, her expression changing from wariness to an eager smile, and then to frozen horror as he let her read a little of the manuscript.

"I don't know, Benny," she said as she passed the pages back to him. "Are you sure that's even sexy?"

"It's certainly provocative."

"It's kinda sick, if you know what I mean."

"Ah, but he's famous."

"I guess that makes it art, huh?"

"Art with a capital A."

"Do you suppose it'll sell?" she said, tapping a cigarette from her gold case.

"If it has the name Alver Guest on the cover, absolutely. If not, we'll have to drum up some controversy."

"Make it known without it being known that you know?"

"Exactly."

She gazed at him through the swirl of her smoke. "Benny, are you going to get in trouble?"

"It's bound to happen sooner or later," he said with a shrug and a hitch in his voice he wished wasn't there.

"That's not much of an answer. I got money riding on you."

"So does Harlan."

"Which is why I'm going to get that girl of yours to whip us up a nice little binding document. My guy'll notarize, and it'll be like it was in place all along."

"Joan, you're a life-safer."

"Just don't mention me in your speech when you win the Pulitzer. Or at your bail hearing."

As she closed the door behind her Ben put his head down on his desk and tried not to crack up. All he'd done by talking to her was bring all his bad feelings to the surface. He had no reason to mistrust Harlan, but then again he had no reason to trust him either. What if he was the perfect patsy, Harlan choosing to bring him this book not because he was discreet but because he was a born sucker? Someone to take the fall when the law got involved: gullible, expendable, doomed.

As a REWARD FOR enduring Joan, he treated himself to lunch. Silly of him to think of basic personal care as a luxury. Hardly a word that adhered to twenty cent burgers from the automat. Sated if not quite satisfied, he was returning to the office when a splash of color in a bookstore window grabbed his eye. Not a store that stocked Baron's books, but he'd made a habit of befriending every bookseller around to keep abreast of the broader world of publishing.

There in the middle of the window display sat a copy of *No Man's Land*. Though Harlan's first book had been reprinted three times, Ben had never seen this edition, with its impressionistic splash of red, the letters intersecting like a crossword puzzle. It stood among other lauded books from the same mid-war era, each with its own bright colorway, glowing like jewels under the shop lights.

In he went, keeping his hands in his pockets to hide their trembling. The shop was not much wider than Ben's office, the shelves towards the front displaying new books, the second-hand stock towards the rear. Hearing the door, the cadaverous owner Spiro emerged from the back room, his wiry hair standing up on one side like he'd been asleep.

"Quirke," he said through a yawn as he buttoned his moth-eaten brown cardigan. "When'd you get out?"

"Out of where?"

"Weren't you in jail?"

"Excuse me?" Ben squeaked, glancing around.

"Didn't something you publish show up on a list?"

"Who told you that?"

"Couple people, I dunno who," Spiro said, scratching his bristly chin.

"Well if it did, it's news to me."

"Speaking of news, you seen this?" Spiro pulled a section of newspaper out of the middle of a pile of papers which promptly fell over.

"Piggins got his butt handed to him pretty neatly," he said as Ben scanned the article, which detailed the outcome of a lawsuit brought by no less a force than Random House against the City of Detroit. Its overbearing police force's in-house censorship board was a constant source of stress for every publisher of Ben's ilk, and more than a few of the upstanding ones, threatening arrest to any bookseller who traded material with content they'd deemed obscene, which in this case had included adultery.

"It's about time a judge put these crooked cops in their place," Spiro said. "If I want a sermon, I'll go to church."

"Of all the books to pick on. *Ten North Frederick* is hardly a low-brow pot-boiler. It was a bestseller for months. They made it into a film."

"More, judge said that them saying they'd arrest the sellers was unlawful intimidation."

"I'd sure be intimidated by the Detroit police," Ben said as he gave the paper back to Spiro. "But tell me, how long has that Avens been out?" He nodded towards the window.

"The new printing? Few weeks. They're there if you want a copy." Spiro pointed to a section of shelving where *Land* and the others stood.

"Some other time," Ben said, fingering his empty pockets. "I have a copy of the first edition."

Spiro's sleepy expression sharpened. "Is that so?"

"It's not for sale, before you ask."

"Well, you let me know when it is."

"Don't hold your breath. How about Alver Guest?"

"In the back. I had to pull 'em off the regular shelves last month."

"Really? I didn't think he was still so controversial."

"I'm too old to put up with these nosy Parkers who come looking for books to complain about," Spiro said with a dismissive wave as he shuffled towards the back room. "Gimme a minute and I'll see what I got."

Armed with a fraying five cent copy of Guest's third novel *On a High Hill*, Ben carried on to the office. He had read the book too young, then again several years after, finding it in the hospital reading room amid a scattering of other New Classics and several tons of third-rate detective novels whose pages tore if you turned them too quickly. Guest's work had made more sense that second time, once Ben had learned the cost of making the wrong choices.

The sort of choices Guest's characters were always making. Living in sin, whoring and drinking, even though the acts themselves were skimmed over, not presented in the sort of lavish detail that filled Baron's output. Racy enough to bother the sort of person who was bothered by racy books. As pure as Laura Ingalls Wilder when put beside that ghastly manuscript of Harlan's.

What did he expect to gain from publishing that horror show? Notoriety? Critical relevance? He was asking Ben to join him on a crusade, confront the law and social reckoning in the name of capital-A Art. Risk his livelihood, his very freedom, when it was all Ben could manage to stay alive.

Guest's manuscript waited for him, haunting his office, consuming his thoughts. If not for Harlan, he'd shovel the lot into the incinerator and never speak of it again. Harlan, who kept leaving him to deal with everything alone. Who kept leaving him.

Landmines

For the next few days Ben threw himself into work, settling old invoices, revising the cover copy for a republished set of sci-fi thrillers. Whatever kept his mind off the book lurking in the bottom of the desk, and the man who had brought it to him.

Easier said than done. Ben had read—and published—plenty of stories of cursed gifts and haunted books that drove their keepers crazy. Keeping his mind off the man was even harder. Every passer-by in a camel-hair coat and a nice hat was Harlan, every footstep in the hall, every knock at the door. Desperate for distraction, Ben splashed out on a transistor radio that he tuned to a popular music station then turned down low, just enough noise that he wasn't jumping at nothing.

Monday morning he was up even before the Erwins after a mainly sleepless night. He'd bought *High Hill* to get reacquainted with Guest's authorial voice, his rhythm and vocabulary, to be sure their manuscript carried a similar style. It had left him even more unsettled, hints of that early abandoned work popping out of the text and infecting his dreams. The ants under the stone, the spoiled milk now seemed lurid, referencing rot and bodily fluids instead of mere ennui.

Hoping the walk would refresh him, he set out early for the office, but the city seemed determined to bring him down. Noxious smells rose from the sewer grates, the morning noises echoing harshly off the skyscrapers, the rumble of a garbage truck's wheels haunted by the roaring echo of fighter planes. The rank smell followed him into the foyer. Dust swirled in the stale air, glinting in the gray beams filtering from the second floor landing, the only windows that hadn't been completely painted over.

As he started up the stairs, he heard a single footfall. Glancing up, he a caught sight of a flash of a tan coat through the third floor railing. He nearly called Harlan's name, but it couldn't be him, not so soon, not when he might never come back at all.

The next step creaked under Ben's foot. As he froze, the noises above him fell silent. Then the person bolted, their shoes scraping against the gritty stairs. Against all logic of self-preservation, Ben took off in pursuit, vaulting up the stairs two at a time. It was only as he burst onto the third floor landing that he asked himself what he was planning to do when he caught whoever it was.

The question was moot, for the hallway was empty.

In the four years Ben had leased this office he'd never seen a soul go up to the top floor. The gumshoes next door claimed it was condemned, and Ben had taken them at face value, given the condition of the rest of the building. The dark vault of the upper floor loomed as he crept past the stairs, their gray carpet of dust undisturbed.

A broom closet and a shuttered lavatory stood between

his office and the PIs' room at the end. Perfect places for an ambush, and he held his breath as he approached. A broken railing from the banister leaned in the corner, and armed with this he tested both narrow doors. Both were firmly locked, but it wasn't until he was himself behind two locked doors that the knot of tension between his shoulderblades unkinked.

And weeks of this to survive. He buried his throbbing head in his arms on his desk and tried not to think. About anything.

AFTER SPENDING THE REST of the morning with his ears perked for the slightest sound from upstairs or the hall, Ben turned up the radio so loud Melody asked him to turn it down so she could hear herself think. The afternoon whizzed past, lost in the to and fro of orders and invoices, deadlines and risk. He was just waking up to the fact that he'd forgotten to have lunch when he heard the front door open.

"Good afternoon, Mr. Avens," Melody chirped. Ben was on his feet before Harlan had answered her, and met him at the door.

"Benny! What a sight for sore eyes." Harlan was all smiles, gripping Ben's arm as they shook hands.

"Mel, why don't you knock off for the day?" Ben said, unable to look away.

"Sure thing, Mr. Q."

As she began to tidy up, he ushered Harlan into his office. "I didn't think I'd see you for weeks."

"I told you I wouldn't be gone long," he replied, handing Ben his coat to hang up. "I was thinking about you, though."

Ben just about dropped the coat. "You were not."

Leaning on the corner of Ben's desk, Harlan blushed, sending Ben's temperature soaring. "It's true," he said roughly. "Thinking how I never should have thrown you out my room the way I did, that night at the Grammercy. The more I get to know you, the more I've hated myself for doing that."

"Please don't hate yourself."

"Figure of speech. But it was a dumb move on my part. I panicked."

"Why? What did I do?"

"Nothing," he replied with a laugh. "I just didn't want you to think I was, you know, on the make. That I'd planned for that, for Lola to do that to you so I could get you up to my room."

"I never once thought that. I wasn't sure any of it was happening, to be honest. It was only a matter of time before I woke up from the dream."

"What dream?"

"Meeting you. Harlan..." And to say his name was still incredible, still impossible, when Ben owed him so much. "Don't you understand how important your book was to me? It was like you'd taken my thoughts right out of my brain and laid them in front of me in black and white. I couldn't get away from them. I was angry with you for so long."

"Angry? For writing a book?"

"For writing *that* book. It overwhelmed me. I couldn't hide from myself, you get me? Even though I had to keep lying to everyone around me. It was the worst kind of secret, knowing that I wasn't what they thought I was, that no matter what the world expected from me, there was never going to be a pretty little wife and white picket fence in my future. It felt like there were landmines all around, and my next wrong step was going to be my last."

"I'm sorry," Harlan murmured. "Sorry to put you through that."

"Don't be sorry. I needed it. Needed to accept the truth about myself. You showed me that I wasn't alone. That somewhere out there, men like me were proud of who they were, proud of who they loved. Otherwise what hope did I have of being loved by anyone?"

Too much, he'd said too much and now he was crying. "Sorry," he sniffled, rubbing his eyes with the back of his hand.

"Don't worry about it," Harlan said softly. "You needed to get that off your chest."

"How much of *Land* is true? Are you—" He caught himself as Harlan stiffened, his flat expression snuffing out the hopeful spark of Ben's curiosity.

"Am I Bull?" Harlan supplied roughly after too long a silence. "Does it make a difference if I am?"

Ben couldn't reply, his throat pinching closed, his mind mired in impossibilities. Some writer he was, to be capable of such shameless prose yet not be able to find a single word in answer. A simple yes or no, but nothing about this was simple. Not from the moment they'd met. Longer, since Ben had first read Harlan's book and found in it a map that had lead him to himself.

And yet it was Harlan who buckled first, exhaling hard as he pushed his fingers through his hair. "Of course I'm not Bull," he said tiredly. "He's stronger than I'll ever be. Strong enough to do things I never could. And if he blew it, well...he was expendable, you get me? I could hurt him, put him through hell, even kill him, and he wouldn't feel it one bit, because he was never real."

He met Ben's gaze again and smiled, and everything was easy and good again, the knot in Ben's chest easing as Harlan chuckled wryly. "Don't mind me," he said. "I'm just jawing, I don't mean anything by it. But listen, I've got someone I want you to meet. The cousin of a friend of mine is a lawyer. He's offered to let us pick his brain."

"About what?"

Harlan's smile widened, his eyes glinting. "About whether or not Geist's filth has any redeeming social value."

Cousins

Harlan's friends were due any minute. When Ben heard the door open, he stepped smartly out to greet them. Stopped short as he recognized the gentleman with the broad, creased brow and curling hair who was looking about at the stacks of boxes.

Breathless, voiceless, Ben leapt back into his office, colliding with Harlan as he flung the door shut and threw himself against the back of it. "Him...he...out there...him..."

"What's gotten into you?" Harlan asked with a frown as he rubbed his shoulder.

A strangled squeal escaped Ben's throat. "Norman fucking Mailer is in my front room. Right now. Here. At this very moment!"

"I told you I had friends coming."

"Yeah, but you didn't tell me who! You didn't tell me that you're friends with Norman fucking Mailer!" Fighting a wave of nauseating terror, Ben clapped his hands over his mouth, sucking air through his whistling nose.

"I guess I take him for granted," Harlan said with a

guilty blush. "He's harmless, I swear."

Ben took a last deep breath then unsealed his mouth. "I'm sure he is, but don't you think you ought to have warned me? And more to the point, where exactly is he meant to sit?" He gestured at the palisade of book boxes lining every wall of what was already a crowded room. "You and I barely fit in here, and you said he was bringing his cousin."

"Let's see what he wants to do."

Ben gestured to the door. "After you."

Harlan eyed him briefly then nodded. "I'll give you a minute, how about?"

Ben replied with a tight smile then closed the door behind Harlan and leaned against it once more. Norman *The-Naked-And-The-Dead* Mailer, and Ben had to go out there and talk to him without acting like an awestruck peasant groveling at the foot of a king. And Harlan blithe as a bee, surprised by Ben's quite reasonable anxieties.

He wobbled to the desk and fumbled a breath mint out of the tin. The sharp flavor burning the inside of his nose, he leaned against the desk and counted down from one hundred, breathing deeply as his shoulders relaxed and feeling came back to his face. If Harlan wasn't ashamed of bringing one of America's greatest living authors to this sleazy rat-hole, then neither was Ben.

He hoped. He only had to make himself believe it for one meeting. Then he could go back to his rightful state of anonymity. If this was what fame felt like, maybe it was better that he not go seeking it. Quietly regretting that he'd given Joan back all her Valium, he wiped his sweating palms on his creased trousers then left his grubby sanctuary.

Harlan took care of introductions, bless him, while Ben grinned and nodded and shook hands with Mailer and his cousin Charles Rembar, a more slightly built man with lively eyes and a clear, strong voice that sounded made for court. Harlan solved the seating problem too, by suggesting they go for lunch.

Trailing behind the trio as they strode down the sidewalk in animated conversation, Ben tried—and failed—not to add up the cost of the other men's clothing and weigh it against his own living expenses. Rembar's shoes were two week's rent on Ben's tenement. Mailer's coat was worth meals for a month. Harlan's haircut alone could have kept Ben alive for days, so he swallowed their proverbial dust and kept a bland smile plastered on his face as they lead him to The Algonquin. Of all places. Another dream coming true, and him completely unprepared, though the Circle had long disbanded and the odds of him encountering a wisecracking Dorothy Parker were slim.

"Don't worry about the bill," Harlan murmured as they crossed the polished lobby. "I'll cover this."

"You can't keep paying for—"

"Don't even start," Harlan said with a chuckle, steering Ben towards the restaurant with a hand between his shoulder blades. "This is a business expense. We're here to do business."

"Right," Ben squeaked, the heat of Harlan's touch radiating down his spine. "Business."

The start of the meeting passed in a blur. His lips tingling from the scalding coffee, Ben tried to focus on the other men's conversation about people he didn't know and places he'd never go, his attention drawn again and again by their rarefied surroundings as he watched the mirrored walls for familiar faces, as if Joan, Lola, anyone might pop out from behind a column and ruin the moment. Make Ben out to be a fool, or rather reveal the fool that he was to two of the most valuable connections he'd ever make.

His ears pricked up on hearing the name *Roth*. Joan had read the jargon-laden public record of Roth's trial and assured Ben that nothing had changed, which wasn't much of a comfort given that he was risking arrest every time he licked a stamp. Since 1873 the so-called Comstock Law had been used to impede anything and everything with the slightest whiff of sexual content, from plain old contraception to 'European' novels to full-frontal stroke mags, trapping the self-proclaimed land of the free in a prurient Dark Ages where your private business was everyone's business. And Ben was caught in the nexus, his livelihood dependent on skirting the postmaster's notice, his personal life hanging on even greater secrecy.

"It's a shame what's happened to Mr. Roth," Rembar was saying. "His conviction notwithstanding, he's doing publishers like our Mr. Quirke here a favor. Between his verdict and whatever happens to Ferlinghetti et al on the west coast, we're finally approaching a benchmark, a legal definition of obscenity."

"How does that help anyone?" Ben ventured to ask as the others nodded sagely.

"Because up until now, it's been assumed," Rembar replied easily. "Obscenity is whatever the plaintiff says it is. Any statement that pushes up against their tolerance for anti-social behavior."

"If obscenity is that which offends, I know a few people who'd call the US constitution the dirtiest rag they've ever read," Mailer said, earning even Ben's laughter.

"You're not wrong," Rembar replied. "It seems to me that one could argue that if a book has some kind of social value, some artistic or analytical merit, like your hot potato," he said, nodding to Harlan, "then any so-called prurient content is not for the purpose of merely titillating the reader but of expressing some artistic intention of the writer. Sex and death are part of the human condition, right? Art needs to be able to talk about these things if it's to have any meaning in our society."

"The world as we know it is about to change," Mailer said knowingly.

"The world of books, maybe," Rembar said with a laugh.

"To me, that is the world," Mailer retorted.

"Again, your point isn't far off," Rembar continued. "Roth's decision could be used to settle all manner of arguments about the social value of art, and more specifically art that happens to have so-called deviant content. Like your books, Mr. Quirke."

"Calling them art is perhaps a stretch," Ben replied carefully as they all turned to him. "I have no intention but to entertain."

"But if we're talking specifically of Geist, then I'd argue the work does have social value," Harlan said. "There's merit in it even if strictly from a historical perspective."

"I'm in agreement with you there," Rembar said to him. "And it's precisely that lever I'd employ in this situation as your defense. It's an historic artefact, in a sense. A little lewd—"

"A little?" Ben blurted.

"But that's a matter of individual taste," Rembar went

on smoothly while Harlan laughed behind his hand. "We as a society need to leave space for dissent in the marketplace of ideas. The majority can't be counted on as the sole determinant of social value."

"In other words, most people don't know what's good for them?" Harlan said, his eyes flashing.

"Your words, not mine," Rembar answered with a laugh.

The talk turned to other books, other names. Ben sipped his coffee and listened as best he could, but he was glad when the party broke up and they left the restaurant.

"So what's up with you?" Harlan said, nudging Ben's toe with his own as the other men's cab pulled away from the curb.

"Nothing's up."

"You seemed real quiet in there."

"I had nothing to say." Even if he did, he'd had no reason to say it. What he thought was irrelevant. He was the front, the patsy that was going to bear the risk. Attract the eyes of the world in the name of printing a book so grotesque he himself wouldn't use for house-training a dog.

Harlan kept pace with him all the way back to the office. Melody had gone home long ago, and as Ben struggled with the rattling lock he thought of asking Harlan to go away. He needed time to think. Distance from the magnetic force of Harlan's attention that held Ben so helplessly fixated.

He said nothing, not even as he fetched the whiskey and a pair of chipped glasses from the filing cabinet. He poured them both a shot and they toasted each other in silence. Wheezing, Harlan set down his empty glass with a thunk.

"Sorry if I threw you in at the deep end," he said hoarsely

as he settled on the corner of Ben's desk. "But I think Chuck has it all figured out, if we ever have to go to trial."

"His sort of argument doesn't do me much good. I haven't published a book with redeeming social value since...ever. Oh God, I'm going to go to jail, aren't I?" Ben groaned, resting his head in his hands.

"Not on my watch," Harlan said firmly.

"You can't guarantee that."

"Isn't that a risk you're already taking?"

"Yes, but..." Ben flopped back in his chair with a sigh. "Guest is famous. Everyone's going to be talking about this book. And I still don't know that I'm the right man for the job."

"Hey, don't worry," Harlan said, getting to his feet. He came around the desk and set his hands on Ben's shoulders from behind. "Everything's going to work out," he soothed, squeezing the cords of Ben's rigid muscles. "I'm not going to let you go down for this. I'll fight 'em every step of the way."

Ben wanted to believe him. Wanted to trust Harlan with everything he had. Wanted this touch to go on and on as Harlan's firm, warm fingers worked into the knotted muscles of Ben's neck. He ought to say something, ought to press for more details, make Harlan sign something, prove his bona fides, swear an oath. Instead he sat in silence and tried not to drool or flinch as little bolts of sensation sparked along his spine.

"You're stiff as a board," Harlan grunted. "I'll introduce you to my guy, down at the steam baths. Writing can take a toll on the body, you know?"

"Mmm-hmmm... I mean...okay..."

Harlan chuckled, his hands stilling on Ben's shoulders.

"Look, I'm sorry if I've come off a little pushy," he said.

"A little?" Ben said with a snort. Before he could apologize Harlan laughed again, then came around to lean on the near corner of the desk.

"The navy will do that do you. I got used to having people do what I tell them. You can't stop to apologize for hurt feelings when you're in the middle of a fire-fight."

"Except that this isn't a fire-fight. This is life."

He gazed at Ben, his lips thin with indecision. Then he sighed. "I know. I'm just making excuses. And I really am sorry for pushing you around."

"Why didn't you warn me about Mailer?"

"You want the truth?" he said. grimacing. "I was worried you'd get cold feet."

"Because of how I act around you?"

"More or less."

"Sure, Mailer's a big deal but he didn't change my life."

"That was all my fault, huh?" Harlan said with a laugh.

"Always will be."

Truth

Ben poured them each another shot, though they took their time drinking it. Watching Harlan swirling the dregs of liquor in his glass, Ben prepared to ask the question that had pestered him for days. Every time he'd thought of Geist's manuscript, which felt less like a book and more like a monster, a slimy presence lurking beneath the surface.

"Harl...why do you really want to publish Geist's book?"

Harlan barely looked his way. "Why wouldn't I publish it?"

"Sure, it's interesting as an artefact, but as a book it's kind of..."

"Weird as hell?"

"That's putting it mildly. I don't know that it'll even sell."

"I don't care if it sells. I just want it out there."

"But why?"

"Does it matter?"

He nearly said no, but that was a lie. Ben's business—his

freedom—was at stake, in a way that Harlan's wasn't. "You're asking me to make myself liable. Lots of people do time for obscenity, you know."

"That's not going to happen," Harlan said firmly.

"That's not exactly up to you, is it?" Ben said as Harlan downed the rest of his drink. "I need to know why this matters so much to you. A book like this could destroy Geist's reputation."

"He'd deserve it," he rasped.

"For abandoning your grandmother?"

Harlan didn't answer. Ben waited, despite his urge to apologize for even asking. Geist's book was a ticking bomb, a liability, threatening them both.

"He knew she'd had a child by him," Harlan said at length, though he still couldn't meet Ben's gaze. "His only child, as far as we know. So you'd think he might have done something to help instead of leaving his only family to lie our way out of the country. The prick took off to Sweden in '28, stayed there until he came to the States after the war. His own daughter..." His voice had risen and he caught himself, let out a ragged sigh. "So I don't give a shit what happens to his reputation. If it pisses some people off, so be it. No one's ever done me any favours."

"Are you sure, Mr New York Times best-seller?"

He rolled his eyes. "Yeah, great, I'm renowned author Harlan Avens. Who still has to hide who he is and what he does." He gestured at Ben, who chose to look past being called a *what*.

"The truth has always been there for those who know to look."

"The truth?" He laughed, not his usual easy chuckle but a harsh spit of breath. "The truth is, everyone's saying I've peaked. That *No Man's Land* was it, I've got nothing else to say."

"That's not true!"

"Tell that to my agent. Tell that to all the acquisition editors who won't touch my new book with a ten foot pole."

"They're fools."

"Fools with money, and not the kind they're parted from in any kind of hurry, if you get me. Publishing is a rigged game, Benny, and it's stacked against us, even though it wouldn't exist without us. Imagine if all the writers went on strike? They'd come crawling back. What's a publishing company without books?" He raised his glass, setting it down hard when he saw it was empty, then lurched to his feet and wandered to the grimy window.

"So what have I got to lose?" he murmured, his gaze distant. "If no one gives a damn what I do, then why shouldn't I do what I want?"

And then he smiled at Ben and it was like he had come into focus. "And right now, what I want is to see if the big, shiny reputation of the legendary Alver Guest can survive his dirty book."

"That's a pretty big *if.*"

"Only one way to find out. If Guest's famous lost book gets banned, then we know where America stands. If it makes it, we'll have changed the rules for everyone. But don't worry, I'm not letting you take the fall."

Words, they were only words, even if they were what Ben wanted to hear. Harlan had fame, and lawyers, and money, but he was only one man. A gay Jewish author, three of the lowest forms of life in today's United States. Unless these words were a lie and Ben was a sucker.

"Hell of a view you got," Harlan murmured, gazing out the window again. As hopeless a view as you could want: a steel fire escape, a soot-stained brick wall, a gray sliver of sky. The murky shadows hollowed Harlan's cheeks and darkened his eyes, reminding Ben for one horrifying moment of those emaciated wretches he'd had to nurse after the troops had liberated that village, and those had been the civilians.

That could have been Harlan, if his family had stayed in Europe. Brave, bold, perfect Harlan: a skeletal corpse in dingy striped pajamas...

"How old were you when you came to the States?" Ben asked before the thought overwhelmed him.

"Eleven," Harlan replied said dully, his eyes distant. "My parents told me we were going on holiday. Except we never went back. I had money in every pocket. In my suitcase, my cap. You better believe we spent every mark. Thank God my folks saw it coming, got out while we were still allowed to travel. Though anyone could have seen it coming, if only they'd been looking. A hell of a thing, watching your nation turn against you. Not that this one was any easier on us. Land of the free, my ass."

Again Ben's mind supplied the imagery, substituting Harlan for all the Jewish kids he'd seen get kicked around school and the playground and streets, feeling his mother's restraining hand on his shoulder, hearing her quiet reminder to stay out of the bigger boys' way, not make them turn on him next. Justice thwarted was justice denied, and before the unfairness of everything in the world crushed him into the dirt, he poured two more shots of whiskey and brought them to the window.

"You and me are one and the same, you know?" Harlan

said, swirling his glass as he gazed out the window. "The minute the US got its thumb out of its ass and joined the war, I was first in line at the recruitment office. I picked the Navy because I wanted to kill Nazis, but I sure as hell didn't want to be on the ground in Europe and have to look 'em in the eye to do it. Any one of those guys could have been, well, someone I used to know, right? I didn't want to ever question what I was doing. Just load, aim, fire, repeat."

He turned to Ben with a ghost of his gorgeous smile on his lips and tears in his eyes. "And there you were in the thick of it," he said. "Putting your life on the line, doing good instead of harm. They gave me a medal. I should give it to you."

They touched their glasses in a wordless toast, the liquor (which was not as top shelf as Ben remembered) stinging his lips and making him cough.

"Don't die on me, Benny," Harlan chuckled as he rubbed between Ben's shoulderblades. "I only just found you."

This set him coughing again, the notion that Harlan had wanted to find him. Had wanted him to be the one to take on this challenge. If Harlan Avens trusted him, who was he to argue?

"God, I'm a fool," he wheezed as Harlan took his glass from his limp hand and set it on the filing cabinet

"That makes two of us."

"Us and how many others. All of that destruction, and what did we even gain?"

"We stopped a madman," Harlan replied, and Ben was fool enough to ignore the edge in his voice.

"But what good did that really do?"

"Are you trying to say the world was supposed to sit back and let that happen?" Harlan barked, his eyes suddenly blazing. "Innocent people murdered by the tens of thousands—"

"Sorry, sorry! And you're right. But...when she was still a young girl, my mother lost every male member of her family save her infant brother to the so-called war to end them all, only so we could go back and do it all over again twenty years later. Except worse, and uglier, and—"

"And it worked, and it's over."

"It's not. It's not over. Trust me, we haven't learned a thing. It only took a generation for us to forget. Another twenty, thirty years, what's to say our kids aren't getting shipped off to fight, I dunno, Khrushchev or the Saudis or Mao? Whoever starts tearing the world apart next."

"God, it makes me so angry," Harlan spat through his teeth, a rage blazing in him to match the sickening sorrow in Ben, his fists clenched but nothing to punch. "Makes *me* want to tear something apart."

His eyes wild, he grabbed Ben by the shirt. For a terrifying second Ben thought he planned to hurt him. Punch him or choke him or throw him out the window.

Instead he kissed him.

The Kiss

Deep in the cracked vault of Ben Quirke's memories, his teenaged self was fucking into his own hand and picturing this very moment. The moment was now and Ben was done for, no will to resist, no matter how crazed it was to let Harlan go on kissing him.

And what a kiss, like the answer to every question ever asked lay in the feel of Ben's mouth under Harlan's, which was crazy in itself because Ben was taller. Or he had been, before his hero, his idol had pinned him against the rough wall of his office to kiss him even harder.

Harlan wanted his mouth, wanted more than his tongue between Ben's lips, and Ben was ready to deliver. Yet it was Harlan with his hands inside Ben's pants, Harlan dropping to his knees as Ben dug his nails into the fiberboard wall and hung on for dear life, too stunned to speak, and then too lost.

Was there anything this man couldn't do with excellence? Whatever relief or pleasure Harlan was getting from this, Ben prayed it equaled his as Harlan's mouth embraced him. Yes, that was the word, a hot, strong, all-encompassing sensation. It felt like caring. It felt like…

"Mother of Christ, that's good."

Harlan laughed, his mouth full of Ben's cock. Then he sucked. Ben bit his hand to keep from shouting, wanting this to last forever, knowing that it couldn't.

Harlan chose that moment to look up, his lips pink and wet and stretched around Ben's shaft, his hands holding him in place. Looked up and fucking winked at him, the smart-ass. Something in Ben snapped, a last link in the chain that had held him hypnotized by Harlan's fame, his strength, his sureness in everything he did. Beyond all that was Harlan the man: on his knees, his mouth there for the taking.

"Suck me," Ben gasped. "Make me come." A command, a prayer, or just desperation? One and the same as Harlan took him deep. Deeper still, a complete possession, but which of them was the one possessed? The man on his knees with a cock in his mouth, or the man overcome, who was biting his own hand to keep from shouting the other's name as the orgasm blew him away…

Echoes of his climax sparking through his limbs, he clung to the wall as Harlan got to his feet. "Why did you do that?" Ben slurred.

"Because I wanted to," Harlan answered, dusting his knees. "And you needed it."

Ben waited for him to step back, turn away, regret what he'd done. Instead he moved nearer, wrapping an arm around Ben's waist, touching his face. A soft touch full of dangerous promise, those lean fingers stroking over Ben's cheek, his jaw, tilting back his head as he traced his thumb across Ben's parted lips.

"Come home with me," he said, such an unlikely thing

to hear that Ben almost refused.

"Why?" he managed to ask.

Harlan gave him that look, that laughing frown that made Ben's insides tingle. "Are you kidding me?" he said with a chuckle in his throat.

"No, I mean...why do you want *me*?" Out of all the men he might be tempting, all the places he could be, why was Harlan Avens in this dirty room doing dirty things with an inky-fingered pornographer not fit to tie his shoes?

"Benny," Harlan purred, brushing his thumb again over Ben's cheek, the dimple of his chin. "If I have to stop to tell you all the reasons I want you, I'll never get to have you."

He leaned near to kiss him but Ben held him back with a hand on his chest. "Harlan, please. You're...you're too much. Don't you understand what you mean to me? I *worshiped* you. I feel like I know you. I can't resist you. I don't want to but even if I did, I couldn't. And if this is going to be the only time you want me, then...oh God, who am I kidding, I'd do it anyway."

"You don't owe me."

"That's not what this is. That's the thing, I don't know what this is. I don't want it to end, but I'm terrified."

"I know, Ben. I'm scared too."

"So what good is there in it for us?"

"More good than we're going to get anywhere else. Ben, I haven't stopped thinking about you since that first night, when I booted you out like the jerk I am. That killed me to do, but I couldn't let you stay, couldn't do all I wanted to do with you, after what you'd told me. It was too much."

"Right? It's too much."

"Impossible."

"A really bad idea."

That sort of silence fell again, overlaid by the beat of Harlan's heart against Ben's hand, a beat that matched the pounding of his own heart, the roar of blood through his veins, the song in his soul.

"How far is it?" Ben heard himself ask. "Where you wanted to take me?"

"About ten minutes uptown."

"You better not screw me around."

"I would never," Harlan answered, his eyes wide.

"Then tell me: what am I to you?"

Everything to lose, but it wouldn't be the first time Ben had lost everything. Why couldn't he just let it happen, let his dreams come true? How could a man so committedly lewd be so stupidly principled?

"I get it, Ben," Harlan said. "This came out of nowhere. But if I wasn't who I am, if I was just..."

"Hermann Metzger?" Ben offered.

Grinning, Harlan rested his head against Ben's shoulder for a heartbeat. "Crazy, right?" he said, raising his head again to meet Ben's eye. "But if I was? Would it change how you feel?"

Was it just his name, his fame? Or was it the man himself affecting him so strongly, making Ben want him? How could he not want this man, with that sideways smile, those fine fingers, that passion, that bravery, in war and in daring to tell the stories he told?

"No. Yes. I don't know," Ben added truthfully. "There's too much to think about. And you're still not answering my question. You know how I feel, and if you don't you haven't been paying attention. You're my hero, Harlan. The most beautiful man I've ever laid eyes on, and the reason I know who I am. So tell me: who am I to you?"

"You're Ben Quirke," he replied, like that meant anything, but he was just so handsome when he smiled that way that Ben couldn't help but believe that it did, that he really did mean something to this man he barely knew who had somehow saved his life. "Benjamin Quirke, the writer. The publisher. A hero on and off the battlefield, even if you're a bit of a martyr. A man dedicated to his causes. And probably too damn good for me. But I can't resist you. And I don't want to."

They kissed again, and it was just as good as the first, Harlan's hands in Ben's hair, Harlan's body against his, pinning him in place, taking him over. Anything Harlan asked, he'd do. Not just now but—

At the peal of a police siren from the street below Harlan broke from their kiss, leaving Ben sagging against the wall. "That's our cue to leave," he said, tucking his shirt back in. "Pull yourself together, Quirke, and that's an order."

The sun had now set and the city was electric, a synergy of light and sound and color: the subway's distant thunder beneath their feet, bolts of neon arcing overhead and changing Harlan's face with every step. Ben had to keep looking at him, wanting every memory of this night to be seared into his brain, disbelieving that any of it was real.

Yet there he was, the man of Ben's dreams, in every sense possible; striding along beside him with a wicked glint in his eye and a grin he couldn't keep off his charming face. In his camelhair coat and fedora he might have been a movie star, leading the young ingénue into a dangerous encounter. Ben being the ingénue, about to be ruthlessly exploited.

He hoped.

He kept waiting for Harlan to hail a cab, and nearly kept on walking when instead he turned up the steps of a clean-looking brownstone just off Lexington. Unlike Ben's clapped-out tenement, this had all its glass round the door and a lamp with a pretty green shade hanging in the foyer instead of a burnt bulb. The strip of thick gray carpet lining the stairs muted their footsteps as they climbed to the third storey. At the apartment door Harlan had to try the key a few times.

"This isn't my place," he said as he turned the key over and tried again. "My friend's away for a few weeks and—got it!" He opened the door then stood back. "After you."

"And you're sure your friend won't mind you bringing—holy mother..."

What remained of the apartment's interior walls had to be there for structural integrity. All the rest were gone, leaving an open space the size of a small cathedral. Low furniture lurking in the heavy shadows, city lights twinkling through the unobstructed windows. Dazzled by the sight, the night, Ben startled at Harlan's touch on his arm.

"I said I'm fine! I mean...oh God."

"It's okay," Harlan said as he took Ben's hands. "You're with me. Nothing's gonna happen."

"I want to believe you."

"Then do. That's the thing with belief. It's a choice. If you want to, you can."

And maybe it really was that simple. A matter of choice, a decision to be who you needed to be, at least in the moment. "I do. I believe you."

"Then come to bed."

Ben nodded, and Harlan smiled, and Ben believed with all his might that the smile was just for him.

Methods

Harlan was intense. He commanded Ben's attention. At every turning point he asked, is this what you want? And Ben said yes, and yes, and yes, as Harlan undressed him, kissed him, stroked him, sucked him to the edge of orgasm then left him there. Then took him over, Ben biting his knuckles raw, his whole body singing, his heart...

He'd think about that later, when thinking was back on the table. When he wasn't face down under Harlan, both of them naked, Harlan's impeccable, Vaseline-smeared cock wedged in the crack of Ben's arse.

"Tell me, Benny," he purred, his fingers woven through Ben's, pressing his hands into the mattress, his breath hot in Ben's ear. "Is this what you want?"

"You can't tell?"

"Oh, I can tell. I want to hear you say it. That's part of the fun, isn't it? Giving in? Letting me have my way?"

"Yes."

"Then give me what I want. Tell me how you want me."

"I...can't."

Harlan nipped at his neck and he moaned, pushing his

hips up to show how much he wanted this, how totally he'd surrendered. Not enough for Harlan, who chuckled darkly as he kneed Ben's thighs further apart.

"I'm gonna keep asking, Benny. Because if there's a way to drive you wild, I want to know. I don't just want to fuck you. I want to *own* you. So tell me how you want it: like this, me holding you down, you sucking mattress? On your knees so I can get deep? Against the wall like the hot piece of ass you are?"

"All of it!"

"Cheater."

"I mean it. Please, Harlan. I'm all yours." Of course he was, for this was everything he'd ever wanted, more than he knew how to resist. And underneath it all, like the ticking of a bomb, the sense that this was the most dangerous thing he'd ever done.

Not that he'd let that stop him. He'd been hurtling towards this conclusion since they met, Harlan's morals the only reason it hadn't happened until now. Ben had surrendered long ago. It was time for Harlan to collect.

"You mean it? You're mine?"

"Yes."

"Then tell me what you want, you cheating son of a bitch." He was laughing, the self-important prick, and Ben didn't give one damn.

"Please, Harlan," he gasped, the other man's hot weight crushing the words from his lungs. "Fuck me. Like this. Right now. Or so help me God, I'll—ohhh..."

At last, at last, impossibly, a dream beyond, as Harlan wound his hips against Ben's backside, teasing him open inch by maddening inch. He'd never had it so good, never this luxury of time, a soft bed, a man who thought of him as anything more than a piece of tail. Never craved the penetration so ferociously, arching his back to receive, trembling with the effort.

Swearing to himself, Harlan released Ben's hands, rising on his arms, moving in waves. Still so slow, taking Ben apart bit by bit, until he was close to sobbing, longing for more, too far gone to ask. Suddenly Harlan rolled off him, leaving him shivering as cold air replaced hot skin.

"What's up?" he said as Harlan stretched out beside him.

"You," Harlan said with a sleazy grin. He pointed to his cock, rising up from his dark curls. "On me. I want to see your face, Benny. I want to know what I'm doing to you."

"But I...that is...oh God."

"What's wrong?" Harlan asked, his smile fading.

"Nothing. Except I've never tried that. I mean, doing it like that. I mean—" With all his paleness and softness and scars on display, his naked want. "I mean that don't meet a lot of well-off men with midtown apartments and great big beds, you know? Or at least none they've invited me to. It's been a while since I've gotten any action, really. And most of that was pretty rough. I don't want to let you down."

"Baby...Benny, come here." Sitting up, Harlan beckoned him near. "You could never let me down," he said, softly touching Ben's cheek. "We'll do whatever you want. We don't even have to screw—"

"Like hell we don't. Lie down. I'll figure it out as I go."

It was simple enough. Gravity did most of the work. All Ben had to do was let it happen, let himself believe that it was possible and relax into the moment, as inch by inch he took Harlan's gorgeous cock.

A thing he'd never dreamed of, in all the dreams he'd

had, all the ways he'd imagined letting this very thing happen, with this man. In his dreams it was always pitch black, it was luck, it was over in seconds. Not this endless opening, this churchlike room, this sea of rainbow stars beyond. Not Harlan the one who surrendered, gasping under Ben, whispering his name, and he held his breath to hear him.

"Please, Ben...let me fuck you. Please...I can't wait another minute."

"Yes. Now."

His hands tight on Ben's thighs, Harlan began to rock his hips, a slow pumping that screwed his cock even deeper. A feeling like nothing before, pain and pleasure spiking through him, chasing each other up his spine and down again. As if everything he'd done before went under the heading of 'fooling around' and this was the first time he'd been fucked.

"Ben...look at me."

And he did, opened his eyes and looked as Harlan broke from his slow, steady rocking to thrust up into him hard. The way Ben needed to be fucked. He didn't need this tenderness, Harlan's whispers, his questions. He needed a cock, deep inside, and he needed the owner to use it with intent.

"Come on, then. Let's have it."

"Benny, you little tease," Harlan said with a devilish smile. "Are you holding out on me?"

"I think you're the one holding out."

"We'll fix that."

And by *fix* he meant fuck, hard, deep, and unrelenting, making Ben match him thrust for thrust by his grip on his thighs, his sheer strength. Too much, it was all too much, as against all odds, against even his own will, Ben came yet again, biting his arm to keep from crying Harlan's name, though Harlan couldn't keep from shouting his as he followed.

His head swimming, unbothered by the smear of semen against his front, Ben flopped forward onto Harlan, who put his arms around him and kissed his forehead.

"Never doubt my methods again."

BEN WOKE THE NEXT morning to the sound of turning pages. The huge room was painfully bright. Groaning, he pulled a spare pillow over his head. He was used to his dark office and apartment, both of whose windows faced walls. This was like waking inside a lightbulb, the sunrise beaming directly through the uncurtained windows and into Ben's eyes when he at last sat up.

"Doing okay?" Harlan asked from a hazy distance.

"I don't know yet," he croaked. "Ask me after coffee."

In the bathroom he ignored the complicated old shower fixture with its multiple spouts and enameled taps in favor of swabbing the bare necessities with a damp cloth then thieving a pinch of Harlan's tooth powder. The light of day revealed the furniture in the apartment: a low, squarely built chesterfield in white leather that was probably even more expensive than it looked, and a round dining table with a set of wheeled chairs that fit cleverly under the edge. Aside from the bed, the bathroom, and the open galley kitchen which took up one wall, everything else was art.

The architect might have left a few more walls up, then they could have spread the pictures around. All by the same artist, whose style seemed to consist of taking two colored shapes and smashing them into each other, then painting the result. Visually exciting if not very meaningful, but fine art generally went right over his head. Too bad, for the prices you could get for it.

Shivering, overly aware of his untanned legs poking out from under his shirt, he wrapped himself in a blanket and toddled to the table, where Harlan sat in his shorts and a t-shirt, piles of pages from Geist's book spread around him, a legal pad by his elbow. Seeing Ben, he grinned and set aside the page he was reading. "How about that coffee?"

"I'll grab something on the way to work. I need to go home first."

"Why, what do you need?"

"A shower. A shave."

"Can't you do that here?"

"Yes, but then I'd have to put my dirty clothes back on, and don't you dare offer to lend me anything of yours," he added as Harlan opened his mouth to do exactly that. "That's too weird."

"Maybe a little," he laughed. "I'll see you soon enough, anyway."

"You will?"

"We gotta keep moving on this," he said, gesturing to the pages splayed across the table. "I've already started dropping hints."

"More hints? About a secret that can't leave my office?"

"You leave that part to me. Hey, what's wrong?" Harlan

asked, his smile fading as Ben fumbled his way into another of the wheeled chairs. More plans that didn't include him. Like Joan and her damned contract.

"The thing is," he started, wishing he'd rehearsed this in any way. "I really, really respect you, Harlan. Your writing, your whole career, it's been an inspiration to me, ever since I first read *No Man's Land*. I owe you more than you'll ever understand."

"But..." Harlan said warily, gesturing for Ben to continue.

"But we really should think about putting this whole publishing deal in writing, don't you think?"

Harlan fell back with a sigh, laying his hand on his heart. "God, Benny, don't scare me like that."

"What did you think I was going to say?"

"Never mind."

"Please, you have to tell me."

Blushing (Harlan Avens blushing! because of him!) he rubbed the back of his neck. "I was a little worried that you might regret last night," he said gruffly. "That you might not want to see me again after that."

"Oh God, no. I mean I do. Want to see you again, that is. Last night was..." *The greatest night of my life. My every fantasy come true. Too meaningful to say aloud.* "Really, really good."

"Good to know. Because I don't want that to be the only time I get to have you."

"Okay. Wait, you can't mean now," Ben murmured, heat blooming inside him as Harlan settled back, spreading his legs to make his erection more obvious.

"Why? You got somewhere you need to be?"

"I just told you. Joan will be expecting us any time."

Harlan glanced at his watch lying beside the yellow legal pad. "Nothing's going to happen until we get there, am I right?"

"Technically, but..." Words failed him as Harlan lurched from his chair to stand in front of him, palming himself through his shorts, his other hand threading through Ben's hair

"What was it I told you about doubting me?" he said, tipping Ben's head back to look him in the eye.

"I'm sorry."

He smiled, and his smile was a miracle. "You're forgiven. Come back to bed, Benny."

"Yes." Yes to everything.

BEN FLOATED HOMEWARD ON winged feet, not caring that anyone who saw him could likely tell from his glassy eyes and relentless grin that he'd just got lucky.

He wasn't used to getting what he wanted. It was usually the first sign that things were about to go wrong. He slowed, fighting an urge to turn around and go back to Harlan. He was several blocks away by now, and as he glanced behind him he realized he had no idea what street he'd come from. Meaning he still had not one clue how to get in touch with Harlan.

No address, no business card, nothing. As if he was keeping Ben at arm's length, not letting get too familiar.

But Harlan would never do that. He wasn't that sort of man. Ben had to hope, for he hardly knew him. Knew his first book back to front, his later books less well, the man not at all. Harlan had thought of him for months, and only thought to find him when he wanted to use Ben's connections. Use him as jail cover, putting everything in Ben's name so his own hands stayed clean.

Something struck his shoulder—a lamppost, for he'd been walking in a daze, lost in his paranoia. Imagining the worst of Harlan when he'd been nothing short of wonderful. Yet why would Harlan butter him up—why take him to bed, indict them both for lewd conduct—if all he wanted was Ben's name on the letterhead?

If Harlan had meant what he said, that he'd been thinking of Ben for months, that it had killed him to make him leave the night they met, why had he waited so long to make a move on him? Why grab Ben like that, like he'd not even wanted to? Unless the words were the lie, a cover for his bad behaviour. Men did bad things when too full of emotion. Ben had done a few himself, when it had seemed harder to not do them. Been cruel, deceitful, shallow, vain. Lied to someone he'd gone to bed with to make them feel better about him never seeing them again.

Ben was a softie, and maybe a martyr, but he wasn't going to let himself get taken for a ride. If, against his sure belief, Harlan screwed him over, he'd find a way to even the score.

Contractual Obligations

BY THE TIME HE reached his street, his mood had sunk to somewhere in the region of his ankles. Dragging his feet up the bare, splintering stairs of the tenement, he began to wonder why he'd bothered coming home. Maybe he ought to swallow his pride and admit how poor he was. Pull on Harlan's heartstrings and beg him to be his sugar daddy. Joan would be happy to have one less expense to explain away to her own daddy.

He went through the motions of washing and dressing, then left again before he could give into his fatigue. Melody was already at the office, poring over a page, a red pen behind each ear.

"Joan called," she said as he passed.

"At this hour?"

"If she calls again, can I say that you're in?"

"Of course. Though she's got a sixth sense, I wouldn't be surprised if she…" They turned as one towards the door at the hammer of her heels on the uncarpeted stairs. As

Melody began patting her rumpled hair into place Ben retreated to his desk. Part of him wanted to tell Joan that he'd scored, but he wouldn't betray Harlan's trust like that. It was none of her business.

She arrived moments later, dressed to dominate in a tailored blue pinstriped suit that covered her to the neck but managed to still bare most of her bountiful cleavage through a Joan Collins-esque cutaway. She paused in his doorway to inspect him, then closed the door behind her and advanced on him, hand on hip.

"So who's the lucky fella?" she asked, pursing her scarlet lips.

"Who said anything about a fella?"

She snorted a laugh. "You don't need to say it, honey, I can read you like a book. Looks like you had a run in with Count Dracula."

He touched his neck, wincing as he prodded the bruises Harlan's kisses had left. "Has it ever occurred to you that I might want to keep some things to myself?"

She snorted again, propping her rump on the edge of his desk. "Since when? You sing like a canary every time the slightest good thing happens to you. So dish."

"No."

"Is it that writer guy Harlan Avens?"

"Jesus, Joan!"

"Bullseye!" she crowed as he covered his face. "Got it in one."

"Sometimes I do mean it when I say I hate you," he said from behind his hands.

"So? Everyone hates me. Is that why you lied to me?"

"When did I lie to you?"

"You told me he wasn't your boyfriend."

"He's not. Or at least he wasn't at the time. I don't know if he is now. But how did you know?"

"Lucky guess. Plus a couple things Mel said last night."

"Last night? Where were you last night that you saw Ms. Masterson?"

"Nowhere special," she said, pulling out a gold compact from her sleek handbag.

"Joan..."

"Okay so we might have gone out to grab a bite to eat. And maybe we did some other stuff afterwards." She was blushing underneath her powder as she inspected her immaculate lipstick in the mirror, turning her head this way and that, preening like he'd seen her do when expecting one of her boy-toys to make an appearance at some function.

"Joan, did you...I can't believe I'm asking, but did you sleep with my secretary? Goddammit, Joan!" he cried as she grimaced. "You're an investor. That's like your father screwing someone from the mailroom!"

"Oh yeah?" she shot back, snapping her compact shut. "Explain to me how it's any different from what you're doing, Mr. Balling Your Meal Ticket, and I don't mean me."

"Oh God, you're right," he breathed as the crushing truth descended on him. He'd finally made something of himself then gone and stuck his prick in the middle of it, put his professional life on the line for a screw. Never mind that Harlan had kissed him first. Ben had let him do it, right here in this office. Let him kiss him and—

"Joan, I'm such a sap."

"Never mind, Benny," she said gently. "I'm just glad someone's treating you right. He is treating you right, ain't he?"

He nodded, because so far it was the truth. Every moment with Harlan was like a dream come true, a fairytale romance.

"Then we got no problem," Joan said with a smoothly villainous smile that must have been devastating from the head of a conference table. "Now, how's about you and me agree to not mind each other's personal life, and then you give Mr. Big Shot a ding-a-ling and tell him to haul his butt in here. We got i's to dot and t's to cross. While we wait, you can tell me all about how you landed him."

"What is he, a fish?"

"You bet. He's a Moby-has-a-great-big—"

"Jesus wept, Joan! You're a lady, you might act like one."

"And you're a great big shmuck."

She had it out of him in the end—the CIA could be so lucky to have her as an interrogator—though he kept mum on the more intimate details. He was describing their night on Broadway when they heard the front door open. Joan gave Ben a stagey wink then threw open his office door.

"Mr. Avens. How good of you to join us. You and me and Mr. Quirke got some business to attend to."

"Sure thing. Just give me a minute with our Mr. Quirke."

"You bet. I'll keep Ms. Masterson company. You don't mind, do you, doll?"

Whether Melody minded, Ben never learned, as Harlan strode into the office, grinning hugely, and shut the door behind him. Part of Ben wanted to leap up and meet him with a kiss. The other part of him wasn't wholly sure that Harlan would kiss him back. He'd been snubbed by lovers in the past, even in private, so he stayed seated until Harlan dropped his briefcase on the desk then grabbed Ben's hand and pulled him from his chair and straight into his arms. Kissed him hard, and a lot, until the ground disappeared from under Ben's feet, leaving him clinging to Harlan's shoulders.

"Did you miss me like I missed you?" Harlan murmured as he turned his attention to the soft place below Ben's ear.

"You sure do ask a lot of questions."

Harlan laughed, his lips buzzing against Ben's skin, making it that much harder to answer. Or think, or stay upright, as he dissolved into Harlan's embrace, letting himself be held like he hadn't been in years. Maybe ever, because this wasn't his mother's quick, fierce hug but something else, full bodied and unrestrained. A lover's touch, and he bit his tongue to keep from breaking down in tears. Not now, not when everything about this moment was more perfect than the real world had any right to be.

Perhaps Harlan sensed his fragility, as he planted a last kiss on the curve of Ben's neck then raised his head to look him in the eye.

"I mean it, Benny," he said, his voice rough with feeling. "I didn't land that kiss on you out of nowhere. That was something I'd wanted for weeks. Months, even. Since I watched you walk down that hotel corridor, wishing you'd turn around so I could tell you to come back."

"You could have stopped me. One word and I'd have come running."

"Still, I'm glad that I gave you the chance to get to know me. So you could tell me to hit the road if you thought I was a creep."

"Never. You're a lot of things, but not that." Harlan was

brave, and noble, and strong, everything Ben wished he was. And yet he'd chosen Ben, out of all the world. They kissed again, Ben's backside tingling as the blood shot to his nether regions. A helpless moan escaped his throat, and Harlan shoved himself away with a husky laugh.

"How about I owe you one?" he panted, glancing at the door.

"Okay. Sure. Yes. Sorry." Stopping to unsnare his shrinking hard-on from his shorts, Ben went to the door and eased it open, but the women were nowhere to be seen. "Hang on, where's my secretary?"

Harlan appeared at his elbow. He pointed at the broom closet. "In there, if I had to guess."

"Why would she be in there?"

"Because you left her alone with that Joan for ten minutes and nature took its course?"

As if in answer, the door sneezed. Or someone behind it, who then stifled a giggle while someone else hushed her.

"Oh God! I can't let them—"

"Relax," Harlan said, catching Ben's arm as he lunged for the closet. "Waiting one more minute isn't going to make or break us. It gives us just enough time for this."

This being another lingering kiss. Or two or three, but who was counting? Ben was feeling much better by the time the women joined them, Joan grinning triumphantly, Melody pink in the face, her clothes even more disheveled than usual. Yet the women had managed before their shenanigans to type up a comprehensive literary service contract between two independent entities. This was about the point in Joan's explanation where Ben's brain shut down. Not that he didn't have contracts with his writers, but those were simple licensing agreements. He and Harlan were involved at a deeper level. They were working together.

At this point he was running out of dreams to have come true. Short of penning a serious novel that won a serious prize, what was left for him to achieve now that he'd met, slept with, and become professionally connected to the biggest influence of his literary life? How about not screw it up, but what were the odds of that?

"I'm a little embarrassed that we never got around to this," Harlan said as Melody took the penciled-in contract out to her desk to retype.

"Well, we did kind of skip that part of the meeting."

"Skipped it a few times, sounds like," Joan said, prodding Harlan with her elbow.

"I couldn't help myself," he said, grinning. "I'm crazy for the kid."

"You don't say."

"Anyway, Joan," Ben said, his voice skittering across three octaves. "Thanks for your help. I literally could not do it without you."

"Aww, you'd find a way, Benny. This kid saved my life, Harl. He's a keeper, he is. And don't you forget it." She went out to check on Melody's progress, closing the door gently.

"Is that true?" Harlan asked, his face full of worry. "You saved her life?"

"I don't know that I'd go that far. I was in the alley behind the Stork Club one night and these two bruisers burst out the back door with this girl between them, kicking and hissing like a wildcat. They didn't notice me, so I clocked the one with a trash can. When I turned around, she'd sucker-punched the other guy in the neck. She grabbed me and we high-tailed it, back through the club and out the front door. And that's how we met."

"What is she, an heiress or something?"

"Worth millions."

"Huh. So she comes by that honestly, does she?"

"Comes by what? Oh, right. Yes, she knows her worth."

"And likes everyone else to know too. But she clearly cares about you. You're lucky to have a friend like that."

"Believe me, I know." He'd only had to save her the once. She'd saved him every day since.

Problematic

JOAN WAS ALL FOR spending the rest of the day at Nom Wah, but Ben declined, in no mood for eating dumplings and drinking rice wine and watching women flirt when he could be getting laid.

"I'm going to have to go out of town for another few weeks," Harlan told him as the women's taxi pulled away.

"When do you leave?"

"Tomorrow."

"And when were you planning to tell me?"

"I only found out today. So will you come home with me? One more night?"

"Yes."

"Taxi!"

Yet despite his eagerness, once inside the apartment Harlan seemed reluctant, carefully hanging his coat and hat before taking Ben's hand, drawing him near, kissing him tenderly.

"I've been waiting to do that for a while," he murmured.

"Do it again."

And he did, stronger, hungrier, threading his fingers

through Ben's hair, his other arm tight around Ben's waist, but when Ben reached between them to find Harlan's belt buckle he stepped back.

"We'll take it slow tonight, how about?"

"Whatever you want."

Ben followed him across the big bare room to the chesterfield and the low bench to one side of it, which turned out when Harlan opened the top to be a stereo console, with a turntable in one end and a liquor cabinet in the other.

"Doubt we'll find anything you like," Harlan said, flipping through the small stack of records standing in the middle cabinet. "Jerry's a true believer in the Church of Coltrane."

"It doesn't matter. I don't mind the quiet."

"Then can I offer you a drink?"

"Nope."

"Then what mmfpph—"

For once Ben used his height, leaning into Harlan and making him arch to meet him. God, he was so good to kiss, tasting of skin and sex, his lithe fingers dancing over Ben's cheeks, tugging at his hair.

"And here I was worried I was coming on too strong," Harlan panted as Ben began kissing his way down his neck.

"No such thing."

"Good to know."

So much for equality, as Harlan grabbed him by the hair and pulled... Damn, had he been a SEAL? One clever move and Ben was on his knees. Not quite, for he'd fallen forward over the arm of the chesterfield, but when he went to stand up Harlan put his hand on the back of Ben's neck.

"Where do you think you're going?"

"I thought we were taking it slow," Ben slurred, his cheek sticking to the white leather upholstery, his cock crushed against the broad arm of the couch, his every nerve alive with wanting.

"That was before you jumped me."

Harlan took him right there, bent over the white leather couch with his pants around his ankles. Made him work for it, anointing him with petroleum jelly then teasing him with the tip of his cock until Ben was shaking, almost sobbing, winding his hips to entice, giving it everything he had. And Harlan took it all, took him deep, his nails digging into Ben's hips as he held him steady. Ben pushed back, arched, wanting him deeper, his own cock riding against the smooth leather, slickened by his pre-cum and feeling too much like skin.

Too much, it was always too much, being with Harlan. Being his, and Ben choked back his shout as he came, spurting over the arm of the sofa and probably the seat. Owned.

"I don't want to stop," Harlan gasped as he held Ben trembling against him.

"Don't stop."

"But you—"

"I said don't stop. Fuck me like you mean it."

"You filthy little—" He bit off the last word with a snarl as he thrust. Again, with such force that Ben's feet left the ground. Too, too much, his arse burning, legs shaking, Harlan's fierce need too wild, too much like danger. Too much for even Harlan, who spilled into him with a hoarse shout that ended on a groan.

"Will you come to bed?" Harlan asked once they'd untangled. And he was such a sweetheart he still worried Ben might say no, his face full of fear.

"You should know you don't need to ask anymore," Ben said as he kicked off his shoes, socks, pants, and jocks in one. "But isn't your friend going to care that I...you know, on the sofa..."

Harlan glanced at the white-on-white stains, shrugged. "That thing's seen worse."

"It has?"

"Now come to bed, you gorgeous thing. I'm not nearly done with you."

"You don't have to keep saying that either," Ben said as Harlan took his hand to lead him to the bed.

"Saying what?"

"You know what."

"That you're gorgeous? But it's true,"

"At least admit you're exaggerating."

"Come on, you gotta like something about yourself. Be honest, if those weren't your legs, you'd think they were spectacular."

"Fine. I like my ankles."

"So do I," Harlan said, waggling his eyebrows. "They're attached to your legs, and at the top of your legs is—"

"Let go of that," Ben said through his teeth.

"No." Harlan gave Ben's cock a gentle squeeze.

"Harlan..."

"Fine. I just don't get it, how a man as...augh, I don't know what to call you. Fuckable? I don't know how you can be so in denial that someone finds you attractive."

"Someone like you, maybe."

"I thought we were past that nonsense."

"Will we ever be?"

Harlan's eyes had cooled. "That's up to you. You're the one with the problem."

The problem being Harlan was more man than Ben knew what to do with. The problem being Ben. "I don't mean your name. But admit it, you're out of my league. You'd be a knock-out no matter what."

"A knock-out?"

"Sure. With those hands, those smoky eyes. And when you smile it's like the sun came out."

He was doing it now, though trying not to, and was he blushing? "You better cut that out," he grunted, grasping Ben's hips to pull him nearer.

"Why, you can't take a dose of your own medicine?"

The heat was back, in his eyes, in the low growl in the back of his throat. "You smart-alecky son of a gun, Quirke."

"Suck it, Metzger."

"Oh, you are in so much trouble."

Someone had trained this man to fight. He spun Ben around, twisting his arm behind him to frog march him the last few steps to the bed. Here he pushed him down, but Ben was looking to get pushed and didn't struggle, even when Harlan dragged him into the middle of the mattress then rolled him onto his front and straddled him, facing his feet.

"I'm sure it's a lovely view," Ben said with a mouthful of mattress, "but the mechanics aren't going to—ow!

"Quiet, you," Harlan said with a dark laugh as he smacked Ben's rump a second time. "You want to know what I like about you? Other than all of you. This. This sexy little dimple on the back of your leg."

Holding Ben's ankles against the bed to keep from getting kicked, Harlan bent down and licked the back of Ben's right knee, a soft, wet, intolerable sensation, tracing the shape of his tendons and muscles. He did it again to the left, then began to work his way up, licking, sometimes biting the backs of Ben's trembling legs until he reached the rise of his ass.

"Should I keep going?" he asked, and Ben said yes, and yes, and yes.

And yet as midnight came around Ben decided to go home. Saying goodbye now saved him the anguish of doing it tomorrow, when he'd had all night to lie awake and worry about...everything. Whether Harlan would still care about him when he got back. Whether Harlan's book was worth the risk they were both taking. Whether Ben would be better off never having met this man, so he didn't have so many things to worry about.

Harlan insisted on calling him a cab then getting dressed to come downstairs and wait with him. Their farewell was an awkward handshake on the sidewalk and Ben holding his breath to keep from bursting into tears. By the time he got home he was numb, and it took him a few tries to unlock his door. Cursing under his breath, he staggered inside and shut the door then leaned against it, blinking in the harsh light of the unshaded bulb overhead.

Though he was sure Joan would put him up if he asked, his pride depended on this unglamorous little room. The only place that felt like his, and he'd done what he could to make it so, plastering the worst of the cracks and hanging scrounged movie posters over the rest. He and Mr. Erwin had wrestled the iron bedframe up the tenement stairs. He'd repainted it a preposterous shade of violet, which needed touching up. Some things couldn't be fixed, like the closet, which only stayed shut if you wedged a bottle cap between the door and frame and which he therefore never used.

It hung open. A prickle of fear creeping across his scalp, he made a circuit of the apartment, touching nothing. His mattress had been pulled away from the wall slightly, the edge of the carpet rippled like someone had looked under it. Whoever had been here had left behind the only thing worth stealing, for his typewriter still sat on the desk. Meaning they hadn't been looking for money.

His head swimming, he sank down on the edge of the bed. Sprang up again, because wasn't it evidence? As if it mattered, as if the police would even care that someone jimmied a lock in a tenement and scrounged around for...what? Geist's manuscript? He'd stopped bringing it home weeks ago, superstitious of its smarmy contents infecting his dreams. Or had Spiro come looking for his first edition Avens? Sure, the old guy was venal but he was hardly a crook.

Tired beyond words, Ben dragged his chair to the front door to wedge it under the doorknob then laid down fully dressed atop the bedspread. Panicked for ten minutes straight. Got up and went to call Joan.

Criminal Intent

FOR ALL HER NIGHTCLUBBING and socializing, Joan always seemed to be home when he needed her the most. He babbled at her in bursts, in between searching the foggy darkness around the phone booth for whoever was persecuting him, from g-men looking to suppress Geist's book to forgotten creditors to the everyday threats of muggers, pickpockets, and whoever else did harm under cover of night.

"But you say your front door wasn't jimmied or nothing?" Joan asked once he'd described the break-in.

"It didn't seem to be. You don't believe me, do you?"

She sighed, fabric rustling as she rolled over, for Joan took all phone calls in bed, day or night. "A turned up corner on the rug and a door that you have to fight to keep close being open is, well, pretty circumstantial as far as evidence goes. I've seen that door open on its own more than once."

"Then I really am cracking up."

"I wouldn't go that far. You're a little jumpy, sure. But that's you all over."

"This is different, though. This might be for real. That book I'm working on...it's not an ordinary book."

"I guessed that. Otherwise Mr. Fancy Pants wouldn't have gotten involved."

"It's not that he's involved, he's *it*. He brought it to me and asked *me* to help *him*, and I couldn't say no, I just couldn't. But I had no idea what was going to be involved."

"That's on you, I'm afraid."

"You're the one who wrote up the contract! I'm not cut out for this sort of thing, espionage and sneaking around and Norman fucking Mailer. Now I'm stuck with him. Oh God, I don't mean that."

He paused to catch his breath, wiping his sweaty steam off the phone booth glass with his sleeve. "I don't know what to do, Joan. I'm positive that I'm in love with him, but I'm starting to hate that damned book. And I think he does really like me, but how long can that last? Even if I do let him do whatever he wants with me. He's got me wrapped around his little finger. Oh God, I let him fuck me on a chesterfield!"

"Hey! Snap out of it, you," Joan barked, popping his panicky bubble. He took a deep, shaky breath, another, clinging to the receiver as he waited for her to finish lighting her next cigarette.

"Benny, are you okay?" she said with a tired sigh, and he could just picture the smoke fanning from her painted lips. "Do you need me to come and get you?"

"No. I mean...no." No more charity, no more deflections, no more dodging his fate. "It's fine. I'm fine. I'll be fine."

"Be careful, baby. Don't break my heart, okay?"

"What do you mean, break *your* heart?"

"Sure, we'll never be an item, but I got a lot of love for you, alright? You're the brother I always wanted."

"You have two brothers."

"Yeah, and they're bigoted dummies with horrible wives, and their big sister is sick of their shit. You, you're something special. I don't want you getting hurt."

"I don't want that either."

"So I'll ask you again: do you need my help?"

"No. Or at least not yet."

"You let me know when you do."

"I will, and Joan, I love—"

"*To continue this call, please deposit ten cents.*"

More money than he had, and he let the line go dead. Joan would understand. She was the only one who did.

It was something like two in the morning and the thought of returning to his apartment made his skin crawl. His last and only safety had been violated, and he didn't even know by whom. He abandoned the phone booth when a police cruiser rolled past. He knew hustlers who worked out of booths round Washington Square, and he didn't need the fuzz presuming he was one of them. Head down, mind ablur, he walked several blocks before he noticed he was close to the office.

Any port in a storm, but once in the foyer he stood for several minutes gazing at the stairs, his feet too heavy to lift, his heart as well. Why was he doing this? Why any of this, working himself to the bone for a meager wage that barely kept him alive, pouring every resource into a business that could be taken from him at any moment at the whim of an eager bureaucrat. Killing himself to write smarmy stroke books for hypocrites, for he knew enough about addresses to know how wealthy some of his mail order customers were. The same men who voted for increased police presence, for anti-obscenity statutes, for harsher sentencing for every sort of deviant. Ben's whole life was a crime and soon enough he'd be made to pay.

Any port in a storm, but as he set his foot on the first stair he heard a metallic clunk from above. He stood like this for several seconds, waiting for the sound to repeat, unable to will himself to take the next step. When it remained silent he started up, hardly breathing, straining to hear the intruder over his galloping heart.

At the last turn of the stairs he paused. They'd be able to see him through the open railings, and he lowered himself to a crouch, crawling up the last few steps on hands and knees in hopes of catching a glimpse of them before he was spotted.

A glimpse of nothing. Had they heard him and split? Were they hiding on that last flight of stairs? Was he simply losing his marbles, jumping at his own shadow? Any of these were equally possible. If someone was up there, they knew he was here. Would be waiting for him, silently in the darkness. Nonsense, no one was there, but it still took all his nerve to creep past the black, echoing void of the staircase to the upper floor.

At his door he hesitated, wondering if the intruders had left fingerprints. Then realized the futility of doing anything about it. Leaden with exhaustion, he hunted up and down the hall but found no sign of trespassing. No footsteps in the dust on the unused stairs, no sound behind any door. Only the doors themselves, clattering on their hinges with every gust of wind that swept down the alley.

In his office he tried several impossible poses in his two chairs before thinking to drag Mel's in to prop up his legs. Curled on the miserably hard seats, shivering in his street clothes, he pressed his eyes shut and thought about Harlan until sleep finally took him.

He woke with a flinch and a groan. Every part of him ached, inside and out, his head thumping with pain. No, the thumping was a sound and it was coming from the door. His watch had stopped, and with the scant light from the alley he had no sense of the time as he dragged himself to his feet and stumbled to see why Mel hadn't brought her key.

Opening the door, his question died on his tongue. Two youngish, pink-faced men in cloth coats and very shiny shoes stood shoulder to shoulder, one of them gripping a manila folder to his chest.

"Can I help you?" Ben rasped, wishing he'd rifled Mel's desk for a breath mint as the two men leaned slightly back.

"We were told we'd find a Mr. Quirke here," the squarer of them said. "Are you he?"

"Who's asking?"

They leaned further back, exchanging a quick look. "My name is Girt, sir, Augustine Girt, and this is my associate Mr. Elmore Lerner. We're charter members of the Alver Guest Historical Society and we wanted to speak with

Mr. Quirke regarding an artefact he may have come into contact with."

"Artefact? Wasn't Guest a writer?"

"Then you're aware of his work?"

"He's known to me, yes. Look, I'm afraid Mr. Quirke isn't available at the moment. I can take your number and have him give you a call." The lie fell from his lips like he'd planned it. Whatever the Guest people wanted, he wanted nothing to do with it. Not without Harlan beside him. Harlan, whose damned book this was. And Ben was Harlan's fool.

The Party

When Ben was at work, he worried about the apartment. When home, he worried about the office. After
three sleepless nights he bought a cot from the army sur-
plus and moved into the office, ducking out in the mornings to shower at the YMCA once Melody had arrived. Just
until Harlan came back, an indefinite deadline that might
be as soon as tomorrow or sometime next year.

Ben only thought about it late at night, when the streets
and the offices around him were empty. The dark and
quiet room, the stiff, too-short bed, the longing: an echo
of other nights long ago. The hostel in Portsmouth after
demob as he waited for the steamer back to New York.
The barracks that first night at Fort Meade. The cabin
at sleep-away camp in Montauk, paid for by one of his
mother's boyfriends the summer he was twelve. They'd
broken up by the time he got home.

The days were easier to fill. With the volume of submissions he could afford to be choosy, and the results
were starting to show in his invoices as sales began to tick
upwards. Better writing made readers come back, though

he was careful to avoid anything too clever, sticking with his reliable themes of spicy spinsters and ray-gun toting supermen.

So easy to stay busy that he let that be the reason he ignored Geist's book. Ben had never thought of himself as squeamish. He'd sawn off men's legs while shells soared overhead. He'd taken women to bed, just in case he liked it. Geist's book had made him feel like he was doing both at the same time. Every now and then, he got up to be sure the drawer where he kept it was locked. Paranoia, pure and simple, and maybe a bit of withdrawal from Joan's pharmacopeia. He'd be better when Harlan came back.

THREE WEEKS LATER, A letter arrived. Not much of a letter, written on a piece of hotel notepaper and terse as a telegram: *back Thursday must see you*. Five words: infinite hope, and Ben begged Joan to take him out that night, to save him from wearing a hole in the floorboards pacing. Waiting. Hoping that *must see you* meant *must kiss you, hold you, fuck you*.

The address at the bottom of Harlan's letter led him to the same brownstone off Lexington. Finally, a link to Harlan's life, and Ben's heart was jumping out of his chest as he pressed the button on the panel by the front door. A man was exiting the building and Ben stepped aside for him, catching the door with his foot as it fell closed.

He slipped inside and started up the stairs, too close to the prize to wait. As he started up the second flight Harlan appeared at the railing above.

"Hey, who let in this low-life?" he said with that gorgeous grin.

"Suck it, Metzger."

"I missed you too, Benny." He came down a few steps and met Ben on the landing, and it took everything Ben had not to grab him and kiss him. Harlan too, his hand trembling in Ben's as they shook. "Thanks for coming."

"Are you kidding me? Like I'd say no to you."

"I'm going to hold you to that later."

"God, I hope so."

Laughing together, they hurried upstairs. They'd start with a kiss, right there in the entry. Then Ben was going to turn the tables, be the one to push Harlan against the wall, get down on his knees and...

"What's going on?" he said as Harlan opened the door, because the apartment was full of people. People Ben had never met, standing around in twos and threes with drinks in their hands and beautiful clothes.

"It's called a party," Harlan said, ushering him inside. "I hear they're all the rage."

"That's not what I meant."

"I know. I wish I could get you alone, show you how much I missed you." He stroked his bent finger softly over Ben's cheek, a tender gesture of unmissable intent. "Hey, it's cool," he said as Ben jerked his head away.

"It most certainly is not cool. I don't know these people from a hole in the ground."

"No one's gonna snitch, Ben. You're among friends."

"Still, I wish you'd told me I was going to be meeting

people. I look like hell."

"You look fine. You look great. God, I missed you."

"I missed you too."

"Good." In one quick move he kissed his fingertips then pressed his hand against Ben's chest. "We won't stay long, I promise. Come on, I'll introduce you to the guy who lives here."

"But what am I supposed to say?" Ben whispered as Harlan steered him towards a gaunt man with gangly limbs and a face that was half freckles who was loitering by the liquor cabinet.

"About what?"

"About me. They'll want to know what I do for a living."

"Tell them the truth. You're a writer, we met at a club in the village, you love shrimp toast—"

"Screw you."

"That's the plan." He waggled his dark eyebrows, his grin fading when Ben didn't respond. "Are you really that uncomfortable? We don't have to stay."

"I don't want to take you away from your friends."

"I'd like it if they became your friends too."

"Me? I can't swing with this sort of crowd. Where everyone's beautiful and they all went to college and guys like me do their laundry."

"Trust me, Benny, none of them started off any smarter or hipper than you or me. Abbie, I've known since middle school. Darla grew up on a turkey farm in Wisconsin. And who am I? Some schmuck from Rockaway Beach who's too embarrassed to use his real name."

"You're not a...schmuck."

"Tell that to my mother."

And then it was too late, Abbie was looming over them, shaking Ben's sweating hand. "A pleasure to meet you," he made himself say. "It's a nice place you've got."

Abbie shrugged. "It's rent controlled, so it's got that going for it."

"Abbie's who painted all these," Harlan said, nodding to the canvases on the distant walls.

"You've got quite a visual imagination," Ben said, hoping he sounded informed.

"Did them when I was fresh outta school. You want one?"

"You don't mean that."

Abbie shrugged again, his bony shoulders nearly reaching his ears. "What do I care? I got another twenty, thirty in storage. I hate them."

"Then why did you hang them up?"

"To remind me I ain't shit," Abbie said in the same heavy monotone. "So many of these young artists think their first work is their best. I don't want to lose sight of how far I've got left to go."

"Spite can be powerful motivation. I mean it," Ben said as Abbie looked at him cock-eyed. "If you want to make a pearl, you start by irritating an oyster, right?"

Abbie blinked at him then laughed, a flat *ha* followed by a little snort. "Hey, Groucho, this kid's alright," he said to Harlan, who had turned to speak with someone else.

"Groucho?"

In reply Harlan waggled his dark eyebrows, miming a cigar between his fingers and winning a round of laughter.

"C'mon, kid," Abbie said, clapping a cadaverous hand on Ben's shoulder. "I'll find you something to drink. What's your name again?"

Abbie made him a whiskey sour then introduced him round as a friend of Harlan's. Most guests asked him if he wrote as well. He always said yes, then immediately asked what they did, to avoid explaining *what* he wrote. Some were poets, some wrote short stories. A middle aged white woman with sun-parched skin and a flowing green robe was a *chronicler of the human condition*. The Wisconsin turkey farmer's daughter Darla was a printmaker and had just finished a showing of linocuts of Manhattan alley-ways. All high-brow stuff of the sort Joan loved and Ben found tedious, but letting people talk about their art kept them from asking him questions as he drifted from group to group making extremely small talk, trying not to finish his drink too quickly, though his mouth was painfully dry. He was however a stranger, and too many conversations were about people he didn't know.

Wandering the margins, he stopped to look at one of Abbie's paintings. Technically, it was the work of a master draughtsman, the lines razor-sharp, the paint filling the angular shapes in smooth, flat planes that suddenly collid-ed in a melting, merging Dali-esque concrescence. Stimu-lating the eye then offering nothing, and he was glad Abbie felt the way he did. Ben had a similar indifference to some of his own creations. Books he'd written then forgotten completely, some of which were still his best sellers. In that Life interview, Harlan claimed to have written *No Man's Land* in two weeks then lost it under his bed for a year. Sometimes genius struck like lightning. Sometimes like a thief.

Across the room, Harlan was in his element, smiling as he raised his glass to toast one of his friends. Ben didn't have an element. He had Joan, and his business, and belief. Tired of feeling conspicuous, he faced the cringing inevitable and went to sit on the sofa where Harlan had fucked him. One end was occupied by a glamourous Black woman in a silver lamé dress. She had kicked off her shoes and tucked her legs under her full skirt, leaning an elbow on the back of the sofa.

"I hear you're a writer too," she said as Ben gingerly lowered himself onto the pearly leather. "Is that how you know Harl?"

"No, that was an accident. We were at a jazz club."

"Oh yeah? Which one?"

"I don't know."

"Well, who was playing?"

"No idea. I don't like jazz."

Frowning, she sat upright. "Then why were you there?"

"I was out with someone."

"I get it," she said as she reclined again. "And you ditched your poor sucker of a date for old Harl."

"Oh, it wasn't a date. Joan's just a friend. And she ditched me first, if we're counting." He was babbling, letting his nerves get the better of him, and he relaxed his grip on his empty glass. "Sorry. I didn't expect you to be here. Or anyone. I'm going to get another drink."

Burning under her cool gaze, he slithered off the sofa. Half a dozen people were standing around the liquor cabinet so he went the other way, leaving his glass on the round dining table. Harlan was talking to Darla, the broad-armed farmer's daughter, and her trim little husband Jerome, who hailed from Mexico. Chalk and cheese, but then who knew what made two people click? It sure didn't make any sense, what he and Harlan had. Whatever it was, and he wasn't about to be the one to rock the boat by asking.

Laughing at something Darla had said, Harlan glanced at Ben. He said something to his friends then started towards Ben, bee-lining straight across the room. Ben looked around but either no one noticed or no one cared. No one cared. Trusting Harlan, believing him, Ben stayed put when Harlan touched his arm.

"How you holding up?"

"I just told your friend Eleanor I don't like jazz."

"So what? Neither does she. You ready to split?"

"Now? But you're having fun."

"I'd be having a lot more fun if it was just you and me."

"But your friends—"

He snorted. "Nuts to them. I see them plenty. I didn't miss them like I missed you."

"Don't say things like that."

"Benny, no one here cares what we—"

"I mean that you're going to make me cry, you jack-ass. Now take me home."

He smiled, that pure and perfect smile that felt like summer. "Let's say goodbye to Abbie. The rest of them can figure it out for themselves."

It was later than Ben realized and the sidewalks were empty, thin clouds streaming across the near full moon, a bite to the wind though it was only September.

"I'm sorry for making you leave," he said as they started along Lexington.

"Don't be. Half the reason I invited you was so you wouldn't think all I wanted was to get into your pants."

"I wouldn't mind. If that was all you wanted."

"I'd mind. I want to get to know you, Ben."

"You do?"

"Why, you got a problem with that?"

"No! Of course not. Please. I'd like that."

The cab ride passed in a haze of suspended desire. Harlan was staying at a smaller hotel, and gave Ben the key and sent him up to the room first so the desk clerk didn't see them together. It was an ordinary room, clean and badly decorated—pea green carpet, banana-yellow drapes. There was no sign it even belonged to Harlan, the bed untouched, nothing on the nightstand or the bathroom shelf. Like that night in Albany, when Ben's easy pick-up had turned out to be a con by the motel manager to extort dumb clucks like him.

Except this was Harlan. He believed Harlan, whose bags were probably in the closet. He wasn't going to look, didn't need to look, trusted Harlan with his life. For no reason at all except he wanted to. But no, he'd been screwed over enough that he'd see it coming. Harlan was pure. He was taking his damn time, and at a soft tapping on the door Ben leapt to answer.

As soon as the door was shut Harlan had him against the wall, his kiss desperate, his hands ferocious. And Ben let go of his fears and grabbed hold of Harlan and kissed him back, just as desperate, just as fierce. Three weeks of living on coffee and paranoia had slimmed him and Harlan's hand slipped easily inside his belt.

"What was that you said about not trying to get in my pants?"

Harlan laughed softly, touching his forehead to Ben's shoulder, and was he blushing? He was too, too much for Ben, too real, too gorgeous as he stroked those fine fingers over Ben's hot cheek, his other hand sliding down to cup his ass.

"I never said I didn't want to, did I? Just that I wanted

more. I want everything, Ben. I want to know what you dream about at night and what you're thinking when you wake up in the morning. I want to know what scares you, what brings you alive. I want to know what makes you happy."

"You do, Harlan. You make me happy."

"I missed you so much."

"I missed you too."

"Come to bed."

"Yes." Yes, and yes, and yes.

The Agent

He woke alone in a plain hotel room. Someone was in the bathroom, and he lay for a panicky few seconds with the blanket pulled up to his nose, trying to remember who. The water shut off then Harlan came out, a towel around his hips.

"Oh, thank God."

"Good morning to you too," Harlan said as he sauntered to the bed. Not even eight in the morning and he was already gorgeous, in a real and honest way, his burnished skin nicked here and there with shrapnel scars, beneath that the lean muscles of a man who took care of himself but didn't make a big deal of it.

"Time to get up," he said with a grin, tugging at the tail of the blanket. "We got things to do."

"We do?"

"We gotta keep working on that book. Unless you brought it with you."

Clamping the blanket under his arms, Ben sat up. "It's at the office. Why don't I go and get it? We can work here." Anything to keep Harlan from seeing how low Ben had sunk.

"Yeah, right," Harlan said with a chuckle. "I'm sure we'll be able to keep our minds on the job with a bed six feet away."

"Speak for your horny self, Metzger."

"I am speaking for myself. Now come on, we'll grab some breakfast on the way."

"I need to go home. Change clothes, maybe shave. Don't offer," he said as Harlan opened his mouth. "Meet me at the office in an hour. You can have me for the rest of the day. I mean...you know what I mean."

The morning rush was over so he hailed the first cab he saw and made it home in record time. He cased the room, but none of his traps had been disturbed: the cello-tape on the drawers and windowpanes, the penny holding the closet shut. He shaved badly, dressed worse, and was out the door with twenty-two minutes to spare.

Twenty-eight minutes later, thanks to missing a train by seconds, he arrived at the office as sweaty as if he'd not even bathed. Harlan was loitering in the hall with a sallow man with slicked hair.

"Sorry I'm late," Ben said, covertly blotting his damp hand against his trousers.

"Don't worry about it," Harlan said with a careless grin as he ushered the man forward. "Rene, this is Ben Quirke. Ben, my agent Rene Conrad." They shook hands, Rene's grip brief and elusive, his face guarded.

Two pairs of eyes boring holes in the back of his head, Ben unlocked the door and let them in. The waiting room felt small and sad without Melody's chipper morning, chief and the tip-tap of her typewriter. As Rene peered around, his fine nostrils twitching, Ben sidled towards his door.

"Give me a second to tidy up," he said. "There's papers everywhere. It looks like hell."

"You don't need to impress me," Harlan said with a grin. "Though I would like a word with you in private."

"You would?"

"Why don't I grab the manuscript for Rene? He can have a flip through while we talk."

"Right." Ben reached behind him and opened the door blind, hoping he could slip through, but Harlan followed him in, then froze.

"Benny..." he breathed, staring about him at the cot and the blankets, the empty cans of beans on the filing cabinet, the stink. "Tell me you're not living here."

"No. Not really," Ben replied as he closed the door. "Just a few nights. I've been so worried that I was having a hard time sleeping at home."

Harlan shook his head. "You can't stay here."

"I'll admit it's not the best situation—"

"It's illegal!" he cried, throwing up his hands. "Did you give up your apartment?"

"Of course not."

"I can't have you living like this. We gotta to find you somewhere better."

"How? I can barely afford the dump I've got."

"Don't you worry about the money."

"Harlan, you can't pay my rent."

"Says who?"

"Says me. It's...weird." Even if he'd daydreamed about this very thing. It was one step from tricking, made him a kept man, which he was too much of already.

"And sleeping here because you're too paranoid to go

home is a sensible alternative?" Hands on his hips, Harlan shook his head again, chewing on his lip like Ben's mother used to do. "No way. You need a decent place to live. Not some flea-bitten rooming house or your damn office but a nice place with a good lock on the door."

And the worst thing was that he was right. How long since Ben had felt safe? When had he last gone to bed without worrying what the night would bring? Last night, as he'd fallen asleep beside Harlan, who was standing before him now expecting him to surrender.

"I'll bleed you dry."

"You won't."

"Do you have any idea how hard it was to find that apartment?"

"Quit making excuses, will you?" Harlan said with a laugh. "It's my money to spend." His fierce expression eased as he took Ben's hand. "I worry about you, Benny. I don't want anything to happen to you. Will you at least think about it?"

"Okay."

"Good. Now, as far as the office goes—"

"Harlan—"

"Quiet, you," he said, giving his hand a squeeze before letting go. "Is it safe to bring someone else in? Lighten your load so we can focus on Geist?"

"I can ask Melody if she knows anyone."

"That's a start. Now you grab the manuscript. I'll take this chair out to the other room."

When they came out Rene was at the window, evidently inspecting the grime around the edges of the panes. Harlan gave Rene the first few pages and they watched him read it, his expression souring like Joan's had the further he got.

He turned the page and grimaced at the next line, then passed the lot back to Harlan. "Is this a joke?" he said, sitting back with one ankle hooked over his knee.

"It's no joke."

"That's a pity."

"I know it's a bit off color," Harlan started.

"Alors, that's putting it mildly." Rene slid a silver cigarette holder from his pocket. "My own tastes aside. Why are you so eager to put your name on such a thing?"

"We could publish under a pen name."

"This is no better," Rene said through a cloud of his own smoke. "Without Harlan Avens or Alver Guest's name on the cover, it's pure pornography. With either of those names, it'll be the talk of the trade. No bookseller will dare. You'll be like lambs to the slaughter."

"Oh God, he's right." Ben leaned forward, covering his face.

"Don't be so dramatic, Rene."

He tsked, waving his cigarette. "And you might try to be pragmatic. Harlan, think. You were just starting to get re-established—"

"Bullshit. I can't sell that book to save my life."

"Yes, yes, no one is biting at the moment, but there are other places to fish. But this..." Eyeing the papers in Harlan's hand, he shuddered. "I wish I'd never seen those words together in one sentence."

"I knew it was too blue," Ben said. He bit his tongue as Harlan shot him a stormy look.

"What if you aren't attached to the deal?" he said to Rene. "We already have a publisher so you don't need to shop it around. There's a good chance it'll flop, so there won't be any money in it for you anyway."

His nostrils quivering, Rene looked back and forth between them and the manuscript. "You realized that you're asking for trouble."

"I'm well aware," Harlan replied.

"And you," Rene said, pointing his cigarette at Ben. "What are your sales like?"

"Climbing steadily. In fact, I've just doubled my workforce."

"Don't worry, Rene," Harlan said firmly. "I've been around, I know how books get made."

Rene stared at him for a long moment, then exhaled heavily. "Please, please don't get yourself arrested."

"I can't promise that," Harlan said with a chuckle.

"Then don't make things worse. If they're going to put you in jail, be sure that it's because of the book and not anything else." Glaring at Harlan, he jerked his head towards Ben, who briefly considered jumping through the window. Was there anyone who couldn't tell?

While Harlan and Rene took care of business, Ben retreated to his sad little office. He had barely started picking up the trash when Harlan came in with the spare chair and a grim face.

"Well, that's that," he said, dropping into the chair. "We're on our own."

"Did Rene quit?"

"Quit, got fired, same difference."

"Harlan—"

"Forget about it," he said with a dismissive wave. "He wasn't getting me deals anyway. Now, how about that breakfast?"

A Slip of the Tongue

BEN SUBMITTED TO BREAKFAST, like he gave in to everything else. Listening with half an ear while the rest of his mind gnawed on the implications, he let Harlan talk about Rene, good and bad. Having never had the luxury of an agent, he had no advice to give, and he wondered if this was how Joan felt on those late night calls as he dumped out his thoughts for her to help him sift through them.

"So you got any other surprises for me?" Harlan asked as they started for the office. "Other than you living at your desk. I feel like we've hardly spoken since I got back."

"That's your fault, dragging me to parties and...all that."

"Next time I'll skip the party, stick to the all that."

"Yes, well, I had a lovely visit from some members of your grandfather's fan club."

"The Alver Guest Historical Society?"

"The very same."

"And?"

"And...I lied. Told them Mr. Quirke wasn't in. It was eight in the morning. I'd had a hell of a night," he explained as Harlan started to laugh. "I wasn't ready to talk to anyone, never mind those two spooks."

"Lerner and Girt? Yeah, they're a treat. I'm starting to think they are the whole Society."

"Do you think they'll come back?"

Harlan sighed, scuffing his heels. "Eventually."

"What am I meant to tell them?"

"Tell them they can talk to me. It has nothing to do with you." A lie, but Ben let it pass. Back at the office, he began sorting through the bills, invoices, catalogs and loose mail that had collected on top of the filing cabinet. Harlan perched on the corner of the desk, flipping through the recently edited pages of Geist's manuscript. At last he dropped the papers on the desk with a sigh.

"Darla's invited us over for dinner tonight," he said.

"Who's *us*?"

"You and me. You remember Darla, don't you? The turkey farmer's daughter."

"I don't know that I can make it," Ben said, an itchy heat creeping across his scalp at the thought of being expected to make small talk with strangers. Even if they were Harlan's friends. If anything that made it worse, made the dinner a trial, Harlan the judge. "I've got loads to do here. Things to catch up on. You know how it is."

"You're not trying to avoid me, are you?"

"Of course not. How could I avoid you? You're right—oh." Right there, pinning him between the cabinet and the wall. "Look, tonight's really no good."

"Then when?" Harlan insisted.

"I don't know."

"That's not good enough."

"I'm sorry, but I don't know else I can say. This is what

it's like being my friend." He gathered an armload of papers then wormed around Harlan to pile them on the desk.

"These people could be good for you," Harlan said, squeezing Ben's shoulder as he began to sort through the heap. "You need to get out of your same old scene, start rubbing elbows with some people worth knowing."

"Because I'm not clever enough to make my own friends?"

Harlan's smile vanished, his hand tensing. "Is that what I said?"

"No."

"Don't go putting words in my mouth." Then he softened. "It's not like I'm asking you to get up on stage. I'm just asking you to dinner."

"That's the thing, though," Ben said, not because he wanted to but because it had to be said. Because Harlan was not just his idol but swiftly becoming his everything, and it felt too much like drowning. "You didn't ask, did you? You just went ahead and made plans then expect me to drop everything and follow orders. I'm sorry but I'm not interested in kissing up to the WASP intelligencia—"

"Hold it right there," Harlan barked. "Those are my friends you're talking about. If you gave them half a chance you'd see how wrong you are."

He'd have no chance at all in a minute, and wasn't that how it always went wrong? With him picking fights, inventing reasons to split up before the other person dumped him. Harlan was playing his part in the drama, shoving his hand through his hair (gorgeous hair, and Ben was going to miss the feel of it) as he blew out an angry breath and stepped back.

"You know what, I'm sorry," he said instead. Not *damn you*, or *what's wrong with your head*, or *I've had it with you*, but *I'm sorry*.

"Why?" Of all the ways Ben might reply, but Harlan just smiled.

"Because you're right, I have been pushing you around. But I would like it if you got to know my friends. You *need* friends, Benny. You'll go nuts trying to get by on your own." He nodded around him at the trash, the grime.

"I've got Joan."

"There's only one of her. What happens when she gets married?"

"She'll never marry."

"She might not have a choice, with her family. And if even if she dies an old maid, she can't be everything you need her to be."

"I've got you," he dared to say, his heart doubling its pace as Harlan smiled and slipped his arm around Ben's waist.

"You sure do," he said softly. "But you could do with a couple more friends."

"I'm sorry to be a burden."

"You're not a burden," he laughed, his laughter shaking Ben, Ben shaken but much less afraid. "The world's not as bad as it seems, you know. Parts of it are, sure. But that means you gotta look harder to find the good. Like you. You're good. Even when you're acting like a stubborn jerk."

"I could say the same about you." And he could, because Harlan was good, so good.

More, he was goodness itself as he laughed then kissed Ben's cheek. "So does that mean I'm forgiven?"

"God yes!"

"Quit calling me that. And don't worry, I'm not going to throw you in at the deep end again. Tonight it'll just be you and me, Darla and Jerome."

The dinner, but if Harlan was vouching, if Harlan was there, how bad could it be? "It'll be hard to be around you and not show how I feel."

"Same here," Harlan said with a guilty smirk (a gorgeous smirk, and it was all for Ben.) "But Darl's no snitch. We've been friends twenty years. The shit she's gone through? Let's just say you and me aren't the only two pansies in Manhattan."

"I'm not a…" Ben's reflex refusal died on his lips. "I'm an idiot, aren't I?"

"Maybe a little, but I still love you."

"Oh. Wow."

A joke. A turn of phrase. Not *love*, not true love. A joke but Harlan wasn't laughing.

"So…" he breathed, his eyes wide, his lips trembling. "About that—"

"Don't explain," Ben gasped. "Just kiss me."

And he did and it was heaven all over again, his strength, his scent, his eager, asking mouth. Asking and Ben answered, sucking Harlan's tongue deep, shivering as Harlan's groan hummed through them both.

Falling into each other, they staggered about the room until Ben collided with the desk. Harlan kept on kissing him until he was half laying on top of him, papers crinkling under Ben's ass. The scrape of the desk legs over the floor woke Harlan, who pulled back enough to look him in the eye.

"I don't care what time it is," he panted. "Come home with me."

"No. I want you now. Right here."

"Ben—"

"Please." He hooked his ankles round Harlan's knees and his arms round his neck, arching off the desk to grind against him.

"But Melody—"

"Fucked Joan in my broom closet. She'll cope."

They kissed again, stronger, hungrier, clawing at each other's clothes, Harlan shivering delightfully when Ben slipped his hand through his open fly. Again as Ben took hold of his shaft.

"Unfair," Harlan groaned, his eyes crossing, his hips moving automatically.

"All's fair in love and war," Ben said with a squeeze.

"I'm going to make you eat those words, Quirke."

With a twitch he jerked his slippery cock out of Ben's grasp, then grabbed him by the thighs and dragged him to the edge of the desk. His backside was suddenly hanging in free space, his trousers slipping off his slimmed hips as Harlan shoved his legs higher. "Is this what you're after?"

"God, yes. There's baby oil in the drawer on the right."

"You dirty little...ah, but it's only ever you in here, isn't it?" Harlan said with that dangerous grin. "All alone at night, pining for me? Biting your arm when you come?"

"How'd you know?"

"I think I'm beginning to figure you out. Won't be long until I've got you wrapped around my little finger."

He already did, owned Ben body and soul, and more with every look, every touch. This touch, Harlan's oiled grip enclosing Ben's aching cock as they kissed again. A touch too good to resist, Harlan's cock sliding beside his, and he wrapped his hand over them both. Moving together, moving as one, joined by their kiss and their hands and what might possibly be love, they came one after the other, swallowing each other's moans.

"That wasn't quite what I wanted," Ben murmured as Harlan hauled him upright.

"I know," Harlan said, taking him in his arms once more. "I'm saving the rest of you for later."

"You are?"

"I want you thinking about me all day. Wondering what I'm going to do to you when I get you home tonight."

"Do we really have to go to that dinner?"

"Afraid so. But don't worry. I'll make it worth your while."

BEN WAS MARKING UP a badly wrinkled section of the manuscript when Melody finally got in, wearing a nicely fitting gray dress and a little black cape that looked suspiciously like one of Joan's. Joan was with her, wearing what she called her penitent's rags—pearl necklace, baby-blue twinset, sensible shoes.

"How's your grandmother?" he asked as she plopped into the other chair, for she only dressed like this to appease her paternal grandmother, who held the purse-strings and made no secret of her expectations.

"If there's a god, on death's door" Joan said dryly, sprawling with her knees apart. "Speaking of, how much longer are you gonna keep this up?" She pointed with her toe at the cot by the wall.

"Don't you start. I had an earful from Harlan already."

"Good, you deserve it. What'd he say?"

"That he wants to find me a new apartment. And he thinks I should hire more help."

"What about me?"

"What about you?"

She cocked her head. "Are you for real?"

"You mean hire *you*? Why? You don't need the money."

"Good, cause you don't have any. But seriously, I got time, I got nothing else to do."

"What about working on your novel?"

"Don't change the subject?" she said through her teeth. Then her smile brightened to its usual impish leer. "Plus, it'll make it easier for me to keep tabs on you, won't it?"

"Oh God."

"See?" she crowed. "It's gonna be swell."

New and Old Friends

WORK KEPT HIS MIND off Joan's looming interference for the rest of the day. That evening he met Harlan at the subway stop in Brooklyn and they walked to Darla and Jerome's, a clean and quiet building on a leafy street. Harlan was about to push the doorbell when he turned to Ben with a strained look.

"You're maybe gonna wonder about Darla," he said. "Wonder if she's who she claims to be."

"I've only met her once, I wouldn't know her from Eve. I don't think I'll notice."

"You might though. So just be cool about it."

"What is she, a lost Romanov?"

"No, dummy," Harlan said with a dry laugh. "She's transsexual."

"Oh. Oh! Really? Wow. I never would have thought...though maybe I...I'll just shut up, how about?" he murmured.

"Now I'm glad I told you in advance,"

"So am I. I'm no good with surprises. I thought you might have noticed that by now."

"I'll take it under advisement," Harlan said, reaching for the doorbell again.

"Me too. I mean, thank you. I mean…Okay, shutting up."

Knowing, it wasn't hard to see in the weight of Darla's jaw, the thickness of her wrists. Every bit of propaganda painted women like her as eroticised deviants but she was simply a woman, wearing a cocktail apron and an updo, passing out canapes to her guests, covering her mouth as she giggled huskily.

Their cozy second storey apartment was worn but comfortable, with ferns hanging in every window, the walls covered with movie posters and postcards and a few pencil sketches of clouds. Darla was farm stock through and through: as tall as Ben, with a spray of freckles across her apple cheeks. She was an easy-going hostess and kept Ben comfortably supplied with whiskey while Jerome cooked the meal and she humiliated Harlan by telling stories of their first years in New York after they'd left the service. Eating cold beans because they hadn't paid the electrical bill; busking with a two-string guitar and a pair of tin buckets for drums so they could earn enough to pay for heat; getting shook down by a pimp because they'd tried it on his corner.

"Couldn't get away with the old routine now," Darla joked, waggling her shoulders and her impressive bosom.

"That's too bad," Harlan said. "You always had great stage presence."

"What do you mean *had*, wise guy?"

"My apologies. Your charm is undiminished, as always."

She saluted him with her cocktail. "And your taste is impeccable. As always." She winked at Ben, who managed not to cough out his mouthful. It was going to take time for him to get used to people knowing things about his love life.

"You know who I haven't seen in a while?" Darla went on, swirling her highball. "That sweet young thing Astrid. You know who I mean, always wears that blue dress, hangs out at Washington Square."

"I'm sure she's doing fine."

"We'd have heard if she wasn't. She'd have had someone's name or number on her, right? Or at least I hope she did."

A name or number in case the cops—or the morgue—needed someone to call. A fine line to tread, a dance with death, for Darla and the other dolls, for Harlan and himself, to simply exist in such a cruel world, where one look, one word was enough to ruin your life.

"It's a jungle out there," Harlan said dryly.

"Forget jungle," Darla said, smoothing her skirt as she stood. "It's trench warfare."

As she left the room to set the table, Harlan took Ben's hand. "Thanks for doing this," he said, bumping his shoulder against Ben's.

"What, sit beside you on a couch?"

"I mean come with me. These people mean a lot to me. So thanks for putting in the effort."

"Anything for you."

Squeezing his hand, Harlan leaned nearer to kiss him on the cheek. Simmering with nervous tension, desperate for relief, Ben turned his head, met Harlan's lips with his own. Froze as behind him someone snorted a laugh.

"Get a room, you two," Darla said, leaning on the doorway. Harlan was laughing too, kissing him and laughing at the same time and was he giving Darla the finger? He was choosing Ben.

They ate squeezed around the tiny table in the kitchen. Ben's experience with Mexican food was confined to late night raids on the local bodega's candy aisle and the smell of the meals cooked by the family who owned it. Every restaurant he'd passed had looked so cheery, so full of friendly life, that he'd never gone in, feeling like an intruder. Jerome's meal looked like a glossy spread in a magazine inviting you to visit the Yucatan, brightly coloured terracotta dishes of rice and beans and vegetables crowded around a platter of shredded roast pork.

"Are you a chef?" Ben asked as they took their seats.

"This?" Jerome replied, as Darla began ladling rice onto his plate. "This isn't anything. Now my mother, she can cook."

"Don't knock yourself, honey," Darla said. "It looks fantastic."

"You always say that."

"Because it's true. Gee, you'd think a fella would take a hint."

After, Ben insisted on washing the dishes while Jerome cleaned the rest of the kitchen. Darla and Harlan returned to the living room, their voices a low hum under the swish of the scrub brush. Jerome was quieter than Darla and went about his work without bothering Ben with small talk or worse, questions.

Then Darla gasped, a wild hiccup of breath. "Oh Lordy!" she cried. "Harl, are you sure you want this in print?"

Jerome threw down the dish towel and hurried for the living room. Ben got there as Darla was handing a clutch of papers to Harlan, both of them red in the face.

"Did you show her the book?" Ben asked. Some secret they were keeping.

"Just a couple of pages," Harlan said quietly.

"A couple too many," Darla said with a shudder. "Ben, have you read this?"

"He had to. He's the one printing it."

Darla wrenched around to give Harlan a look straight from the Book of Joan. "Are you sure you know what you're doing?"

"As much as I ever do."

"Then maybe I need to ask if *you* know what you're doing," she said, turning the look on Ben.

"Don't worry about him," Harlan said quickly. "I've got everything under control. Ben's used to dealing with racy topics."

"This isn't racy, this is..." Glaring at the pages crushed between Harlan's hands she paused, then with a groan sagged against the arm of the sofa. "I guess it's none of my business. As if I could ever keep you from doing what you want. But please, when you get hauled in front of a judge, don't call me as a character witness."

Harlan was quiet on the way back to his hotel. But when Ben touched him he came alive, and their first screw was a desperate clinch against the wall, Harlan's thigh between Ben's, his head on Ben's shoulder, his eyes clenched shut as he worked them together. There was more, and more, and Ben said yes to it all, wanting Harlan to be free. And so he didn't say the other thing, the words whirling round his head and thrumming on his tongue and threatening to bring an end to everything.

Harlan had said it first but there were so many ways

to say it. A jest, a joke, a hyperbole. *I love this crazy kid.* Not love. Not true love, no matter how much this felt like love was meant to feel. This was just sex, just their bodies colliding, just everything Ben had ever dreamed of. He didn't need Harlan's love when he already had so much.

THEY PLAYED AT THIS for two more nights, meeting Abbie at a tea house where he and Harlan traded schoolboy insults over dim sum while Ben felt irrelevant. The next night they stopped in at a cocktail party at Eleonore's, where Ben met two dozen people whose names he immediately forgot. Riding back to the hotel, he found he didn't want to look at Harlan. It was all too much, being so conspicuously *with* him, showing off what he'd always kept so carefully hidden. Not that he'd ever had someone worth showing off. You didn't get attached to a man whose name you didn't know, whose face you'd barely seen before admitting with as few words as possible what you wanted from him.

He didn't know what he wanted from Harlan. What they had couldn't last. What he dreamed of couldn't be. They had only these moments. It was enough.

And though he threw himself into lovemaking, when Harlan had him on his knees, he lost his nerve. "I'm sorry," he sniffed as they lay together, Harlan's arms around him and his head on Harlan's shoulder.

"Shhh. It happens. It's been a long week."

"I missed you so much."

"Then you're not going to like what I say next."

Ben raised his head. "You're going away again? For how long?"

"I don't know. I have to go back to Europe."

"You'll be gone weeks."

"I'm sorry."

"I guess that's how it is with a famous writer."

"Don't start with that," Harlan said with a dry chuckle. "And I'm not always this busy. Most of the time I barely leave the house. I'll have more time for you soon, I promise."

Ben laid his head down again as a wave of dizzy hope washed over him. It was too much to believe, that this wasn't the end, in case it really was.

He woke while the sky was still black. Harlan had an early flight and was in the shower, though he finished before Ben found the courage to join him. He dressed while Ben showered, and when he got out was packing his typewriter into its case.

"I wish I'd had time to look for an apartment for you," he said as Ben toweled himself.

"You know, we don't have any idea why someone broke in. Maybe it was just a burglar. A typewriter's not the kind of thing you can fence in a hurry. They'd want something they could pocket."

"I'm still going to worry about you."

"Somehow I think you'd do that no matter what."

At the office Ben did his best to focus on the work in front of him and not listen for Harlan's tread on the stairs. He got all the way home that night before realizing he'd forgotten to eat, but he was exhausted by the very thought of leaving the apartment, navigating the streets, choosing a meal...

If he went straight to bed he'd be up with the birds, for it wasn't even eight o'clock. Another long and lonesome night, and you'd have thought he'd survived enough of them to be used to it by now. Every lonely night was the same as the one before yet wholly unique, full of untold traps and pitfalls, chasms of misery, oceans of self-loathing. He'd only ever found one way out, one lifeboat in the storm. The only hope a man like him had of living happily ever after.

For everything he loved in *No Man's Land*, he had never been comfortable with its abruptly equivocal ending. Did Sterling jump from the cliff or not? Did Bull get to him in time? Questions for Harlan, though he might not answer. Writers didn't owe anyone an explanation. Ben had thought of and in many cases written every possible outcome of that heartrending scene. He'd burned the lot, as he'd burned most of his first work. At best the stories were juvenile rantings, at worst evidence in an indecency conviction.

Fragments still lived in his mind—a scene in a train carriage traveling through Switzerland, a section of dialog, a description of Sterling's back and the movement of his muscles as he rowed. The clumsiness of his prose, huge chunks of it taken up with political rants and ham-fisted philosophizing as a way to justify the frenzied emotions and even more frenzied acts. Burned or not, what better training for his current occupation, which was to write about the unspeakable?

There sat the old reliable on the table, a fresh ream

of paper beside it. An escape hatch, a time machine, a lifeboat. Moving automatically, he dropped a page onto the typewriter's paper guide and cranked it into position, his fingers on the keys before his backside had hit the pine.

Interventions

HE RAN OUT OF words around midnight and dragged himself to bed, only to be kept awake by phantoms of the words he'd write tomorrow. He stumbled through his morning, downing two cups of coffee before he was straight enough to put in his order with the waitress at the diner.

Climbing the stairs at the office nearly killed him. Sweating, speechless, he greeted Melody with a grunt as he staggered past.

"Mr. Q?" She'd accepted the moniker as a compromise, refusing to use his given name in case she said it in front of a client.

"Hold my calls. And my mail. I'll look at those later," he said, flapping his hand at the stack of manila envelopes brimming with other people's dirty thoughts waiting on the corner of her desk.

"Sure thing, Mr. Q. Here, I brought you a coffee."

"Lord above, you're an angel. A blessed fecking angel."

"Gee, Mr. Q. It's just a coffee."

"They say it's the thought that counts."

He toddled to his desk where his nemesis waited, lurking in the bottom drawer. Geist's book, whose lurid imagery had crept up on him more than once while in bed with Harlan. A cursed object, drawing them together yet forcing them apart, and he left the drawer locked, cradling his coffee as he sat back with a sigh.

He could open the next chapter of his own book like this, with Dale in a diner, thinking through the fight with Roger. *With a nod of thanks to the waitress, Dale breathed in the scent, the steam softening the tension he'd held in his jaw since...*

"MR. Q?"

"Hmm?"

Melody lingered by his door, a tentative hand on the frame. "Mr. Q, are you alright?"

"I've been better," he said as he slapped the carriage return, "but I'll survive."

"It's just you haven't stopped once, and I just wanted to be sure you didn't need anything before I left."

"Left for what?"

"For the day. It's five o'clock."

"It is?" And he hadn't felt it happen, hadn't felt the time pass. Until now, pain sparking up his forearms as he flexed his hands. "I'll just finish this chapter then head home."

"Sure thing, Mr. Q. I'll see you tomorrow."

This chapter, which led so naturally into the next that he was a fool not to catch every one of the words pouring out of him. Too tired to struggle through the streets, he slept at the office, slinking out at first light to shower at the Y so Melody didn't ask if he'd slept at the office. A lucky break, for when he got back Joan was with her, fresh as sunshine in a dress so white it hurt Ben's eyes. He waved away their questions, shut himself in his office, and slept for another hour before waking from a dream with the solution to one of the plot problems he'd been unable to solve last night.

He glanced up as Joan came into his office. "You know, the polite thing is to knock."

"The polite thing is to notice that someone's knocking," she shot back.

"Sorry, I couldn't hear you."

"You sure you're not ignoring me?"

"How can I? You're right there."

"Then stop typing for a minute, you clown."

"I'm almost done."

"Like hell you are. For Pete's sake, will you talk to me for a minute?"

"I'm right in the middle of this really important scene—excuse me, put that back!"

"In a minute," she said, holding the page she'd yanked out of the typewriter away from him. "I've been sitting out there all damn day waiting for you to explain what I'm meant to be doing here. I mean, it's a nice view and all, but you can't just want me here to keep Mel company."

"You're the one who chose to work here."

"Because you said you needed help. What you really need is a night off."

There was no way to stop her. Besides, she was right, and

so he meekly followed her and Melody to the Heidelberg, where he ate a schnitzel the size of a road map then the end of Joan's sauerbraten while the women made kissy faces at each other. His sides aching, his head thumping, he hailed a cab and nearly fell asleep in the backseat on the way home.

Upstairs, he managed to get his shoes off before dropping into bed. He woke with a start, but it was just the Erwins at each other's throats again. Not needing to be back at the office for a few more hours, Ben got up, undressed, laid down again, and started thinking of Harlan.

It was nearly noon in Western Europe. What was Harlan doing? Digging through musty boxes? Signing boring documents? Sitting beside a canal with a coffee and a sweet pastry with cream, reading a pocket book he'd picked up on his way through a train station? Eyeing the charming waiter who was taking another customer's order? Or had he already scored with someone better?

Terrible thoughts, and once unleashed they kept coming, of who Harlan might fuck without Ben ever knowing. Any man alive who wanted it, with those eyes, that laugh, those nimble fingers. Terrible, pointless thoughts, and only one way to stop them.

When midday came and Joan hadn't shown up, he figured he wasn't needed at the office and kept writing. To stop for even an afternoon was to risk never starting again. Every word he wrote now was one less word to write later. And wouldn't that be a coup, to finish it before Harlan came back? To say to him, *here is the story I wrote for you. The story I wrote* because *of you.* His love revealed on the pages in Harlan's hand, so that he never had to say the words out loud.

IT WAS THE MIDDLE of the next day, or maybe the day after that. Returning from the bodega with a six-pack of Fanta and a bag of ice for his sore wrists, he found Joan on his doorstep, arguing with his empty apartment.

"Nobody's home."

She whirled about, her finger at the ready. Froze, her mouth falling open as she looked him up and down. "Lordy..." she breathed. "Ben, are you okay?"

"Why wouldn't I be?"

"You look like you saw a ghost. No, like you *are* a ghost."

"I'm fine," he said, putting down the soda to fumble for his keys. "Just busy. What's up?"

"This," she said, eyeing him strangely. "You. You haven't been to the office in a few days. You still work there?"

"Of course. It's my company, isn't it?"

"So?"

"So what?" he replied as she followed him into the apartment. "Everything's in good hands."

"No it damn well isn't!" she cried, stomping her foot and making him jump. "Poor Mel's losing her mind trying to run that place by herself."

"Aren't you helping?"

"Helping how? I don't know shit about your business. She's got all kinds of jerks calling her up, hollering at her over the phone, wanting answers she can't give them because you're not around!" She checked herself, exhaled stiffly. "Look, I don't like being mad at you," she went on more kindly. "But what the hell am I supposed to do when you act like this? I worry about you, Benny. We all do."

"Oh God, don't cry." Joan never cried except at the movies. "I'm sorry," he said as she dabbed at her mascara. "You're right. I'm an idiot."

"You're not," she sniffed. "I don't know what you are, but please don't disappear on me. Don't go where I can't find you."

Joan never cried; he cried too much, but God, she was right. What good was pouring out his heart if it killed him? As they hugged she gasped.

"Jeez, Benny, you're skin and bones."

"I keep forgetting to eat."

"Maybe you are an idiot after all." And then they were laughing and crying at the same time. Saint Joan, the real life saver.

"Will you at least let me buy you dinner?" she said when they'd caught their breath. "Anywhere you like. Doesn't have to be nothing fancy."

"I wouldn't mind a sit-down meal."

"What about Bruno's? They do a mean chicken pizzicato."

"Just give me half an hour to wash up, find some clothes. How about I meet you there?"

"You better not stand me up."

"I wouldn't dare."

He boiled some water and washed his face and neck, using talcum on the rest of him to manage the itchy stink. He was halfway through shaving when the start of the next chapter began to unfurl in his mind. He darted to the typewriter as the imagery took shape, his eyes half shut to dodge distractions, his hands finding the keys by instinct.

SOMEONE WAS KNOCKING ON the door again. Other people had shoved notes under it, which he hadn't opened. He was almost out of aspirin, which meant he'd have to go out soon, but not before he got through this next scene.

The knocking stopped. After a little it started again. More like pounding, but if the cops wanted in they could show the warrant to the building superintendent.

"Ben, if you're home, please open the door." Not Joan. Not a cop. Harlan Avens, at his door.

"Go away!"

"Are you kidding me?" Harlan said after a pause.

"I look like hell. I haven't showered. Or shaved. And how do you know where I live?"

"Open the door this instant," Joan said in her don't-try-me voice, "or we're going to go find the super and tell him you're a dope fiend."

"Easy there," Harlan said to her.

"Screw you and your *easy there*," she spat. "I want god-damn answers. He's taken my money, he's stood me up, he's hurting my lady friend *and* you with his selfish bull-shit. Enough is enough."

"Shut up, the both of you! Shut up and go away! I can't concentrate! I...Shit!" So much so that he'd typed what he was saying. He rolled back the page and dashed out the words while Joan and Harlan (Harlan Avens! here! right now!) argued with each other:

"How could you let this happen?"

"How is it my fault?"

"I thought you were his friend."

"You're the one who keeps leaving town."

"You think it's cause I want to? Unlike some of us, I got bills to pay."

"You better watch your mouth, buster, or I'll—"

"For God's sake, shut up!" Ben yelled, ripping the ruined page from the machine, for he'd begun to type their words too. "Shut up and leave me alone!"

"To hell with this," Harlan grunted. Of course. As if he'd want anything more to do with Ben now that he knew the depths he could sink to.

"Hey, what are you doing?" Joan said with interest.

"What does it look like?" There was a rattling and a click and the door swung open.

"You gotta teach me how to do that," Joan said as Harlan stood up, pocketing a slip of metal.

"Sure thing, after we...my God." Both of them were staring at Ben like he'd stepped off a spaceship. "Benny, what have you done to yourself?"

"Why are you here?"

"Why do you think he's here?" Joan spat. "You're too stubborn to listen to me so I had bring in the big guns."

"I'm okay. I'm fine. I'm busy. I'm nearly done. If I just had a few more days—"

"In a few more days you'll be dead."

"No. No, I'm fine. Honest. I should have something to eat but I'm fine. I'm busy."

"Everyone's been worried sick about you," Harlan said gently as he moved to stand by Ben's elbow at the desk.

"How do you know? You weren't even here."

"That doesn't mean I wasn't thinking about you, and...are you writing this down?"

"No."

"You are. For God's sake, Benny, you're cracking up."

"I'm fine—hey!" He snatched for the page Harlan had ripped out of the machine. "That was a good bit!"

"No, it wasn't. Come on, at least get up and give me a hug." He jerked Ben's chair away from the table, nearly spilling him out of it. Harlan caught him under the arm and hauled him to his feet.

"Yeugh...what the hell have you been eating?" he asked, screwing up his face as he smelled Ben's breath.

Ben looked around for a clue amid the coffee cups and soda bottles. "I...don't know."

"Is he like this all the time?" Harlan said to Joan, who was picking through the heap of dirty clothes on Ben's bed with an expression of mild horror.

"Only when he's being an asshole." She dropped the shirt she was holding then sniffed her hand. "Forget about packing, can we split? I think the laundry starting to turn."

"I haven't had time to do laundry," Ben said as Harlan marched him to the door.

"You haven't *made* time, you mean," Joan said over Harlan's shoulder.

"Well, you're making time for me," Harlan said firmly. "I've been on the go for a day and a half but I'm here for you now and we're going to start by going to dinner."

"That's nice. You two have fun."

"I meant you and me, you jackass."

"But—"

"But nothing."

"But I haven't even shaved."

"We'll work around it. Keep moving."

An enormous gold-hued sedan was idling at the curb. A uniformed driver came around to open their door.

"Where are we going that we need to arrive in this?" Ben asked as Joan got in.

"Trust me," Harlan said, steering him around to the other side. "And don't worry about your clothes."

It was easiest not to argue. Once they got to where they were going, he'd leave. Manhattan wasn't so big he couldn't get home on foot.

Waking

HE WAS DRIFTING. LOST at sea, tossed by the waves, but he wasn't afraid. The blessing of dreams, and knowing he was dreaming, he woke. Not in his bed or Harlan's or the army cot but on a woven vinyl lounge chair in the glassed-in back porch of a clapboard cottage on the beach.

Everything was gray: the light, the sand, the wall, his hands. The water was merely a shushing rhythm and a slate blue streak in the distance. Like he hadn't woken at all. No, because in dreams he never felt pain and right now he ached all over.

He heaved himself off the squeaking lounge, then squeezed past the clutter of weathered beach furniture crowding the narrow porch, eased open the old wood-framed screen door, and slipped outside. The waves were louder, the light brighter and coming from every direction. Another cottage stood among the dunes about a quarter mile to the right, its windows boarded over, its seaward face the same blistered dead-blue color. As for Manhattan, not a sign. Nothing to see but the sea and the sand and the thin blades of dune grass bent flat by the wind. Like the world had been washed away.

Maybe he was still dreaming, though the pain said otherwise. Maybe he was dead. That made the most sense. He had died—by accident or otherwise—and this was Purgatory: gray, formless, friendless.

"It's about time you got up."

Ben whirled around, his vision catching up a second later, so that Harlan's ghost shimmered as it drifted around the corner of the cottage.

"Oh no, not you too."

Frowning, the other ghost pulled up short. "What's that supposed to mean?"

"Was it a car crash? Did Joan survive?"

"Of course she survived. Benny, what are you talking about?"

"We're dead, aren't we? And we're ghosts and this is what it's like and—"

And then Harlan was touching him, holding him, and he wasn't a ghost, was hot and strong and alive, and for no reason at all Ben shattered. Almost, because Harlan was holding him, touching him, whispering to him, words he couldn't hear over the shush of the waves and his sobbing.

"I'm really glad we're not dead," he eventually mumbled as he nuzzled into the tear-soaked curve of Harlan's neck.

"Me too," Harlan said with a soft chuckle Ben felt in his chest.

"You don't understand. I really thought we were."

"I believe you. Come inside, you can get cleaned up, have something to eat."

The rented cottage was spare and tidy, every wall painted the same pale shade of bleached gray. The pitted mirror in the tiny bathroom showed a gaunt, ragged inmate of a work farm, his hair standing out every way, his cheeks hollow. Facing the other way, Ben peeled off his creased clothes and inserted himself in the shower stall, which had apparently been plumbed for a family of leprechauns, the spray hitting him in the sternum. After bashing his elbows and kinking his neck he gave up and sat on the stall floor and let the water rain down on his head.

Wrapped in a threadbare beach robe, he shaved with Harlan's kit. Carefully, his hands shaking, his cheeks slack. A pair of toothbrushes stood in a glass on the edge of the sink. Harlan had thought of everything.

Sitting at the gray Formica table, Ben ate three roast beef sandwiches in a row while Harlan filled in the gaping hole in his memory of the night before.

"You were snoring before we even hit Queens," he said, screwing lids on jars as Ben chewed. "Me and Joan had a hell of a time getting you out of the car. I figured you'd wake up on the lounger in an hour and be banging on the door to be let in."

"Why are we here?"

"You needed a break."

"So you kidnapped me?"

Harlan shot Ben a fatherly glance, one dark brow lowered. "Are you saying I should take you back to that firetrap of an apartment so you can go on starving yourself to death?"

"No, but—"

"Look, there's nothing to worry about. We've got an icebox full of food, beer if you want it, sun and sand and no distractions."

"Good. I can get some writing done."

"Oy..." He ran his hand over his uncombed hair. "Ben

you need to take a break."

"Impossible."

"It's not. You gotta learn how to relax."

"Relax? I don't have time. I have a business to run. Geist's book to edit. Orders to fill. I need to get back to the city."

As he rose from his chair, Harlan put his hands on his shoulders and shoved him down again. "Sit your ass down, Quirke. And that's an order."

"Who put you in command?"

"I did." He gave Ben's shoulders a squeeze. Again, pressing those firm, wicked fingers into the knots of Ben's muscles. "You have nothing to worry about. Geist's book will keep, and Joan and Melody have everything else under control."

"But what about my book…" And then it didn't seem to matter as much as with another quiet chuckle Harlan ran his thumbs firmly down the sides of Ben's neck.

"If the ideas are any good, they'll wait. At least until I'm done showing you how much I missed you."

"I missed you too."

"Then give me a kiss, you nut."

As Ben twisted to face him, Harlan bent down and took that kiss. Took it hard, took Ben's breath away. Took command of him, and why shouldn't he let him? Why fight what he wanted so much that it had nearly killed him?

Harlan's kiss was fierce, but his every other touch was soft. He asked no questions, for he knew what Ben liked. He knew Ben like no one ever had.

Lying together under a gray wool blanket in the gray little bedroom, they kissed and petted and whispered to each other empty words full of feeling. *I missed you, I need you, I want you. I'm sorry,* Harlan for leaving, Ben for not believing that he'd come back.

But he had and he was here and Ben didn't know when he'd ever felt so safe, like Harlan's arms were a fortress protecting them both. "Thank you for this," he murmured, shifting nearer, their foreheads almost touching.

"We haven't even done anything," Harlan said with that little laugh Ben felt in his chest.

"I meant thank you for coming to get me. For...for saving me from myself. I'm sorry you had to see that."

Harlan's face fell. "Ben, why didn't you ask for help?"

"Because I never felt like I needed help. I didn't notice a thing. When I get like that I forget everything but the writing."

"Baron's not worth killing yourself for."

"I wasn't writing a Baron book."

"What was it?"

"I...can't tell you."

"You can't tell *me*?"

"I don't talk about my works in progress. It's bad luck."

"So it *is* a book. You can at least tell me that, can't you?"

"Yes, it's a book. But please don't ask me any more about it."

"Sure thing. It's not like I don't have plenty to keep my mind occupied."

"Why, what are you working on?"

"Who, me? I'm working on you."

"What do you—oh God." And the manic days, the hunger, the fear: everything faded like gun-smoke and drifted away as Harlan slowly, gently, enclosed Ben's cock in his hot grip.

"You don't need to do a thing," he murmured, stroking

his thumb along Ben's shaft as he squeezed. "Let me take care of you. Just lie back and relax."

Whimpering, half-blind with need, Ben nodded. Let himself sink into the bed, let Harlan coax him to unbearable hardness.

"It could be like this all the time," Harlan said as Ben moaned. "Me taking care of you, you letting me."

"I love—I'd love that."

"Good, cause you might not have a choice."

Whatever Harlan meant, Ben wasn't going to get an answer from him as he slid down the bed to take Ben in his mouth. And then answers didn't matter. Nothing mattered but the moment, and the moment was sublime.

On The Shore

DAMN HIM, BUT HARLAN was right again. Ben had need-ed this break. Fed and well fucked, they wandered the beach until they found a place where the dunes formed a hollow. Out of the wind, shielded from view if anyone happened onto the beach, they sat without speaking and watched the tide rise, the sky fading from misty blue to a dark pearly gray as the sun dropped behind them.

"Well. This was really nice," Ben said. "Thank you."

"Anything for you," Harlan said, putting his arm around Ben's shoulder. "I mean it. Don't ever be afraid to ask for help."

"As long as you know I'm not always smart enough to know I need it."

Laughing, Harlan pulled him closer and kissed him on the cheek. Held him tighter when Ben moved to get up. "Where do you think you're going?"

"Shouldn't we think about getting back to the city? It'll be dark soon."

"So? We've got nowhere to be. This is us for a week." He gestured to the crashing surf, the twilit sky, the empty beach.

"A week?" Ben shoved Harlan's arm off. "Are you kidding me?"

"Relax. Like I told you, it's all taken care of. Melody and Joan—"

"Damn it, Joan. I knew this was her fault."

"It's nobody's fault," Harlan said as Ben got to his feet. "We're only trying to help you."

"Well, stop. I'm a grown adult, I can take care of myself."

"Really?" He looked Ben up and down, taking in the dirty clothes, the uncut hair, the terrible shave, for he'd missed that spot by his dimple, like always. "And how's that working out for you?"

"Don't be an asshole,"

"Don't be an ingrate."

"I'm not, I'm—" He blew out the breath he was holding. "Look, I'll admit things got a bit...hectic. And maybe I let it get to me. But I don't need you mothering me. I'm done with being everyone's pet project."

He stood panting as Harlan gazed at him, his face blank. Then Harlan sighed and got to his feet. "If it will make you feel better, we can go up to the store so you can call Melody and she can fill you in on the details."

"You mean there's not even a phone here? What if there's an emergency?"

"Like what?" Harlan said, brushing the gray sand from his gray slacks.

"I don't know, drowning, or you cut yourself and I have to go for help while you're bleeding to death and—forget it. I shouldn't even say it out loud." He snatched up his shoes then slid and skidded his way down the slope. Harlan caught up as he reached the smooth beach.

"Nothing's going to happen, Ben," he said as they started for the cottage.

"You don't know that."

"We'll just have to be careful. Stay out of the water, avoid knives and matches. Maybe we shouldn't even get out of bed."

"I see what you're doing."

"What, trying to help you feel more comfortable?"

"That's not the point. I didn't ask to come here. I didn't ask for any of this."

"It's for your own good. Besides, I thought you were okay with me telling you what to do."

One day Ben would play Harlan at cards and take him for all he had, his lips twitching obviously as he tried to hide his smirk. "Don't you dare turn this into a joke."

At once he grew serious. "I'm sorry, Ben. And you're right, I didn't ask. But you were so spun out last night, I couldn't have gotten a clear answer out of you for anything." Protected by the gray mist of twilight, he took Ben's hand. "It hurt me to see you like that. I care what happens to you."

"Really?"

That little laugh, a sound of surprise, as Harlan squeezed his hand. "Of course."

"But why?"

"Why do I care about you? Because you don't lie to me."

A thought so preposterous Ben gasped, wounded by the mere thought that anyone might betray this man. "Why would I ever lie to you?"

"Maybe because I'm a famous writer and you want to kiss my ass?"

"But you *are* a famous writer. And I *do* want to kiss your arse. Though not like that."

"No?" Harlan said, grinning as he tugged Ben nearer. "Then how?"

Forgiven, just like that. "How about I show you some time?" he said, his palms tingling with expectation.

"How about right now?"

Giggling, they stumbled through the unlit cottage, stubbing toes, knocking shins. In the bedroom Harlan shoved him hard against the wall, kissed him harder, and Ben gave in, gave him everything. This was how he'd always thought it would be, a frenzied clinch in a dark, nameless place, his idol not asking but taking as Harlan jerked open Ben's pants, which slid off his slimmed hips and fell to the floor.

"I was going to say come to bed," Harlan said, pressing his thigh between Ben's, his cock rubbing against Ben's hip. "But I think I want you just like this."

"Anything."

"Turn around."

How did he know? Because he knew, had already fucked the truth out of him, knew Ben liked it best when Harlan took over. Shaking, barely breathing, his arms braced against the coarse gray wall boards, he let Harlan shove his feet apart, pose his hips just so. "You're so ready for me," he purred in Ben's ear as he stroked his softened ass, still slippery from the fuck of barely two hours ago.

"Always. I'll always want you." And then it was all about the getting, Harlan stripping himself one-handed in seconds then taking him there against the wall, the only sound the slap of raw flesh and their frenzied breathing, the only light a faint gleam from the sea.

BEN WOKE AS HE often did these days, with a scene forming in his mind. Reciting the critical plot points in a whisper, he rummaged through the gloomy cottage searching for paper and a pen. A notepad, last year's laundry list, anything to capture this idea before it evaporated in the push and pull of the day.

At last he swallowed his ethical cringe about touching other writers' work and opened Harlan's typewriter case. It was a sweet little machine, and he found several sheets of blank bond underneath it, along with the stub of a pencil. He replaced the machine, put the case back in the corner of the sitting room, and snuck out of the cottage through the back porch, pinching a crumbling foam kick-board from the clutter of old beach toys in the corner to use as a writing desk. Harlan needed sleep, and Ben needed solitude, needed not to be thinking about someone looking over his shoulder while he wrote. Definitely not *that* someone, who would read into every word.

The sky was clear for a change, the sun a mere suggestion beneath the shimmering horizon. Aside from a few lone fishermen whipping their long, flexing surf-fishing poles back and forth half a mile to the south, the beach was deserted, and Ben found the sandy hollow without much trouble. He wriggled his butt into the sand until it felt like a chair, propped the faded yellow foam board on his lap, and got to work.

After a scratchy start the words came easier, moving effortlessly from the place where stories came from and almost falling onto the page, as if he was discovering them, not inventing them. As if the story already existed and all he had to do was remember.

He stopped when the pencil was too blunt to use. A good morning's work, as long as he could read his own handwriting. Harlan wouldn't mind him typing it up. Harlan could suck eggs. Ben was a writer. He wrote. Wherever, whenever, vacation or no.

He settled back against the warm sand. Sticking the kickboard behind his head and the pages under the board so the wind didn't steal them, he laid his arm over his eyes against the golden glare of the sun.

"BEN. BENNY, WAKE UP," Harlan said, shaking his shoulder. Curled up on his side, his head pillowed on his bent arm, Ben swatted at him. "Be my guest, but you're gonna get a sunburn, you stay out here much longer."

Why was the prick always right? Stiff from lying on the hard sand, Ben pushed himself upright with a groan. The kickboard had slid down the slope a little and uncovered his cache of papers, and as he watched in horror, the wind off the sea lifted the top two or three pages and carried them fluttering out of his reach.

With a cry he grabbed for the pile. Harlan went jogging

after the pages, which were caught in the fine grass further up the dune. Ben fanned through his draft but only those three had gone astray. He looked up as Harlan chuckled. He was reading.

"Can I have that back?"

"Sure," Harlan said vaguely, his eyes flashing over the page.

"Please don't read it. It's not finished."

"But it's really good."

"That's not the point," Ben said as he lurched to his feet. "I said don't read it!"

"Hey, take it easy," Harlan said with a frown as Ben whipped the papers from his grasp.

"Forget about easy. Quit pushing me around."

"What are you talking about?"

"You know exactly what I'm talking about. I asked you not to read it and you did it anyway. I wouldn't ever do that to you. You ask and ask when you know I'll say yes, but when it's something that's important to me you don't even listen. You just do what you want and I'm meant to be happy and I'm not."

"Ben, you're a fine writer—"

"That's not the point! And did I ask for your goddamn opinion?"

Harlan was staring at him in shock. His head thumping, his heart on fire, Ben skirted the sandy hollow and took off up the beach, wanting to get as far as possible before he fell apart completely.

All this for a book. All this frantic self-martyring, these angry words, this breakdown for a fucking book. He ought to burn the pages crushed in his hand. Burn the damned contract, forget Geist had ever existed. Close down Baron and get an ordinary job stocking shelves. Grow the hell up.

The beach ended in a tumble of coarse, ash-colored rocks at the base of a sandy cliff. Gulls wheeled above the rocks where they jutted into the water, diving in ones and twos to stab at sea things stuck in the crevices. He sat where the sand was dry and watched them, their heedless drops and cawing ascents back to the sun-bleached sky. Far across the water, a freighter trailed a plume of pale smoke as it chugged towards the open sea.

What happened if you walked out and just kept walking? Would self-preservation take over, send him scrambling back towards land? No one would care either way, if they even noticed. He'd be doing them all a favor, freeing them from the burden of keeping him alive.

Whether the Catholic in his blood or the infinitesimal chance that maybe, possibly, Harlan might be disappointed to hear that he'd died, something kept him sitting on the sand until the distant ship had vanished over the horizon. When another half an hour had passed and Harlan still hadn't come to find him, Ben had to accept the fact that he likely never would.

The road that had brought them to the cottage would eventually lead him to a town. Montauk if he was lucky, where he could call Joan and...

No. He'd leaned on her too long, let her cover for his weaknesses until he was made of nothing else. He'd get his own arse back to Manhattan then tell her all about it, that time he thought a famous author was in love with him.

Because if he was—if Harlan loved him like he'd accidentally said he did—why had he let Ben walk away?

An Apology

He'd wandered farther away from the cottage than he thought. All the way back the sun beat down on his neck and the clump of folded paper in his pocket scraped against his leg while he felt stupider and stupider for letting his imagination get the better of him. Imagining that this was normal, that bottom-dwelling smut peddlers like him had equal footing with proper novelists, that Harlan wasn't going to get fed up sooner or later with Ben's low-brow inclinations.

Who knew what kind of trash he'd been spewing? Every time he'd sat down at the typewriter it was like someone else had been moving his hands, the words appearing on the page without him having thought them. Which meant he had no idea if he'd written a single coherent sentence since Harlan left. Even so, he couldn't shake the sense that it was something extraordinary. A mythic message, and he was merely the scribe. If on the other hand it was gibberish, he could burn it and spare the world. Either way, it was none of Harlan's business.

Nearing the cottage, he considered walking on by, going

on to the next one, begging to use their phone. So what if Joan found out he'd screwed up again? Just one of the many benefits of being friends with Ben Quirke: every now and then you got to watch him fall to pieces. Before he made up his mind, the screen door of the cottage slammed open and Harlan came running towards him. He skidded to a stop a few feet away, breathing hard.

"Ben, I'm so sorry," he gulped. "I didn't want it to be like this."

"Neither did I." He'd wanted his hero to see him, believe in him. He'd stupidly wanted forever, not a handful of nights and this disaster.

"So can I try to make it up to you?" Harlan said, stepping closer. Smiling as he reached for Ben's numb hand.

"What do you mean?"

His eyes creasing, Harlan chuckled, the sound swallowed by the ceaseless surf. "I mean I'm sorry for pushing you around. For thinking that was the best way to do this. It scared me so much, seeing you like that. I thought that if you got out of the city, got some fresh air, didn't have everything piling up around you that you'd feel better. That's all I wanted."

"And here I am, all ungrateful and yelling at you and being a jerk and—"

"Don't," he said, jabbing a finger into Ben's chest, though they were still holding hands. "Don't you dare take the blame. None of this is your fault, Benny. This is all on me. I'm the one who should be sorry. Me and my big ideas."

"You only wanted to help."

"Ben, you're miserable. Worse, I *made* you miserable."

"I'm pretty sure I was doing that all by myself."

"Then let me make you happy."

"You already have. Harlan, I thought...I thought you'd be gone."

Too, too much: too much happiness, too much Harlan, and the joy spilled up and out of him and he fell on Harlan's shoulders and began sobbing yet again. Ugly, helpless tears and Harlan holding him close, stroking his back. Here for him.

"Did you really think I'd ditch you because you told me off?" Harlan said as Ben sniffled against his neck. "Give me a little credit, will you?"

"I'm an idiot, aren't I?"

"No. You're just damaged goods."

"I'm sorry."

And Harlan laughed, not cruelly but with the tired laugh of a man used to loving a fool, and kissed Ben's wet cheeks. "You didn't do anything wrong, but I forgive you. So what can I do to make this right? Anything in the world."

The simplest question, the simplest answer, and it stuck in Ben's throat like a bone. He ought to be grateful. He ought to take this for what it was, make the best of their time here, not knowing when they'd have the chance again. Harlan was waiting for him to speak, his expectant smile fading.

If only he didn't have to speak. If only there was a page between them, a blank space where Ben could explain what he wanted and what he expected and why the two things never aligned. He'd filled half a book with that explanation and yet here he was face to face with the thing he most wanted and how could he expect anything except to lose it?

Maybe there was nothing to lose. Maybe Harlan's waiting silence was enough. Harlan, who wanted to hear Ben's words so badly he had to steal them. Who was here with him when he ought to be miles away, and wanted him to be happy.

"I want to go home."

"Sure," Harlan said, that sideways grin creeping back onto his gorgeous mouth. "What, you think after all that I'm going to say no?" he said as Ben stared at him.

"I don't know. I'm sorry. Can we really go home?"

"You bet. Now come inside, maybe before we hit the trail I can cheer you up."

"How?" Ben asked as Harlan began leading him towards the cottage. "Oh. I really am an idiot, aren't I?"

"You're too hard on yourself, is what it is," Harlan said with a laugh, opening the screen door for him. "So when someone treats you with respect you don't know how to cope."

"You're right. I shouldn't doubt you."

"You should if you don't feel safe around me."

"I do, though." To Ben's sun-blind eyes the sitting room was a mass of blur and shadow and he paused in the doorway. "It's when you weren't around that things got...unsafe."

"Then I'll just have to stick around, won't I?" Harlan said, slipping his arms around Ben from behind.

"To protect me from myself?"

"If that's what it takes." Holding him close, he laid his forehead on Ben's shoulder in that way he had when he had too much feeling. "You matter to me," he said, the words muffled by Ben's shirt. "I don't know what I can promise you but I want to..."

"Go on."

"I want more of this. A lot more. I missed you when I was away, and I kind of liked it. Missing someone. I liked thinking about you, about what you were doing that day, though I guess I got that wrong. And don't say you're sorry," he added, giving Ben a squeeze as he opened his mouth to do just that. "You didn't go off the rails because you wanted to."

"No. It's never on purpose."

"Does that happen a lot?"

If they were having this conversation Ben needed to see Harlan's face. Harlan felt him stiffen and loosened his embrace so he could turn around. "Define *a lot*."

"More than a few times?"

"A year? No, not that often."

"Shit. That's still too many," he said, frowning.

"Joan seems to know when I'm about to hit bottom."

"I'll talk to her about it. I don't ever want that to happen to you again."

"There might not be much you can do about it."

"That's not going to stop me from trying. I want to make you happy, Ben. I'll do whatever it takes."

What it took was a lot of kissing and a teary-eyed but magnificent fuck, Harlan's body stretched over his, teasing and teasing until with a snarl he hoisted Ben up onto his knees and took him in a single brutal thrust. And this was what made him happy, and damn anyone who said it shouldn't be so.

THEY FELL ASLEEP ENTANGLED. When they woke the cottage was dim, the noontime sun a copper penny behind sand-coloured clouds. "We don't really have to leave," Ben said, feeling helpless as he sat on the bed and Harlan packed their few things into his calfskin bag sitting open on the flaking rattan dresser.

"You ass," Harlan said, shooting him a look. "Don't change your mind just because you think it's what I want. This is about what *you* want. If you want to go home, I'll take you home."

Half a home, at best: a room, a bed, a door. Even this dingy little cottage on the ugly end of Long Island was nicer than Ben's miserable apartment, never mind the cot in the office. Both of which had never been meant as anything but a temporary stopping place until he found where he was meant to be.

Harlan closed the bag with a click of the brass clasp then came and sat beside Ben and took his hand. Just like that, and Ben took a deep breath and closed his eyes and spoke without stopping himself, said what was in his heart, despite the ragged fear that his heart was a liar.

"I want to go home with you. Wherever that is."

"We can do that," Harlan said, squeezing Ben's hand. Just like that. And then Ben was crying again, like an idiot, trying to mash the tears back into his eyes with the heel of his hand, wrecking the beautiful moment. With a soft laugh and a sigh Harlan put his arms around him.

"Thank you," Ben gulped, laying his head on Harlan's shoulder. "I'm sorry. But thank you."

"Enough of that," Harlan grumbled, though there was humor in his voice. "Besides, you might not want to thank me by the end."

At this Ben sat up. "Why, what's happening?"

"There's something we gotta do before we leave," Harlan said with a grimace of something like pain. "Sorry."

"No need to apologize."

His face hot, he winced again. "Yeah, well, we'll see."

Mrs. Metzger

THEY WALKED UP THE sandy road to the corner store, its weathered siding the same blistered blue-gray as the cottages it served. The ghostly letters on the faded billboard on its roof offered fresh bait and cold beer.

"You might as well wait here," Harlan said as they stepped onto the warped plank porch. "I just have to borrow the car."

"The man at the bait shop is going to loan you his car?"

"Rex and me go way back. I'll just be a sec." He glanced around then kissed Ben quickly on the cheek and went into the store.

The wet of Harlan's lips cooling on his suddenly hot cheek, Ben sat on the bench in front of the dusty store window. The day had been so full of highs and lows and it still wasn't over. Harlan had been cagey on the walk, leaving Ben with nothing but his imagination. Who were they about to see? A relative? A mentor? An old flame?

Restless, he got up from the bench and wandered around the corner of the building. The sky was still hazy, and he leaned against the silvered wooden siding of the store and let the pearly light and empty sound sedate his restless thinking.

He trusted Harlan. They'd fought and made up. It might happen again or might not, and Ben had to trust that Harlan would forgive him if it did. He wanted to trust him, wanted to feel at home with him, feel safe. For too long he'd lived this way, on the edge of everything: poverty, his friendships, his business, his sanity. Harlan was in the center of life, a fixed, solid thing Ben could cling to.

Joan was sweet, in her way, but ephemeral, there when she wanted to be. She was likely to infect Melody with the same instability. Nothing in Ben's life was uncomplicated, and he shut his eyes and let his head fall back against the siding. He startled upright at the cough and rumble of an old engine starting. Harlan whistled, and Ben came back to the front to find him waiting by a battered old Packard. Once maroon, it had been faded by sun and salt air to a pale tomatoey brown, which at least hid most of the rust.

"You didn't tell me Al Capone worked at the bait shop," Ben said as he grappled with the stiff door handle.

"Don't talk like that about Luanne," Harlan said, pointing a serious finger at him over the curving hood. "Just because she's a bit rough around the gills doesn't mean she's not still beautiful."

Ben kept his comments to himself as they rattled down the macadam road, Luanne popping and sputtering and finding every pothole. The road improved after a few miles and they drove for about fifteen minutes, Harlan's fingers drumming incessantly on the wooden wheel. They pulled off onto another side road then stopped in front of a small house with freshly painted yellow siding and a screened front porch, in the middle of a row of similar houses.

"I don't know how you're going to take this," Harlan said, staring at the house. "In fact I probably should have told you this a lot sooner." His face was white, his jaw trembling, and as he turned to Ben the gut-wrenching thought occurred that they were breaking up after all.

Time slowed, like it had in the field, when you could see the shells incoming and your heart was the tick of a clock meting out your last seconds of life. Ben had seen Harlan's bleak expression on the face of a young surgeon the first time he'd had to tell a soldier about his impending amputation. Harlan opened his mouth then paused, staring over Ben's shoulder with a look of horror. Just like in the restaurant when he'd seen Lola. Ben twisted around to see a small woman in a blue floral house dress and immense, thick lensed glasses standing in the porch door.

"Are you going to sit there at the end of the driveway all day or what?" she cawed, waving a thin hand. As she hopped down the steps in her slippers, Harlan rested his head on the steering wheel.

"Is that your mother?" Ben asked. Harlan nodded. "Yeah, you should have definitely brought this up sooner."

"She's harmless," Harlan muttered. "More or less."

Mrs. Metzger was waiting for them at the bottom of the steps. Five foot tall if that, her hair mostly gray and held back in a snood like a wartime bride, she reached up to pinch Harlan's cheek.

"So?" she said as he rubbed the red mark.

"So what?"

"So introduce me to your friend."

"Ma..."

She tilted her head to glare at him over the goggle-eyed glasses. Harlan glared back, then groaned, his shoulders sagging.

"Ben, may I present my mother, Mrs. Eileen Metzger," he grated. "Ma, this is Ben. Ben Quirke."

Ben shook her hand with all the care he'd show Joan at a society do, with a gentle clasp of her fingertips and little bow. "It's a pleasure to meet you, Mrs. Metzger."

"Oh, a mick, are you?" she said, looking him over with more interest. She waved away Harlan's protest and took Ben's arm. "You know I don't mean nothing by it, don't you, Mr. Quirke? Come in, come in, I'm just about to make coffee. You drink coffee?"

"Er, yes?"

"Good. Me, I don't care for tea. Looks like dirty water. Tastes like it too, don't it?"

"Er, sometimes?"

The house was pin-tidy and smelled like cinnamon, a tabby cat of the caramel persuasion flicking its tail as it watched from the back of a doily covered armchair in the living room. Though he wanted to poke around for photos of young Harlan nee Hermann, Ben followed Mrs. Metzger to the gleaming kitchen. As she rattled around, fussing with the percolator and talking to herself about where the sugar was and if she still had any cake left from Gloria's sister's kid's wedding, Ben shifted his chair towards Harlan's.

"Why are we here?" he asked under his breath.

"Because if I set foot on Long Island, she knows," Harlan whispered, following her with his eyes. "And if I don't stop by, she'll never let me forget it."

"She's sweet."

"She's what?" he said, jerking away with a look of horror.

"On a personal level, I mean."

"Yeah, I got that, but—"

Harlan startled as his mother slapped his shoulder. "You're in my seat, bubbe. Besides, I want to sit next to your nice young friend."

Face ablaze, Harlan surrendered the chair to his mother. "Can you grab our coffees?" she asked with a dismissive wave, her charm bracelet jingling on her slim wrist. As Harlan sputtered she turned back to Ben and laid a soft but implacable hand on his arm. "So tell me, is he doing alright?"

"Who?"

"My boy Hermann."

"Ma, I'm right here," Harlan gritted through his teeth.

"Yeah, but you lie to me," she said with another wave. "I want the facts. And my coffee, if you don't mind."

"I do not lie to you," he said, his voice swooping.

"Everyone lies to their mother," she said, still gripping Ben's arm. "So tell me, is he staying out of trouble?"

"He's fine," Ben replied, very carefully not looking at Harlan. "A bit flighty, but he's good to have as a friend."

"Flighty, that was his father, see? Couldn't settle on anything. Gee, I loved him. He had the tightest little—"

"For the love of God, Ma!" Harlan set her coffee on the table with a clunk, sloshing a bit over the edge. Mrs. Metzger looked from the brown spill to her son and back to the table. With a groan, Harlan grabbed for the dish towel that was hanging on the front of the oven.

"Uh-uh," she said, the charm bracelet winking as she wagged her finger. "I just washed that. Use the sponge on the sink first."

Ben sipped his coffee and kept a straight face as Harlan

mopped up the spill then dried the table. "Why don't you take that wet towel through to the breezeway," his mother said as he made to hang it back on the oven rail. "On the rack with the others."

She winked at Ben as Harlan stomped out of the kitchen. "He acts tough but don't let it fool you. But you might know that already. How long you been friends?"

"A few months, on and off."

"There he goes with the on and off," she said, her lips thinned. "I told him, it doesn't matter who it is, he has to do right by his friends. So tell me, is he doing right by you?"

"Er, well...I suppose he is."

"He brought you to meet me, so that's something. I don't usually get to meet his friends."

"Have there been many? Friends, that is."

"I hear things," she said, her glasses shifting as she wrinkled her nose. "Nothing for a while. He's been keeping you a secret. But looks like the cat's out of the old bag now. So are you hungry?"

"A little."

"Great, I'll fix you something." She hopped up and went to the fridge. By the time Harlan came back, a steady smile which failed to reach his eyes plastered on his lips, Ben was halfway through a plate of potato salad.

"What happened to you?" he said around a mouthful as Harlan slid into the seat beside him.

"I took a little walk to cool my head."

"Don't take it so hard. She loves you."

"I know. I'm lucky she's still around," he said tiredly. "But she doesn't make it easy."

She fed them until Ben was sweating, a parade of dishes emerging from the fridge like she'd expected them (and several other people) to visit. Gloria's niece's wedding cake was found, though how Mrs. Metzger had lost a five pound slab of cake in her modest Frigidaire was too much for Ben to think about. Throughout the meal, she kept up a narrative of young Hermann's life: his Cub Scout years, his tenure at the school paper, his habit of wetting himself as a small child when talking to certain grown-ups in the neighborhood, which made Ben wince and had Harlan choking on his coffee.

Rumbling back to the bait shop with the windows down, his body heavy with food, Ben realized he was happy. Simply, comfortably, as if this was how he felt all the time, and that restless lurking sense of doom he'd come to accept as his natural state was the error, a bad dream and not the truth about life. The truth was, there was no truth. There were no perfect choices, always a price to be paid. Something you had to give up if you wanted something better to take its place. For once, the thought didn't frighten him.

Twitterpated

When they reached the bait shop Harlan pulled up in the shadow of the building and stopped the car. They sat for a few minutes, the car pinging and tinging around them as it cooled, the crash of the breakers on the sand a gray flickering in the distance.

"Can we—"

"We can—"

Grinning, they both fell silent again. "You first," Harlan said.

"Can we stay another night?"

"I thought you wanted to go home," he said, his forehead creasing.

"I did. But there's no rush. This is enough, being with you. Wherever you are, that's home." Trusting in the quiet solitude, Ben slid across the seat to kiss Harlan's cheek. That was his plan, but Harlan met him in the middle, met Ben's mouth with his own in a wild kiss like it was the most natural thing ever. And maybe it was, and everyone who disagreed was lying to themselves and the world. This was real, full and real: this love in the shadows, this kiss, as fierce as it was natural. They belonged together, as much as any two lovers could.

"We'll do whatever you want to do," Harlan said, cradling Ben's face, his thumb stroking softly over Ben's cheek. "It was all for you anyway."

"Okay, but don't expect any more action tonight. I'm stuffed. I kind of just want to lie down."

"We can work with that."

"God, I love—being with you."

If the near miss frightened Harlan he didn't let it show, giving Ben one of those heartbreaking smiles before kissing him one last time then getting out of the car. As they walked into the shop, a middle aged man with a heavy paunch and a bloodhound's sagging eyes looked up from the newspaper spread on the counter.

"Hiya, Herm," he grated in the gargling voice of a life-long smoker. "How's your ma?"

"Same as ever, Rex," Harlan replied, dropping the car keys on the paper. "Thanks for letting us borrow Lu-anne."

"Any time," Rex said as he scooped up the keys. "Oh, and some lady's been calling for you."

"For me?"

"Harlan Avens is you, right? Your nom de plume?"

"So who's calling?"

"What's her name?" Rex mused. "Meredith, Mona..."

"Melody?" Ben offered as the cracked black phone beside the ancient brass cash register began to ring.

"Yeah, that was it, " Rex said, his jowls wobbling as he nodded. "You might as well get that, it's gonna be her again."

With a shrug Harlan picked up the receiver. "Mel? It's

Harlan. What's going on?" He gasped, his eyes darting to Ben. "Where are you? Alright, we'll be as quick as we can."

"What was all that about?" Ben asked as Harlan hung up.

"I'll tell you in a minute," he said brusquely. "Say, Rex, any chance we can keep the Packard for a few more hours?"

"Where you wanna take her?" Rex asked, cocking a grizzled eyebrow.

"Back into town."

"Manhattan? Not on your life."

"Rex, old pal, you gotta help me out."

"I'd love to, Herm, but she can't make it to Manhattan. She don't even have plates. Best I can do is run you into Montauk but then you're on your own."

"Good enough."

"How are we going to get to the city?" Ben asked as he followed Harlan to the door.

"The train, if we're lucky. Or a taxi."

"That'll cost a fortune!"

"As your financier, who gives a damn?"

"Right, right."

"We'll work it out, Benny. Trust me, nothing's so bad it can't be fixed." The phone rang again and Harlan groaned, clutching his forehead.

"You get that," Ben said. "I'll run to the cottage and grab our things."

"Right."

Determined not to panic, Ben jogged back to the cottage, stopping there long enough to scout around for any loose papers. Laden with the bag and Harlan's machine, his shoes filling with dry sand, he was waddling in what he hoped was the direction of the bait shop when Harlan appeared out of the haze.

"Come on, soldier, shake a leg," he said tightly, taking the typewriter from him. "Ma's going to let me borrow her car."

"What's going on?" Ben panted.

"Let's just say, if we don't get back to Manhattan soon you might not have a company."

"To hell with Baron. Let it burn."

"I wish it was that easy, Benny," he said with a grim smile. "I really do."

Rex drove them over, Ben rattling around on the back seat as the Packard's wheels juddered on the sandy road. When they arrived at the little yellow house, Mrs. Metzger was waiting on the steps wearing a tan duster coat, a scarf printed with green and white daisies tied neatly over her hair.

"Where do you think you're going?" Harlan asked her as they got out of the car.

"With you. Where did you think?"

"Why would you come with us?"

"How else am I going to get my car back from Manhattan? Wait for you to get off your tuchus and return it?"

"But Ma—"

"No buts. Don't worry, I'll still let you drive. You were always such a good driver. Just like your father."

"Well that settles it," Rex said as she handed Harlan the keys. "I'm coming with."

"Why on earth—" Harlan started with a groan.

"I'm not about to stand by while a lady of her, how should I say this?" He pondered, snapping his fingers to jog his memory.

"My advanced age?" she offered pertly.

"By no means, madam," he enunciated with a toothy grin. "I was going to say *sophisticated constitution*, and I would be remiss if I allowed such an esteemed lady to drive to and from the city all by herself. Not at this late hour."

She drew herself up—the effect was diminished by how little she had to work with. "How very noble of you, Mr. Schiff," she said with a lift of her chin.

"Please, Mrs. Metzger," he said as he offered his elbow to escort her to her car. "Call me Rex."

MRS. METZGER'S FORD '49 made for smoother ride than Rex's rusted out Packard. Harlan sat slumped in the driver's seat, one hand on the wheel and the other resting on the gear shift, his face unreadable as they streaked along the blacktop.

Ben wanted to touch him, lay his hand on Harlan's to reassure him, though he wasn't sure of what. Some show of support, but as he uncrossed his arms to reach out Harlan exhaled heavily and shifted in his seat, switching hands on the wheel to lean against the window.

Avoiding him. No, it was coincidence. It was nothing it all. It was Ben's brain spinning out on fear and desperation, reading into Harlan's distress, blaming himself for causing it. Behind them, Rex was showing Mrs. Metzger pictures of his grandkids from a photo booth in Coney Island.

"Aww, the little one looks just like you," Mrs. Metzger cooed.

"Yeah, bald as a cue ball and missing half his teeth, the poor kid," chuckled Rex.

"Now, now, don't sell yourself short. You were a real looker back in the old days. A regular Rudy Valentino."

He chuckled again. "Shucks, you think so?"

"Sure I do. Just because I was married didn't mean my eyes stopped working."

"Shucks, Mrs. Metzger, you got me all twitterpated."

"Oh, go on with you, Rex. Behave yourself."

Sighing deep in his throat, Harlan pinched the bridge of his nose. "God help me," he muttered under his breath.

"Don't worry," Ben said, folding his hands in his lap. "We'll be there soon."

"But will I survive?" He cringed as his mother laughed again. Ben bit his lips, trying not to laugh along.

"Geist and his damn book," Harlan hissed. "I'm starting to I wish I'd never found it."

"You could have saved yourself a lot of trouble."

"But then I wouldn't have had an excuse to see you again."

"As if you needed an excuse."

"How was I supposed to know that?" He spoke sharply but when they passed a streetlight he was grinning. "I'm glad you're with me, Benny," he said, resting his hand briefly on Ben's knee. "I mean it. I'm glad you agreed to help me with this nutty scheme."

"I don't know how I could have said no to you."

"If you had, I would have understood." The banged up Chevrolet in front of them finally turned and Harlan zoomed through the junction in a burst of speed.

"Level with me," Ben said when he'd got his breath back. "You're connected. You know lots of people in publishing. You could have even formed your own company. Instead you came to me. And I know we have a contract, but for a while we didn't. And I just wonder...why me? Even among the pulp presses, I'm a nobody. What did you see in me in those couple of hours that made you trust me with so much?"

Harlan glanced behind them at his mother, who was dozing against Rex's shoulder, snoring softly. "I wanted a partner in crime, I guess you could say. Not just someone to proof and typeset it and leave it at that. I wanted someone to talk to about it. Someone who cared enough about books to be open to stories that weren't always the prettiest, as long as they were real."

"Real? Are you kidding me? I write about spacemen and sexually insatiable dormitory monitors."

"But your stories make people feel real things. Real emotions. Passion and fear and triumph."

"So do you. Your books, I mean. *No Man's Land* isn't pretty either but it's real. Realer than anything I'd read before."

"So many people hated it," he said under his breath.

"Does that matter? Lots of good art has very few patrons. How many rubes are lining up for the opera or the ballet when they could be at a tractor pull?"

"So you're saying I'm a singing Spaniard in tights?" Harlan asked, his lip twitching.

"Would you rather be a rodeo clown?"

"Either way, sounds like I'm about to get trampled by a bull."

As Ben started laughing, Harlan set his hand on his

leg again. He left it there until they hit Queens and he needed both hands to drive. The change in speed woke Mrs. Metzger, who kept up a commentary of New York landmarks as they crossed the 59th St Bridge and wove their way downtown.

"Ma, I'm going to drop you and Rex off at Darla's," Harlan said to her in the rearview mirror as they waited at a stoplight. "She'll take care of you until I get back with the car."

"Oh no, mister,' Mrs. Metzger replied, crossing her arms. "You're not driving my car around Manhattan. You know New York drivers. They don't value their lives the way sensible people do."

"But Ma—"

"But nothing. You said you needed to get to the city. You never said a thing about needing the car once you got here."

"Ma, you're killing me."

"Oh Hermann, you're always so dramatic."

"We'll grab a taxi," Ben said as Harlan groaned and rested his head on the wheel. "It'll be hard enough to find parking at Darla's."

"Fine," Harlan mumbled. "We'll take a taxi."

The light had turned green, and when the car behind them honked, he sat up and drove on. They soon reached Darla's street, where a teal blue Meteor was luckily pulling away from the curb a few doors past her building.

"Do you know Darla?" Ben asked Mrs. Metzger as they waited on the sidewalk in front of the building for Harlan to finish parking.

"Sure I know her. Harlan introduced us years ago, when she went by a different name. I'll break it to Mr. Schiff gently, don't you worry. And you boys be careful, you hear? New York always has something up her sleeve."

"We'll be fine," Ben replied, hoping she didn't notice the tension in his smile. "Your Hermann is a...er...fine person."

"Isn't he just? He's a real catch, he is," she said with a significant look, nudging Ben with her elbow. "Smart money says hold onto him. He's an original."

"He's a great writer."

"See, he won't let me read his books. Tells me they're too blue. Say, you're a writer too, aren't you?"

Harlan joined them, saving Ben from answering Mrs. Metzger's treacherous question. If *No Man's Land*, with its elisions and allusions, was too racy for her, Ben's books would send her into conniptions.

"Thanks for loaning me the car," Harlan said, passing her the keys.

"All you gotta do is ask, bubbe, you know that," she replied, pinching his cheek while he rolled his eyes. Harlan had phoned Darla from the bait shop to alert her, and they left the unlikely pair, the compact Mrs. Metzger and the barrel-bellied Rex, waiting for her on the stoop.

"Are you ever going to tell me what's going on?" Ben asked as he and Harlan marched towards the main drag.

"I will when I know."

"Is there something you're not telling me?"

"We'll talk about it when we get there, okay?"

Before Ben could reply Harlan stepped into the street, whistling sharply as he raised his hand to flag the oncoming cab. In the backseat he sat slumped against the door, gnawing on his knuckles as he gazed sightlessly out the window. Again Ben wanted to speak to him, touch him, reassure him, but what could he say? Even if they were alone, he had nothing to offer.

His hands lay slack on his knees, the knuckles standing out, his wrists so slender he'd run out of holes on his watch band. With Mel and Joan at the wheel of Baron, he'd been left to his own devices, and it had just about killed him.

"How long were you away for? This last time," he added as Harlan blinked at him like a man waking up. "When you came back and found me…you know."

"Three and a half weeks."

Nearly a month of barely eating, barely sleeping, never once thinking of his business or the people running it. All for a book, some words on a page. And yet it had felt so necessary. As if writing those words was his life's purpose, the reason he had survived all that had come before.

"I won't let it happen again," Harlan said softly. "If it means I don't leave town, so be it."

He didn't reply, afraid to say anything in case he said it all: that nothing Harlan did would be enough to protect Ben from himself. He was the weak link in the chain, the reason everything had gone wrong. Instead of taking responsibility for himself and Baron, he'd let Harlan whisk him away to the seaside, leaving the girls up to their necks in his dirty business.

More like Harlan's business, as he still hadn't told Ben why they'd left in such a rush. "Are you going to tell me what's happened?"

Harlan's eyes flicked towards the cabbie. "In a minute."

They pulled up at Ben's building soon after. Harlan threw a handful of bills over the seat and sprang from the cab. Ben followed more slowly, catching up with him halfway up the stairs.

At the office Harlan paused; the door stood open a sliver, and he pushed it open with his toe. Mel's desk was bare, as she left it every night. The rest of the room as well, the closet hanging open and empty. Using his shirt sleeve to cover his hand, Ben opened the door to his office.

"Oh God..." Where were the boxes of books? His cot? Even the filing cabinet had been ransacked, the drawers standing open, loose pages spilled on the floor. "Harlan, I'm ruined."

Desperate Measures

RUINED. THE WORD REVERBERATED in his head as he rifled through the few pages littering the drawers of the plundered filing cabinet. A piece of paper lay on the floor and he scooped it up, but aside from a typed date of six months ago it was blank, and he let it fall.

No more Baron, no more Geist. Everything was gone, taken while his back was turned, while he lay in the sand and ate roast beef. His stomach roiling, he covered his mouth. Harlan was speaking, his words a blur, and Ben shook his head to clear his ears.

"Don't worry, Benny," Harlan soothed, rubbing his back. "Everything's going to be okay."

"How can you say that?"

The squeak and clang of the heavy basement door swinging shut echoed up the stairwell. As footsteps started up the stairs, Ben dashed from the office, Harlan on his heels, to peer over the banister. A woman was on the first landing, her slim hand gripping the rail, a diamond bracelet twinkling on her wrist.

"Joan?" he hissed.

"It's me, Mr. Q," Melody replied tiredly, leaning out to wave at him. She was red-faced and sweating, her blouse half unbuttoned, tendrils of hair stuck to her cheeks.

"Will someone tell me what in God's name is going on?" Ben said she started up the last flight. "Starting with where's Joan."

"At the police station," Melody said, breathing hard.

"Oh God." Everything he had and everything he'd sacrificed, and this was how it ended. He grabbed for the rail as his knees buckled, his guts churning with a nauseating wave of fear.

"You told me she got arrested," Harlan said to Mel, frowning.

"She didn't. Just answering questions. Two plainclothes guys. No warrant, though, so no search. Joan wouldn't budge."

"Bless her," Harlan murmured. Saint Joan to the rescue, yet again. "Which precinct?"

"The ninth."

"Right." As he started for the stairs Ben grabbed his arm.

"You're not going down there, are you?"

"Don't worry, Benny. It's going to be okay." He clapped Ben to his chest in a fierce hug, planting a kiss on his cheek then letting go. "You keep him out of the way," he said to Mel, pointing at Ben. "I don't care how, but you are not to let him leave this building."

As he darted down the stairs, Mel ushered Ben into his office, steering him to his desk like a nurse with a doddering old man.

"It's ok, Mr. Q," she said, petting his arm. "You'll see. We'll figure it out."

"What happened to all the boxes?" he murmured, pointing at the vacant room.

"Of books? We sold out of those last week. While you were AWOL."

"And my bed?"

"I shoved it in the hall closet after the cops left. The files too, before you ask. What I thought was worth keeping, at any rate. The rest I've been burning. We got it covered, Mr. Q. We're gonna be okay, you'll see."

"Okay."

Wishing she'd left the cot so he could lie down on it forever, Ben sat at his desk, rested his head on his folded arms, and tried not to lose his mind. *Stop panicking. You're imagining things. You haven't ruined his life. You haven't done anything wrong.* He told himself this again and again in a hypnotic inner chant, until he just about believed it, while Melody moved about the rooms, picking up loose papers and being her generally useful self.

Looking down through the cage of his arms, he could see the bottom drawer of his desk. No point letting that indictable junk linger, and he felt for the key, stuck to its magnet under his chair. Except that it wasn't. He hadn't heard of anyone in the business getting charged with the mere possessing a manuscript, but it was several breathless seconds before he could find his voice enough to call for Mel.

She appeared at the door at once. "What is it, Mr. Q?"

"Do we know where the key is?"

"One sec." She disappeared briefly and returned with her blouse untucked. "That drawer was next on the list," she said, laying the warm key on his palm.

"I won't ask where you were keeping that. Where's the

wastepaper basket?"

As she fetched it, he flipped through the stories he'd ferreted away and would now burn, as he should have the minute they arrived. Stories about man-eating plants and sex farms, gay street-walkers and the cops they blackmailed. Works so blatantly intended to arouse that they had no hope of passing that lawyer Rembar's test of social merit.

Geist's book belonged with them in the incinerator. Could that rotten box of scraps even be called a book? Or was it merely Harlan's wishful thinking, his last grasp at relevance as his star faded from the firmament of American literature?

Whatever it was, it was missing.

Ben leapt from his chair, knocking it over as he scrambled for the filing cabinet, but the rancid box, its contents, and the manuscript Harlan had transcribed were nowhere to be found. He snatched up the waste basket and upended the contents on his desk to search through the dog-eared submissions one by one.

Finding nothing, he strode out to the waiting room, where Mel was sitting slumped with her chin on her folded hands, watching an antacid dissolve in a glass of water in front of her nose. She sat upright at the sound of voices in the hall. As Ben lunged to lock the door it opened and a trio of men entered: Girt and Lerner of the Guest Society, and older man in an expensive overcoat, with a leather attaché under his arm.

Mel stifled a groan. "Sorry, Mr. Q. With our luck today I should have known."

The Guest men shared a dirty look. "So you are Quirke," Lerner said, propping his fists on his hips.

"Yes? What of it?"

"You were here the other morning. You lied to us!"

"I don't know what you're talking about."

As a slim, bookish child whose unwed mother had refused to soften her broad Woodlawn Heights accent, Ben had dealt with uncountable bullies growing up. What burst their bubble the quickest was a sharp poke of undiluted hostility. "What is it you want?" he said curtly, cutting off Lerner's sputtering.

"We want the truth!" Girt cried, stabbing the air with a finger. The third man cleared his throat, and he closed his mouth with a snap. Smiling smoothly beneath sterile gray eyes, the man stepped forward, producing a business card from an inside pocket.

"My name is Jeffers, Nyland Jeffers, and I represent these gentlemen on behalf of the Alver Guest Historical Society."

Ben pocketed the card—Harlan would want to know everything—but said nothing. Damn them if they thought they were drawing him into this dance. After a moment Jeffers cleared his throat and went on: "The fact of the matter, Mr. Quirke, is that you're in unlawful possession of my clients' property. Now the last thing we want to do is get the authorities involved—"

"Not that we won't!" Girt cried, brandishing his finger again.

"Mr. Girt, please." Tension pinching his eyes, Jeffers turned back to Ben with the same placating smile. "With that in mind, Mr. Quirke, I'm sure you'll agree that it would be much simpler for all parties if you simply surrendered the property."

"And which property is this?"

"Guest's manuscript, you thief," Girt blurted.

"Guest?" Ben said as the others hushed him.

"Yes, Mr. Quirke," Jeffers said, a muscle beginning to twitch beneath his right eye.

"As in the renowned author Alver Guest?"

"Who else?" sputtered Girt.

"I wouldn't know. And there's no manuscript here by Alver Guest."

Melody drew a breath but Ben threw up a hand to keep her from speaking as Girt rolled his eyes.

"Fine. Alfred Geist, then," he huffed.

"None of his either."

"They're the same man!" he cried, throwing up his hands.

"Mr. Quirke, we could play this game all day," Jeffers said through his teeth.

"Speak for yourself, I was on my way home."

His eye twitched again. "In which case it would make sense for you to hand over the documents so we can conclude this business amicably and be on our way."

"I would if I could, but I haven't anything to give you. Besides, I see no evidence of your claim. Anyone could have business cards printed. Are you even a lawyer?"

The three men answered at once in a shouting jumble:

"Now just a minute—"

"If you'd care to call the bar society, you'll find—"

"It's one thing for you to lie to us, but this, sir," Girt said shrilly over the others, pounding his fist into his palm, "this will not stand!"

"Are you threatening me?" Ben said, looking from the man's hands to his face.

"Ye—no," he corrected at a hiss from Jeffers. "No, I am

not threatening you, Mr. Quirke. I am merely stating my displeasure. With force."

"Duly noted. Now if we have no further business—"

"We can't be brushed off so easily, Mr. Quirke," Jeffers said. "Your associate Mr. Avens has usurped my clients' right to the estate of the author known as Alver Guest, and that amounts to theft. You can either surrender the manuscript or expect to be subject to criminal investigation, if not reported to the state department for misappropriation of recovered wartime artifacts. Hand over the book, however, and this all goes away."

How he wished it all would go away. Geist's book was an albatross, a ball and chain, dragging behind him everywhere he went. Just minutes ago he had thought about burning it, along with the rest of the trash. Putting an end to everything, even if that meant letting Harlan go.

Wasn't that the sensible choice, the responsible choice? He couldn't keep living this way: riddled with paranoia, clinging to the edge of his sanity, never having a moment without worry. His work had suffered, and his art. For all he knew, the story he'd nearly killed himself to write might not be worth the paper it was typed on. Inspired by a man he met by chance, a man so enmeshed with Ben's personal mythology that even now he couldn't say if he knew Harlan at all, or if what he loved was only the idea of him. The man of his dreams, not figuratively but in truth.

"Well, Mr. Quirke?" Jeffers said, the other two flanking him like a firing squad. Whatever he said, they'd never believe him

"All right. I'll give you everything."

"Mr. Q.," Melody murmured, "shouldn't we wait for—"

"I don't remember asking your advice, Ms. Masterson," he replied sharply, hoping she'd forgive him later. "This doesn't concern you."

She met his gaze then bowed her head. "Yes, Mr. Quirke."

He was only buying time and he knew it, but that was the best he could do. By the time these men realized they'd been duped, he would have seen Harlan, found the real book, made a real plan. He hoped.

He led the trio into his office, indicating the heap of paper on his desk with a sweeping gesture. "It's all yours."

"Is this some kind of joke?" Jeffers said, glaring at the pile.

"Like we told you, this was how it was recovered, in pieces," Girt said primly. Lerner had picked up a page and started to read, his eyes popping out of his head. Girt slapped the paper out of his hand.

"Keep your mitts off, Elmo. That's archival."

"You could have just asked," Lerner replied, rubbing his hand.

Melody was sent to fetch a box while the Society men stacked the papers in a slightly neater stack and Ben paced his office, trying to look furious, needing them to leave before he crumbled. Or worse, before Harlan came back and everything got complicated.

"Thank you for your cooperation, Mr. Quirke," Jeffers said, offering a greasy smile and a brief if crushing handshake once the papers had been shuffled into the box. "I'm glad we could see eye to eye."

Ben smiled tightly but said nothing as Mel opened the door for the trio, Lerner stealing downward glances at the contents of the box in his arms. As their bickering voices died away, Ben toddled back into his office. His head swimming, he felt his way around his desk and fell into his chair. Mel followed, pausing in the doorway.

"Gee, Mr. Q," she breathed with something like admiration. "I didn't know you had it in you."

"Neither did I," he croaked. And then he didn't, as a cold sweat erupted across his brow and back. As the room began to tilt to one side he snatched up the wastepaper pail, seconds before Mrs. Metzger's brisket made a horrid reappearance.

Blood he could deal with, the pain and gore of military triage. Fear on the other hand felt like dying, and he added many tears to the mess in the basket as the adrenaline ebbed from his veins. Eventually Mel took the pail from him and gave him her handkerchief and a glass of water she had fetched from the restroom downstairs.

"I'm not made for this," he said, dipping the clean end of the handkerchief in the water to mop his face. "I don't know why I thought I could keep going."

"Whatever made you start this company?"

"I didn't. I inherited it."

"From who?"

"It's a long story."

"I'm all ears."

Company Man

NNO ONE KNEW THE whole story. Not even Joan, other than the barest facts. No one knew how close he'd come to meeting his maker after he'd lost his mother's piecework job.

"There were three of us at first. Friends I made in...in hospital."

"You were injured in the war?"

"No, this was a few years later. And I was only sick in the head. Good old Bellevue. After we were discharged, we started meeting every week or so for coffee. First just to stay in touch, but then to read each other's writing. We got so many rejections from agents and editors that one night after we'd had a few drinks we more or less dared each other to write the most ridiculous story we could and submit to a new science fiction magazine."

"And?"

He smiled, remembering the shock, then the joy, of opening the magazine's reply. "And they printed everything we submitted, and paid us by the word. I wrote so many stories from them I eventually got to know the owner. They had a book department too, and after I'd sold him five or six novels he asked if I wanted a job in the editing department. Turned out I *was* the editing department, but you know what that's like."

"So you worked your way up?"

"No. He...he died suddenly. Drove his car into the river."

"Gosh! That's quite the accident."

"That's what they called it at the time. Later we found he was being blackmailed."

"For what?"

"Being a pansy." The bluntest of statements but it said everything as Mel gasped then shook her head sadly.

"The poor fella. Why something like that's anyone else's business I'll never know. So what happened to his company?"

"The blackmail fell apart when there was no one to extort. He'd left his house and most of his money and personal effects to his wife and children, but it turned out that he'd left Baron Press to me."

"No shit! Sorry, Joan's lowered my vocabulary."

"She'll do that."

"He didn't happen to leave you any money, did he?"

"Good guess, because no. It nearly bankrupted me. It was in all sorts of debt, writers were drying up, in part because he'd stopped paying them so he could pay the blackmailer. I gave up the offices, let go everyone on the staff until there was only, well, me."

"And still you kept going?"

"God knows why. To give me a sense of purpose, I guess. A reason to keep getting up in the morning. And here we are."

At the end of everything: his business, Harlan's book, Harlan's love. There was no hope of carrying on. Baron had survived as long as it had by going unnoticed. It was now a known entity, of interest to the NYPD and the State Department and God knew who else. Geist's book would put the publishing world's eyes on him and everything he did from hereon. His business, his personal habits, the company he kept. Joan, who only remained his friend as long as no one knew. Every aspect of his life would be exposed to the public, all for that creepy book about a dead man's lover.

Unless he refused. Got Joan to help him get out of the contract she herself had forced him to sign. Said good-bye to Harlan and his impossible dream of getting away with a crime in plain sight. Said good-bye to Harlan. Now, before they got any deeper into trouble.

"We're going to work it out, Mr. Q, I just know it," Melody said, patting his shoulder as he scrubbed at his teary face. "Don't ask me how, but just believe me, okay? Believe that things are gonna be okay. You'll see him again."

"Will he want to see me?"

"Why wouldn't he? He's pretty stuck on you, Mr. Q."

"How do you know?" Ben sniffed into his soggy handkerchief.

"A woman knows these things," she said, giving him one of Joan's more maternal looks. "The way his eyes follow you around the room. The way he smiles when you're speaking, even if you aren't talking to him."

"Are you sure?"

"As much as any woman who trusts her intuition. Give it time. You'll see." Time: the greatest luxury, the one thing he never had enough of. The one thing that was always running out.

A loose page lay on the desk. As she began picking up the other fallen pages Ben turned it over, revealing the first lines of *Truck Stop on the Road to Hell*:

The road's a lonesome place. Some men will do anything to break its monotony. Take any risk just for the thrill of it. Jimmy Pace was one such man...

Trash. Pointless, soulless, indictable trash, and he crushed the page and tossed it aside then slumped on the desk, his head in his hand. "Mel, where's the Geist?"

"The box or the transcript?" she asked, her voice throttled from bending over.

"Either. It wasn't in the drawer or the filing cabinet. If you haven't seen it, and I haven't seen it, then where did it go?"

She stood upright slowly, her eyes darting. Her head snapped around at the sound of Joan's heels. Blushing furiously, she snatched up the soiled wastepaper bin and whisked it out of the room, bobbing her head at Joan as she passed.

Joan was alone and seemed unharmed, not a wrinkle on her periwinkle suit, not a russet hair out of place. "Don't you worry, Benny," she said, patting his cheek. "Everything's under control."

"What's going on?"

"I said don't worry."

"That's not an answer. This is my company, I should know what's happening to it."

"Look, it's none of your business, Benny."

"How can my business not be my business?"

"It's just not, alright? Jeez, you gotta learn to trust me."

"Excuse me, when have I not trusted you?" he said, following her into his office. "Is it always going to be like this? You interfering in my life? I'm a grown man, you know."

"Then act like it for once," she cried, stomping her heel. "Quit jerking us around, hiding in that rat hole cold water flat, writing like you're racing against the clock. Ignoring me, ignoring Mel, ignoring the man you keep telling me you're in love with."

"I never said I was—"

"Don't you even start with that," she hissed. "I could cite you numerous occasions—you know what, that's not even important. What matters is what me and Mel had to go through while you were off writing your magnum opus. Cops and lawyers and those dingbat antiquarians from the Alver Guest Society," she said, counting them on her fingers. "And that's before we get to the five crates of books we had to write-off because they fell off the back of a truck in the rain. I put my neck out for you, Benny, and nearly got it chopped off. And all that's on top of me worrying that I'm never gonna see you alive again!"

Laying her hand on her heart, she stopped to catch her breath. "I love you, Benny, but goddamn it, I'm tired. Deep in my soul, I'm tired. I don't wanna give up on you but you ask for the sun and the moon and I'm tired of reaching for them."

"I'm sorry," he said in a small voice. She was right, and he was wrong, and it was time he stood on his own two feet.

"I know you are, baby," she replied with a sad smile. "But *sorry* isn't always going to cut it."

"I know. I treat you more like a mother than a friend. It's not fair to you. I should leave you alone."

"I never said that. I don't want that, not at all. If anything I want more of you, Benny. I don't want to lose you."

"Same. You're a lifesaver, Joan. Really you are. I couldn't have done any of this without you."

"Ah, you would have figured it out."

"No, I don't think I would have."

"Then repay me by not screwing it up with that man of yours."

Ben bit his lip, refusing to get sucked into the whirlpool of terrible thoughts, clinging to the one that mattered most. "What's happening with Harlan?" he asked. "The police can't charge him with anything. One look at the business license and they'll know he has nothing to do with Baron."

Joan winced like he'd stomped on her foot. "Yeah. See, there's something you need to know about that."

"What's there to know? My business license hasn't expired. I renewed it myself in April."

"The license isn't the issue," she went on with the same pained expression. "It's Baron as a whole. The thing is, while you were...you know, incommunicado, Harl and I had a talk. About you, about me, about Baron."

"Go on."

"And we kind of wondered whether you were really the right man for the job. I don't mean for writing and editing and working out the covers and all, for that you're a natural. But you've said it yourself, that you feel like you're drowning. I see what you put yourself through for this business. Me and Harlan both. Maybe you aren't cut out for, you know, running a publishing company."

"You wouldn't be the first to think so."

"Which is why I might have forged your signature a

couple, few, maybe six or seven times, max. But you know my guy will notarize anything I put in front of him."

Ben inhaled a slow breath, his nostrils whistling, his heart very loud. "And what exactly did you put in front of him?"

"The transfer of your share of Baron Books."

"The transfer of my share?"

"Yep."

"To Harlan?"

"Mm-hm."

"Of Baron."

"The very same."

"You sold it. You sold my company. Baron Books is my company and you sold it? You sold it to *Harlan*?"

He fell back in the chair, grabbing the arm rests as the room tilted sideways again. Nothing: he had nothing. A room he leased by the month, an office with nothing in it, the clothes on his back, his damned self, and a hundred pages of a book he was killing himself to write.

"I'm sure he'll sell it back to you," Joan said, wringing her hands, her voice coming from far away. "Now that you're, you know, compos mentis again."

He shook his head like a dog and the world snapped into focus. "What the hell does that mean?"

"It means you were out of your stinking mind!" She caught herself, then sighed, sagging against the desk. "Benny, I had no idea. No idea how hard it is to make a living in your stinking industry. No wonder it's killing you. Melody hadn't been paid in three weeks. Kid was living on cold coffee and dehydrated soup."

"Why did she do that?"

"Because you weren't there to sign her paycheck. Look,

I know this business means the world to you, but you can't keep going like this. Even with me and Mel. Something has to give."

She was right. Joan was always right. Everything she said was true, was something he'd said to himself. "Was I really that far gone?"

"The fact that you don't remember should tell you something. Ben, I love you. You're the best friend I've ever had. The only person who isn't always trying to get something from me. You never ask for help, even when you need it."

"I don't want to be a burden."

"Of course you don't," she said kindly, her eyes bright with tears. "But the longer you hold out, the worse you are when it all goes to pieces. This isn't the first time. Hell, this isn't the first time this year that I've wondered if...well, if you're gonna answer the door, or if I'm gonna find you dead because you forgot to eat."

"You don't mean that."

"I do. You've put me through a lot this year. Me and everyone else who cares about you. Harl was...well, he was heartbroken."

"How so?"

"You looked half dead when we dragged you out. Never mind look it, you *were* half dead."

"I know."

"And I had to, *we* had to deal with it. Your boyfriend didn't go back across the pond for kicks, Benny. He's been reading wills and identifying skulls and shit. Then he comes back and finds you losing your mind."

"I know. I'm sorry. I should be giving Baron more time."

"No, I really don't think you should. Baron was never

your baby. You did your best with it, but you can't keep going like this. You can either write, or run the business, but you need to admit that you can't do both. Me, I'm no writer—"

"No, Joan, you're a great—"

"I mean that I'm no pro. I can put a few lines down on paper and make them sound pretty, but you, you're a natural. But you gotta quit this whole starving artist shtick. I mean, you ever see the gut on Hemmingway? That guy knows how to eat."

How did she do that, turn the worst moment into joy? "You're right. Again. Like always."

"Not always. Just usually."

"I don't want to fight you, Joan. I just want this all to go away. I'm not...I'm not good under pressure."

"Don't I know it. Look, everything's gonna be okay. Just, I don't know, think of Gary Cooper in all them war flicks. Cool as a cucumber."

"Easy for you to say, you're not the one who's in a pickle."

"See? You still got a sense of humor, so how bad can it be? And you're wrong. I'm in it as deep as you."

"Why?"

"I didn't sell him my share. I sold him yours."

The End of the Book

Finished. Not ruined but not anything else either. Just a man with nothing to his name, sitting numbly behind his desk with his brain leaking out of his ears and his heart in pieces as Joan went on to explain the situation with Geist's book. Something about Cleveland, and probable cause, and extra-judicial overreach.

"Forget Cleveland," he said at length, throwing up his hands. "What's going on with Harlan? What's going to happen to me?"

"Nothing's gonna happen," Joan soothed. "There's nothing they can do."

"How do you know?"

"Because it's not up to the NYPD to interpret the law. Just because some sergeant has his jocks in a twist over a book he hasn't even read doesn't mean he can charge someone with obscenity. Particularly when he's got no evidence."

He wanted to believe her. His life depended on it, but as she began detailing the finer points he lost the train of explanation. Whatever happened, to him or Harlan, it wouldn't change the fact that he had failed.

He'd had gold in his hand—new business prospects, new friends, new love, a new life—and he'd let it slip through his fingers. Let himself disappear down the rabbit hole into the imaginary world of fiction, where he could make his characters be everything he wasn't: strong, clever, indestructible. Where a man's problems were solved with the stroke of a pen; make him braver, make him smarter, make him disappear.

Living people kept on living, kept on hurting. Kept on thinking about everything they might have done differently, every choice they wish they could make again. Life wasn't a story, it was a strip of film—single exposure, no edits. No mercy.

He muddled around for a little once Joan left, picking through the last scraps of paper while Melody swept both rooms. He thought of offering to help, but something in the grim set of her jaw made him leave her alone. If Baron folded, she was out of a job. Doubly so, given the number of his books she'd authored.

He was startled by a knock on his open door, but it was only Melody. "Mr. Q, are you going to be okay?"

"I don't know. Is anyone?"

She chuckled, folding her arms as she leaned on the doorframe. "Feeling existential after all that, huh?"

"Melody, what makes you a writer?"

"I dunno," she said, twisting a toe in the dust. "I always said anyone who wanted to could call themselves that."

"True, but I meant, why do you write? If you never sold another book in your life, would you still be a writer?"

"Probably. I've been writing since I was nine. I don't know what else to do with myself."

"Work. Marry. See the world."

"I can do those and still write. I'd say, doing those sorts of things might make someone a better writer. Otherwise there's nothing in here," and she tapped herself on the forehead. "You gotta fill the well, Mr. Quirke. Be in the world, love the world, for all its stupid glories. Go out and find a story worth telling. Someone will want to hear it."

"Hopefully."

"And what about you?" she asked gently. "If you didn't do it for a living?"

"Of course I would. I nearly destroyed my business because I couldn't stop writing. I'm sorry about leaving you to deal with it. And for not paying you. That was inexcusable."

"Joan had my back. She wouldn't have let anything happen to me."

"Oh God, she didn't adopt you too, did she? How many pet writers does one woman need?"

Melody blushed, erasing the shape she'd drawn with her toe in the dirt. "You know, she's the first person who didn't call me nuts for wanting to write. After you, that is."

"All writers are a little bit nuts." He had to be, to have chosen this life. And then to have it taken from him...

"Is there anything I can do for you?" he asked to keep from sinking into his sour thoughts. "I've been dead weight this whole time. And now Baron's not even mine."

Harlan owned it. Like he owned every other part of Ben: heart and soul and body, for better or worse. Sunk, and he covered his face, too much of a gentleman to bawl in front of a woman, despite the tears leaking between his fingers.

"It's okay, Ben," she murmured. "Everything's going to work out, I just know it."

"How do you know?"

"I just do. And when I know something, it's for real. Like when I first met Mr. Avens. I thought to myself, Mr. Quirke doesn't stand a chance with this one."

"You did?" he sniffled, rubbing his teary face with his upper arm, his sleeve the only part of him that was clean. "You could have told me."

"Told you what, that I'm psychic? I'd only been working here a few weeks. Last thing I needed was you thinking I was off my rocker. Or that I was prying. That's your personal business. I can't keep the thoughts from popping up, but I do know how to keep my mouth shut."

"Well, if you have any other bolts from the blue, let me know. I could use all the help I can get."

"Don't we all," she replied dryly. "You ought to go home. I'll be alright by myself."

"If you're staying, so am I."

"In that case, give me a hand. You're tall, you can reach the cobwebs better than I can."

Night had well and truly fallen, and he tuned the radio to a station playing crooners then helped Melody clean the office, mopping the floors and pulling down several years' worth of cobwebs from the corners of the ceilings. By the time he had dumped the last bucket of water down the cistern on the floor below and hauled himself back upstairs, he was ready to curl up under his desk and sleep for a week.

They had resorted to playing tic-tac-toe on the back of that page of *Truck Stop* to keep themselves awake when they heard Joan and the lawyer's voices echoing up the stairwell. Harlan wasn't with them. Ben knew that timbre, the cadence of his speech, his quick step. Knew it by its absence, and as Melody went to meet them he stayed where he was, behind her desk. He didn't have the strength to stand, knowing that Harlan wasn't free. Knowing that he'd let him take the fall, bear the blame for Ben's shady business.

"I'm telling you, Mel," Joan was saying as they neared the door. "What a bunch of...you know what? Never mind. Cops are cops, am I right?"

"I wouldn't know," Mel replied, "but I'll take your word for it."

In they came: Melody, her cheeks crimson; Joan, grinning fiercely; her lawyer Mr. Dwyer, a petite man in pinstripes with a gold-cornered briefcase; and Harlan.

Ben leapt up, hissing as he bashed his thighs on the edge of the desk. Just like that first day Harlan had walked into his office. Unlike that day, Harlan barely met his eye, his hands deep in his pockets as he lingered by the door, shuffling his feet.

Watching him, Ben hardly heard a word of Joan's report, waiting for a glance, a smirk, any sign of Harlan's feelings. Any clue of what to do or say to mend this brokenness between them.

They couldn't go on as before. Everything had changed. The thing that had brought them together had finally pushed them apart, and so he waited, saying nothing, in case he made things worse.

"We won't need you again tonight, Mr. Avens," Dwyer said, closing the latches on his briefcase. "You might as well head home and get some sleep."

"You too, Benny," Joan said, beckoning him to his feet. "You boys need my guy to drive you?"

"I'd rather walk. Blow off some steam," Harlan said in a

dull voice.

"Whatever you need," Joan replied, patting his arm. "Give us a call tomorrow, alright? I'm thinking the three of us got a few more things to work out."

She plucked Ben's hat from the stand and plopped it on his head. Put his jacket in his hand then steered him out into the hallway and shut the door. Harlan was waiting by the stairs, his face in shadow. As Ben neared, he started downstairs, pausing on the landing to look up at him blankly.

"You coming or what?" Without waiting for Ben's answer he kept walking, his footsteps ringing hollowly. Ben followed, their shadows bending up the walls, thrown by the unshaded ceiling fixtures shining through the railings. The disillusioned maestro and the ingénue, his innocence betrayed by the flawed truth of human nature; two tired men who once thought they had a future together.

That was what this was. Ben had never let himself fall for anyone, never let himself believe that any of the men he'd fooled around with had a permanent place in his life. Mel was right, he'd never stood a chance against Harlan. Had been half in love with him before they'd ever met. Loved him through his writing, and he was a fool for expecting anything more.

They walked in silence, Harlan with his head down and his hands in his pockets, his shoulders up around his ears. Ben didn't ask where they were going, not wanting the end to arrive any sooner. Wanting more time to memorize Harlan's face, the way it changed in the changing light, sometimes seeming older, sometimes younger, but always perfectly Harlan. Perfectly the man Ben had imagined years ago, gazing at that photograph from *Life* pinned to his bedroom wall, wondering how a stranger, a man he'd never met, had known so much about him.

It was somewhere around midnight and the city was as quiet as New York could be, only a few dark figures hurrying along the bare sidewalks, the occasional flare of headlamps streaking through the streetlights' geometric constellations. Harlan's stiff posture had eased as they walked, his pace slowing as they approached the vast dark shape rising before them, which turned out to be the footings of the Williamsburg Bridge. Walking in its shadows they came to the river, divided from them by FDR Drive, the lights of Brooklyn twinkling across the black water.

There was nowhere left to go. With a sigh Harlan leaned back against the nearest piling, his gaze drifting upwards into the darkness beneath the bridge. "That's it," he murmured, closing his eyes. "I give up."

Seeing the incoming punch didn't make it hurt any less. In truth, Ben was lucky to have had so much, to have loved a man like Harlan, even if he lost him. And what more could gay men expect? A hotel reservation in only one name. Books that got you thrown in jail. Farewell after farewell after farewell, until you had nothing at all.

"Well. Thanks for everything," he said, hating the shake in his voice, the heat rising to his cheeks as he retreated a few steps, not wanting to crowd the man who'd just given up on him. "And don't feel like you need to speak to me if you see me. It's easier that way, if we pretend we've never met."

"What are you talking about?" Harlan said, frowning.

"I mean if we run into each other. You know Joan, she's always dragging me somewhere."

"Wait, do you think I'm trying to dump you?"

"Please, don't think that I blame you," Ben said, retreating further as Harlan took a step towards him. "It's all me. I know I'm not very good with...friends. People. Anyone."

"Benny..." Laughing softly, Harlan shook his head. "I don't mean you. I meant Geist's book."

"But...really?"

"Not a moment too soon, either. I've been losing my mind over that damn thing. Trying to turn that pile of garbage into a work of art has gotta be the worst idea I've ever had."

"You mean all that work, and you're just going to walk away?"

"What's it worth to you?" Harlan said, spreading his hands. "I mean it. Would you be sad if Geist's book disappeared tomorrow?"

"But doesn't it matter to you?"

"Not like it used to. Not if it means putting you in the line of fire. And what for? To get revenge on a dead man who probably never knew I was alive."

Sighing, he turned to gaze across the inky river towards the cold stars of Brooklyn, the city hidden by the bridge, Harlan swallowed by its shadows. "I thought that book—Geist's secret book—could exorcise these ghosts that haunt me," he said, Ben's breath catching in his chest at the ache in Harlan's voice. "These memories from so long ago I can't tell if they're real, or made of all the nightmares I've lived since. All these things I should have buried years ago."

"Isn't that what Geist means? Ghost?" Ben asked quietly.

"Shit, you're right," Harlan chuckled, feeling for his handkerchief to blot his teary eyes. "And there you've been, through all of this. You never once questioned me. You let me think I was going pull it off."

"I'm sorry."

He laughed again. "You don't need to apologize for supporting me. Half the time I don't know why you even put up with me."

"Because I love you. Oh God." Except Harlan didn't flinch, didn't draw back in alarm. Instead he smiled, with tears in his eyes and that perfect smile that was only for Ben, and though they stood side by side in the cold of the night Ben felt a heat spread through him as if he lay in Harlan's arms.

"I love you too," Harlan said, a catch in his throat as he leaned his shoulder against Ben's. "I don't know how I ever got along without you."

"Are you serious? After all the trouble I caused you?"

"I caused it all. Don't say it's not true, because it is. If I hadn't tried to push that book on you, made you sign that contract—" He broke off as an approaching car's headlamps lit up the wet pavement.

"You can blame Joan for the contract," Ben said once the car had gone.

"You should thank her for trying to protect you. Honest to God, I'd half started hoping we'd get busted so it would all go away. Not you, just the rest of it, all this sneaking around and Geist's smutty trash. But I couldn't stand the thought of you suffering. Of seeing you take the blame for something I was making you do. The thought I could have put you in jail..." He rolled his shoulders uncomfortably. "I couldn't do that to you, put you through that. Ruin your life to prove a point."

"I could have said no anytime."

He chuckled, bumping against Ben's shoulder again. "When have you ever said no to me?"

"True."

"Which is why it wasn't fair for me to play around like that. I should have been man enough from the start to admit that all I wanted was you."

Ben shivered as Harlan's hungry gaze ignited a scorching heat within him. "So," he breathed when breathing was once again possible. "What should we do about that?"

"We should go somewhere that we don't have to worry about getting busted," Harlan replied, leaning into Ben with a wicked grin. "Because I plan on us breaking several indecency laws."

Comfortable

Us. There was an *us*, there was a *we*, there was Harlan adjusting his hard-on as he peeked around the bridge piling. "Coast is clear. Let's find a taxi."

"Where are we going?" Ben asked as they started back towards the city.

"Grammercy Park?" he said with a grin.

"Is Knopf paying for this one too?"

"No, but I'll bet the Park takes American Express. Unless there's somewhere you'd rather go," he added more seriously.

"You've seen my apartment. You tell me."

"The Park it is, then."

Ben didn't care where they went. As long as they went there together. Traffic picked up After a few blocks and they were able to hail a cab. They rode uptown in simmering silence, Ben sitting on his hands to keep from reaching for Harlan. At this hour there weren't many guests around, and Ben skulked around the elevators while Harlan booked a room. They had the elevator to themselves, sneaking glances at each other like the co-conspirators they were. Their fifth floor suite was the junior of Harlan's penthouse from their first meeting, the satin draped bed filling most of the room.

"I need a shower after all that," Harlan said. "Why don't you make yourself comfortable?"

"Right. Okay."

Comfortable: was that a thing Ben knew how to be? He undressed slowly, hanging each item in the closet with care, his hands moving in the opposite direction from his mind. Harlan had forgiven him, but had he forgiven Harlan? There was asking for help and then there was having help forced on you, having other people make all your choices for you. All his life he had let himself be led by other people's decisions, out of fear of making the wrong one on his own.

As if he was the only fallible dupe on the planet. Everyone was equally damned, equally saved. Anyone could make bad choices, even a man who you'd worshiped for half your life.

Harlan was a man and nothing more. Carrying the weight of a bitter grudge, worried that his art meant nothing, as frightened by the emptiness of his future as Ben was. A man, not a mythic hero, as broken as any other. Yet real, and really here. Not a dream but a real and living man on the other side of the bathroom door. A man who loved him, as impossible as that seemed.

Sitting on the edge of the bed in his t-shirt and shorts and one sock, Ben felt dizzy, from the day of near disasters as much as from bringing up that enormous meal of Mrs. Metzger's. A century ago, yet it had only been today. As he was counting back the hours, someone knocked at the door.

"Room service."

"Oh. Yes. Just leave the tray. Please," Ben called through the door a flush of guilt for shorting the maid on the tip. He watched through the peep hole until she was out of sight, then brought in the tray. Under the silver cloche was a plate of greens and sliced cucumber.

"When did you order a salad?" Ben asked as Harlan came waltzing out of the bathroom, nude except for the towel around his waist.

"At check in, when I chickened out on asking if they had any Vaseline." Grinning, he plucked the cruet bottle of salad oil out of the little stand and took it to the bedside table.

"And when were you going to tell me that you bought my company out from under my feet?"

Harlan stiffened, then turned to him with a carefully blank expression. "I didn't know if I should bring it up while we were away. You needed to relax, not be thinking about Baron."

"Then when? When we got back from Long Island? Or were you going to string me along until after Geist's book came out?"

"We did what we thought was best," he replied, shifting uncomfortably. "I know you feel like we ignored you—"

"You goddamn manipulated me! How hard did you try to get my attention? Or did you just take Joan's word for it when she waved a contract at you?"

"I wasn't trying to steal your company," Harlan said sharply. "I was trying to save your life."

Chastened, Ben looked down at his skeletal hands. A dying man's hands, but if he was already halfway dead he had nothing to lose. "I know you were only trying to help.

But I've been passed around like a bad check for years. Everything I have came to me because someone else didn't want it. I didn't start Baron, but it was mine. The only thing that's ever been mine. And thanks to Mel, I was finally in the black again, for the first time in forever. I was finally getting ahead. I thought that maybe I wasn't out of my mind for trying to make a living this way."

"And then I came along and blew it to kingdom come," Harlan said, shaking his head. "What a self-centered ass I am."

"Please don't feel bad."

"I should, I treated you like a child. I should have told you about the deal with Joan right away. No, I should have done more to help you at the start. Made sure you had people taking care of you."

"I had Joan."

"There's only so much she can do. She's got a life of her own. Besides, she was already running your business, and doing a damn fine job."

"She's a godsend."

"But she's not your mother."

"Neither are you."

"No, but I do have one to give away if you're interested."

"I'm going to tell her you said that."

"She knows," Harlan said with a guilty smirk. "And I shouldn't have kept you in the dark. That was wrong and I'm sorry, but Ben...honestly, I didn't know what else to do. No one had spoken to you in days. Joan was bawling her eyes out."

"Was she really?" Ben hadn't thought she knew how, her tears never more than a sparkle on her lashes, quickly blotted before they ruined her makeup.

"I wasn't doing so hot myself," Harlan went on, his voice cracking with emotion. "You scared the life out of me, Benny. It made me realize what I was doing to you."

"You didn't do anything."

"Like hell I didn't," he said with a bitter laugh. "All this time, I told myself I was doing you a favor, you and your little press, bringing you this plum deal. I was going to make you famous. I just made things worse for you. I put you in an impossible situation. And then I went and fell in love with you."

"Oh. Wow."

"That part I don't regret," he said, sinking onto the bed beside Ben and taking his hand. "But I should have done things differently."

"They always say not to mix business with pleasure."

"They do. I'm a fool, Ben. I did everything backwards. I put you through hell. It's no wonder you cracked up."

"That wasn't your doing. That was all me. And it'll probably happen again."

"Even if it does, just know that you won't have to go through it alone." He raised Ben's hand and kissed the back tenderly. Glancing up through his dark lashes, he turned Ben's hand over and kissed his wrist. Again, tracing his tongue over Ben's pulse point. Distracting as hell, right when Ben needed clarity.

"Harl..." he murmured as Harlan began to kiss his way up Ben's forearm.

"Hmm?"

"Are you going to tell me where the book is?"

"Geist's?" he asked, sitting upright. "In a suitcase in a locker by the men's room in Penn Station. Joan's idea," he said as Ben gaped at him. "If you're game, we could try publishing it again in a couple years."

"Be my guest," Ben said with a shudder. "I want nothing to do with it, from hereon. I'm going to be on some frightening lists for a while."

"What if we cleared out of the States? Baron could open a branch office in Paris."

"As in France? You're nuts."

"Nuts over you."

"Harl, be serious."

"I am a hundred percent serious."

"What about your mother?"

"She's not invited."

As he started to laugh, Harlan slipped an arm around him, catching his chin to hold his gaze. "Ben, I've faced death," he said. "I know how precious life is. I will spend my whole life on you, if you'll let me. Just be with me. Wherever it is I end up. Be mine."

"You don't know what you're getting yourself into."

"Bullshit," he chuckled. "I know exactly what I'm getting myself into. And what kind of jerk runs out on the person he loves just because they're down in the dumps. It's for better and for worse, isn't it?"

"But we're not—"

"Hush," Harlan said, putting a finger to Ben's lips. "Trust me, Benny, if I could, I would. Drag you down to City Hall right now and make this official. So what if you hit a rough patch? As long as you never give up. And know that I won't ever give up on you. You're worth too much for that."

"Me? I'm no one."

"So? Who am I?"

"You're Harlan Avens."

"No, I'm not," he said with that sunshine grin. "I'm Hermann Metzger from East Rockaway, remember? And I want to know," he purred, a heat kindling in his dark eyes, "why you aren't naked yet."

As he leaned nearer for a kiss, Ben pulled back. "Because I'm still not sure this is a good idea."

"What's up?"

"Me. I've been working myself to the bone. I've barely slept in days. I was sick to my stomach. There's been so much going on I don't know whether I'm coming or going. My God, I can't even take a vacation without it ending in a disaster."

"There was no disaster, Ben."

"It was a near miss, and you're still not in the clear. And me, I have a lot to sort out. My whole life, more or less. So trying to keep up my side of a relationship...can't you see that it isn't going to work?"

"What are you afraid of?"

"Everything. Harlan, I'm not good at...life. I left too big a piece of me overseas. I've been trying to stitch that hole closed for fifteen years and I just keep bleeding. I can't be saved."

"Bullshit. Ben, you don't need to change a thing about yourself. It's you I love. Not some perfect Ben Quirke I expect you to turn yourself into to suit me, but you, this guy here." He tapped Ben's chest. "Who sometimes forgets to eat because inspiration matters more. Who's never had anyone to give him the love he deserves. Until now. Believe me, Ben, I'm here because I want to be. Even like this, fighting over which of us is the bigger asshole."

"That's not what this is about."

"Then tell me, why are we arguing?"

"It's because you think I'm wonderful, or something, and I can't see how that can be true."

"How about you try taking my word for it? Me, I haven't spent a lifetime listening to you talk yourself down. I have no preconceived notions about you."

"So?"

"So who *you* think you are isn't who *I* think you are. Because I happen to think you're wonderful. So either I'm at least a little bit right about you, or I have a big beautiful Benjamin Quirke-shaped hole in my judgement that you're exploiting, to fool me into thinking you're better than you are."

"I'm not trying to fool anyone."

"I know that. You're just being yourself. And I really like who that is. Not for what you ought to be. Just as you are. Trust me, you're no worse than the rest of us. You want to talk demons, I could break your heart with some of the shit I've done. So stop beating yourself up over nothing. I mean it. I don't want to hear you say another bad word about yourself. If you have to think it to yourself, that's your problem, but take my word for it: you're adorable, and smart, and brave, and worth it. Me, I'm an arrogant prick and you know it. Do you think I'd hang around if I didn't want to? I'd have split long ago."

"You will, though. You'll get tired of me in the end."

"How dare you?"

"What?"

"You heard me," Harlan said with a laugh. "How dare you judge my loyalty?"

"That's not what I meant," Ben stammered. "But I know I'll never be enough for you. I hate parties, and dinners, and shrimp toast and all of it. And you, with the people you know, the artists and parties. Tell me how I fit into your world."

"My world? I don't have a world. I mean it," he said as Ben tried to protest. "I've been thrown out of every club that's had me as a member. I lost my homeland, I got shit on by the US Navy, I can't even go to a country club without lying about who I am. And sure, I have friends, but don't you think it's kind of strange that you don't? And big sister Joan doesn't count."

"It's not my fault my friends keep dying."

Harlan's face fell. "Benny, what do you mean?"

"Not everyone. But most of my friends from school who enlisted died in combat. I've lost touch with the rest. The friends I've made since the service are either dead or in prison."

"All of them?"

"Two of them took their lives. Another was murdered." By his mother, more than Harlan needed to know.

"Shit. Benny..." he sniffled. "You've been going it alone for too long."

"I'd don't mind. I've got—"

"Don't say Joan," Harlan warned.

"Who else can I count on?"

"How about me?"

"Harlan..."

"I mean it, Ben. Don't pretend that you don't feel this too."

"I do, but..."

"But what?"

"You sure you're not just putting up with me?"

He chuckled, shaking his head. "We all have to do that to get along, don't we? Believe me, Benny, I screw up plenty.

But I trust the people who care about me to forgive me when I do."

"I do. I forgive you. You didn't do anything wrong. I'm sorry. Oh God, I'm pathetic." As yet more tears pricked his eyes he tried to cover his face, but Harlan grabbed his wrist and held on.

"Don't say that," he urged. "It's not true. You're just a good man who pushed himself too hard." His grip softened as he slid his other arm around Ben's shoulders.

"I hate to break it to you, Benny, but you're incredible," he said, pulling him closer. "You're brave and devoted and you have the sweetest little smile. And you're loved. By a whole bunch of people. Me included." And then he turned Ben's face towards him and kissed him on the lips, waiting until Ben opened his mouth to pull him closer, take him over.

Loyalty

Naked at last, they lay in bed and kissed and kissed. Ben couldn't get enough of Harlan's mouth, a kiss something to be shared with someone who had time for you. He hoped. He hoped that this really was the start and not the end, because even with Harlan's kisses, his touches, his sweet words, Ben could barely keep his eyes open. He felt like he'd climbed a mountain, his arms leaden as he clung to Harlan. Too many things had happened today, too many highs and lows, from the fugue of his writing session this morning to his anger at Harlan for reading his raw work to reconciliation and the chaos that preceded it. He had met Harlan's mother today. Harlan's mother knew Darla. Harlan's mother was stranded at Darla's with Rex from the bait shop...

Harlan pulled back to look him in the eye. "What do you need, Benny?"

"I don't know. Nothing really."

"Is there something on your mind?"

"Nothing important. Just things. The day. The future. You. Everything."

"Is your brain always going a mile a minute?"

"You could break the sound barrier if you cracked open my skull. Wow, that was in poor taste. I must be delirious."

"Maybe we should take it easy."

"Maybe. And didn't we fool around earlier?"

"Right, that was today, wasn't it?"

"The longest day of my life."

"You said it. But I don't mind if you want to go to sleep. I'm happy just to be close to you. We have the rest of our lives for fooling around."

"The rest of our lives," Ben sighed, studying Harlan's face. The face he thought he'd never see again. "Imagine that."

"You don't have to imagine it," Harlan replied intently. "Honest to God, if I could, I'd be down on one knee asking you to marry me."

"Oh, stop."

"Why? Don't you believe me?"

"It's not a matter of believe, it's—wait, where are you going?"

Harlan had scrambled out of bed and was kneeling before him on the carpet, beaming like the sun. Feeling hot, feeling cold, feeling like he had better pay attention, Ben sat up. "What are you doing?"

"Following standard procedures." He scooted closer then took Ben's hand.

"Harl..."

"Quiet, you. Because this isn't going to take long. Please, Ben, be mine. From now until forever. Let me make you happy, every day until I pass from this earth."

"Oh, I do. I mean, I will. I mean, oh, just kiss me, please."

Blinking away fresh tears of purest joy, he held out his

arms, expecting Harlan to return his embrace. Instead he sprang at Ben, tackling him to the mattress.

"You ought to know I'm going to hold you to that," Ben murmured as Harlan began planting kisses up the side of his neck.

"That's kind of the point of getting engaged," Harlan chuckled.

Ben shivered at the tickle of his lips. "I mean it. If the chance ever comes, it's you and me and city hall."

"It's a date. Now how about we practice for the honeymoon?"

Ben laughed, because wasn't it funny? Wasn't it wonderful? To love someone so much you want them beside you all your life? To break the law to do it, and to simply not care, because of this man, this love: both improbable, both his.

"Are you okay?" Harlan asked as Ben blinked away a few last tears.

"I'm just happy."

"Are you sure?"

"Do you ever ask a lot of stupid questions." Throwing his arm around Harlan's neck, he pulled him into a kiss, his cock sliding beside Harlan's as he swiveled his hips. Harlan groaned, his weight pressing Ben into the mattress.

"How do you want me, Benny? Tell me."

"I want to see your face."

He bit his lip in indecision, then laid beside Ben. Some careful positioning of Ben's legs over Harlan's and he was sitting in his lap, Harlan's oiled cock riding between his buttocks. Slowly, sweetly, Harlan fingered him open until they fit together.

"Benny, you're a treasure," he purred, rocking his hips

as Ben arched to take him deeper. But slowly, so slowly, Ben watching his lover, the changing light in his eyes as he climbed towards climax, the tip of his tongue between his teeth, his cheeks flushed, his hand stroking Ben's naked skin. And then enclosing him, those clever fingers wrapping around Ben's leaking cock.

Moving together, moving as one, and wasn't it wonderful to be loved so wonderfully? To feel safe in surrender, to give up trying to hold his head above water, knowing Harlan would never let him drown.

Except in ecstasy, as Harlan shuddered and Ben felt the echoes, clenching his muscles around Harlan and making him shudder again.

"You're too good," he gasped, letting go of Ben's shaft to grip his thigh, angling his hips to thrust deeper. Harder. Faster and absolutely perfect as Harlan spilled into him. Working his own cock, Ben followed seconds later.

"What did I tell you?" Harlan breathed, grinning foolishly.

"To never doubt your methods?"

Laughing, he kissed Ben's bare shoulder. "And don't you forget it."

THEY FELL ASLEEP SOON after, and woke too early. Harlan ordered room service and they ate in bed while Harlan told a few stories of his trip overseas. Light moments, like forgetting the German word for towel when he called the front desk, or the colors of the sunset over the sea on the Reykjavík-to-Gander leg of his flight home.

"I wonder when the Guest men will come back," Ben said as Harlan poured himself another coffee from the carafe on the little cart.

"The who?"

"Lerner and Girt, from the Alver Guest Society. They showed up last night while you were at the precinct. I forgot to tell you in all the...everything."

He snorted, rolling his eyes as he settled on the bed beside Ben again. "And what did they want this time?"

"The manuscript. They had a lawyer with them and everything. I might have panicked a little, because I gave them that slush pile."

Harlan nearly spat his coffee. "What in the world did you do that for?" he asked with a laugh, wiping his chin.

"I don't know, I just wanted them to go away. I knew they'd be back, but you were at the police station, and so was Joan and...I didn't know what else to do."

"It's okay, Benny. You're not the only one who's let that damn book turn his brain to mush."

"What are we going to do with it?" Ben asked as Harlan set his cup aside.

"Let them have it."

"Really?"

"What do I want with it? I say, let's hand it over, and if they can salvage something from that wreckage, they're welcome to it. We're better off without it. Besides, I got what I wanted out of the deal." Smirking, he raised Ben's hand and kissed the back.

"Fair enough," Ben said as Harlan began to kiss his way

up the soft skin of his inner arm. "But if you want my time, all you have to do is ask."

"I'll keep that in mind."

"Like right now. If you wanted some of my time..." He slid his hand up Harlan's thigh, both of them shivering as his fingertips brushed against Harlan's stiffening shaft.

"Watch it, Quirke..."

"Maybe it's not my time you wanted."

"You know what I want."

Even tasting of coffee, Harlan's kiss was sublime, savage yet sweet as they fell into each other. Joan could wait. Melody too. And the Guest men, and all the rest of the greasy, grabbing world. Ben didn't have time to spare for any of that right now.

He was too busy being in love with the man who had saved his life.

Hollywood

To some people, writing comes easy. They show up with the story alive in their heads, and all they need to do is take dictation. For the rest of us, writing is a bit like poking your heart repeatedly with a sharp stick until it bleeds some insight about human experience onto your page. It hurts. I can't avoid feeling all my characters' emotions, and I only hope it makes my writing better. I have no other purpose in life. No, that's not true. I have one other calling, and that's loving Benjamin Quirke.

I could make it a full time job if he had the bankroll. I never knew it was possible to forget food exists, but there's plenty of days when, if I didn't feed him, he wouldn't eat. I don't think of it as a burden but a service. An act of love. Taking care of the small things so the man I love can focus on what matters to him.

Because damn him if he isn't a better writer than me.

Prolific, sure, but when he lets himself write from his heart, there's no touching that bewildering mix of bold, decisive dialog and the poetic inner life of his characters. As if he can see beneath the world's hard shell into another universe. I don't even want to tell him how good it is, in case he does it again. Disappears into his own head, forgets about his body and the world. But that won't happen on my watch. His future is my future.

As futures go, it's a sweet life. Joan's twice the agent Rene ever was. Knows twice as many people as he did, and she never hesitates to grease the wheels of commerce. Selling Baron was her idea, and though I argued at the time, she was right. Let DelRay deal with the headaches, the edits and cover artists, the censors and paranoia. Ben was never meant to be a businessman, and the money not only paid off Joan's investment but covers the rent on our apartment just off Sunset Strip.

Joan's fault as well, that I moved to Hollywood of all places, though after my first winter in California I don't know that I'll ever want to live in New York again. We'll see once I've sold a screenplay, which she figures is due any time. Like always, I don't ask too many questions of my management. I'm just the talent

Today I'm the errand boy. Ben's nearly done the first edit of *Stone Horizon*, and I'm happy to keep the household running so he can stay on track. I miss the book's original title *The Thief of Genius*, but like I said, I'm not the one steering the bus. Whatever the title, it's going to ruffle more than a few feathers, I don't doubt.

I can't say much more—it's not my book, after all. Every writer has their superstitions, and if Ben works best when he writes in secret, so be it. I've done some strange things to get through a draft, so I let him be.

On my way home from the supermarket, I stop by the post office to pick up our mail. The apartment has a slot but most of our stuff comes to the P.O. box. There's not much today, just a letter from my mother and a bigger envelope from Joan, sent express. I read Mom's letter as I walk. She and Rex...God help me but they're getting married in the fall. Along with her letter, she's sent a strip of pictures of the two of them clowning it up in a Coney Island photo booth. An odd couple, but it gives her something to do, whipping him into shape. Better him than me.

Speaking of, am I ever glad to be done with that damn book. It's now in the hands of the Alver Guest Historical Society, who've picked out some of the least smarmy fragments to display in their in boxy little museum in his old house in Baltimore. Good luck to them if they aim for anything more.

Walking home by rote, I shiver again at the thought of what I might have lost if I'd persisted. Does that make me unprincipled, that I chose love over moral vindication? Or is this love of ours its own kind of victory? A stance against the stifling oppression that lurks beneath America's veneer of freedom.

I've given this country so much already. Thousands in taxes, years of service, my innocence. The least it could give me was the right to love as my heart tells me to, not as some other man's faith commands. Questions to ponder with Ben over a drink on the balcony later, as the California sunset sets the world aglow.

Or is it Ben who glows? The west coast has done him a world of good. He smiles more, and doesn't flinch at loud noises, and when I ask what he wants in bed he tells me. How could I put that on the line, drag him into court with me over that stinking book, put our relationship on trial in front of the world? If that makes me a coward, I'll live with it.

Because of this man, sitting at the desk with his head down over a manuscript, a cup of coffee gone cold to one side, a pile of finished pages to the other. Maybe it's California that's doing him good, but it could as easily be me. He brings out my mothering instinct, with the way he forgets to eat or sleep and his terrible housekeeping habits. I try to help him more than scold him. He needs my support, not my opinions. I keep myself busy around our breezy little apartment until he sits up, groaning as he bends his neck side to side.

"It's probably time I took a break," he sighs, leaning his head back against my chest I massage some of the stiffness from his neck and shoulders

"A little R and R?"

He laughs softly, letting his shoulders drop as I drag my thumbs down the sides of his neck. "I wanted to make a dirty joke but I can't think of a word that starts with 'r'."

"I can think of one that starts with a 'd'," I say, wishing there wasn't a chair back between us.

"Desperate, you mean?" he says, stretching his arms up and back to encircle me.

"Takes one to know one." I slip my hand under his chin and he gasps. As if he's surprised, but doesn't it knock me out, like it does every time he surrenders.

"They did say the devil would assume a seductive form," he murmurs as I start to unbutton his shirt with my other hand.

"Don't pretend you don't like it, Quirke."

He laughs and I have to kiss him. Too full of feeling to say how I feel. Lost for words, because mere words can't encompass this mystery: that out of all the people on this earth, all the souls alive, this man is mine.

Married in Massachusetts

2005

FOR AN EVENT NEARLY fifty years in the making, the wedding was a quiet affair. Just the two of them, and the handful of guests who had made the trek up to Cambridge, where the USA's first legal same-sex marriage had been performed only a few weeks ago, along with dozens of others across Massachusetts. He and Harlan had watched the news footage from Harlan's hospital room, where he'd been recovering from falling in the shower.

They'd witnessed so many momentous on-screen events: the moon landing, the fall of the Berlin Wall. Others had been less glorious, like the explosion of the Challenger. This event was the first that had changed their lives.

"We could have waited instead of making this a big deal," Harlan said yet again as the porter helped him down from the train. "New York'll fall any day now."

"Hush!" Ben said, holding Harlan's wheelchair steady. "Don't say that out loud."

"I'm not going to jinx it, you superstitious old..." Muttering, Harlan eased himself into the wheelchair. He'd refused to rent one at home, arguing rightfully that it was too big to store in their apartment and too inconvenient to use in Manhattan. Faced with an overnight trip and unknown amounts of standing up, he'd surrendered to the indignity, but he'd always been a terrible patient and was making no exception.

"I'm not taking any chances," Ben said as Harlan set his feet on the flaps. "We've only got so many days left, you and me. So quit complaining and take it like a man." Leaning on the handles, he got the wheelchair moving.

"You've been waiting your whole life for a chance to push me around, haven't you?" Harlan said, twisting to look back at him.

"Watch out or I'll point you at the tracks and let go."

"You nut," he chuckled, settling in the seat. "You remember we already cashed in my life insurance, right?"

The rest of the wedding party were waiting at the city hall: Joan and Melody's adopted daughter Electra and her husband Sandy; Darla, but not Jerome, who had passed from heart failure some five years ago; and Abbie's nephew Marty and his date, a sweet-faced young man from Utah who kept looking over his shoulder like his Mormon relations were hot on his trail. Ben had so wanted Joan and Mel to be here, but with Joan in the middle of chemotherapy, he hadn't even asked. Just promised that he'd send them a DVD of the ceremony.

Aging was a hell of a reward for surviving. Some part of him always hurt. He was always a little bit cold. He ate sparingly or suffered indigestion. Being alive still beat the alternative, hands down. Every day he was alive was another day he had Harlan to love.

Marty pushed Harlan's chair up the long ramp at the city hall. Ben took his time following, stopping now and then to dab at his tears, if only so he could see where he was going. Electra was waiting for him in the lobby.

"Where's Harl?"

"You'll see," she said, taking his elbow and matching his tired pace. Harlan was right, they should have waited for New York to amend its laws so they could have wed in their own living room instead of dragging themselves and everyone two hundred odd miles to this fluorescent-lit government office for the sake of a piece of paper he and Harlan had lived without for forty-seven years.

And then Electra opened the door, and he saw Harlan waiting for him, and he knew that this was the right thing to do. Forty-seven years of secrecy, of indignities, of watching their friends die before their time in one holocaust or another: from violence, from misery, from a disease that ravaged gay communities while the rest of the world hid their heads in the sand. He and Harlan had survived it all, weathered the storms and done it together, loving one another as truly as any two people ever loved. To declare that love in public, freely and legally, was to change the world.

As Ben and Electra drew near, Harlan set his hands on the arms of the wheelchair and attempted to rise. "I'm not disabled," he said firmly as Marty began to protest. "I'm injured, there's a difference. Just gimme a hand, you turkey."

Using Marty's arm and favoring his left leg, he got shakily to his feet, but as he took Ben's hand his back straightened, his lips curving in that sideways smile that was so indelibly Harlan. Still the handsomest man Ben had ever known, the years doing nothing to dim the light in his eyes, even if his hands shook as he slid the plain gold band over Ben's bony finger.

Prompted by Electra, Ben said some words, his heart beating so loudly he couldn't hear Harlan's replies. The same words as any couple spoke, to love each other for better and worse, in sickness and health. A commitment that he and Harlan had made every day for four and a half decades, not as an obligation but as a sacred duty.

"By the power vested in me by the State of Massachu-setts," said the beaming officiant, "I now pronounce you husband and husband."

Harlan was still the best kisser, too.

FOR THE WEDDING NIGHT they'd booked a room at a bed and breakfast near the college. Though the place didn't serve dinner, Darla had taken charge of catering, arranging for a local restaurant to provide a hot buffet. Ben had thought it a bit much for the seven of them, but he hadn't bothered making a fuss. What mattered was the ceremony, and the man who had stood with him.

"We made it," Harlan said, clinging to Ben's arm as they crossed the few steps from the parking lot. "We lived through every kind of hell, but we goddamn made it."

"Mind your mouth while we're in there, though."

"You never change, do you?"

"It's a bit late for that."

"I love you, Benny," he chuckled. "I always have."

Ben pressed his hand in answer, not trusting his voice. Marty was waiting at the bottom of the old porch and helped Harlan up the stairs. He retreated with a laugh as Harlan waved him away and grabbed Ben's arm again.

"Young know-it-all," he muttered. "Thinks just because he's my agent he can push me around."

"You better tell him that's my job."

"And a temporary one at that."

Marty had slipped around them and was holding open the door. "You can get mad at us about this tomorrow," he said, grinning. "For tonight, just go with the flow."

"Kid, if I could go with the flow I wouldn't have to see my proctologist every three months," Harlan said as they shuffled past. "As for getting mad at you, I'd sooner...well, I'll be."

It felt like everyone they knew was there in that room. People Ben hadn't expected to see, whom they had told once about the wedding but hadn't invited because the whole thing was so casual and so far away. A tumult of faces, of memories, and he laughed until he cried and laughed again, and all the while Harlan was by his side, even though he had to ask for his chair after the first toast.

Speeches were made, tears shed. A hat was passed, taking donations in the couple's names for the GMHC. Instead of a cake, which neither of them cared for, there was a mountain of cookies, rich and buttery and dense with chunks of dark chocolate, just how Harlan liked them. Ben ate more than he needed of everything, and had a glass and a half of champagne, both of which he'd pay for tomorrow.

With no one demanding his attention for a change he was dozing in his seat when someone nudged his foot.

He roused himself to find Harlan in the wheelchair. "You want to split?" he said, nodding towards the lobby.

"Leave our own party? That's a bit gauche."

"I thought you hated parties."

"I do, but…" He glanced around but every guest was absorbed in one conversation or another. "I suppose they won't mind. Wait, shouldn't we say goodbye?" he asked as Harlan started wheeling for the door.

"Not unless you want to be here for another hour."

"Good point."

They'd booked the B&B before Harlan's fall. He had insisted on keeping the booking, which meant leaving the wheelchair in the lobby and climbing the turning staircase of the old Victorian home to reach their room.

"Remember when we used to have to sneak around?" Harlan wheezed, leaning on the rail. "You'd go up first then I'd come up ten minutes later so they didn't think we were together."

"The good old days."

He snorted, gripping Ben's arm as he climbed another step. "Kids don't know how good they got it now."

They took turns in their tiny bathroom, Harlan moving a little easier in the room now that he had his cane. When Ben came out, he was stretched out on the bed in his pajamas, his hands folded on his chest. As Ben lay beside him he groaned.

"I may never eat another chocolate chip cookie again. Screw that, I'm not moving again."

"You mean to tell me you're going to leave our marriage unconsummated?"

He cracked open one eye. "Seriously? You have the energy to—"

"No. I can barely move, myself. It's enough to have you here with me." He leaned over and kissed Harlan. His husband. Not in his imagination but in law. Against the odds, the centuries of secrecy and oppression, the loss of thousands, millions of lives, the gay men and women and gender outlaws whose resistance had made this future possible.

They'd fought the odds and won. Their prize was each other.

"What's on your mind?" he asked as Harlan sighed.

"I was thinking we should stop at the cemetery on the way home and buy two adjacent plots."

"Really? That's a bit morbid."

"You asked," Harlan said with a shrug. "I don't ever want to be apart from you, Benny. I never want to let you go."

They kissed again, holding each other close, as they had so many nights, as they would every night as long as they were able.

"I love you so much," Ben whispered, doing nothing to stop his tears, unashamed to be crying. For joy. For loss. For the unlikeliness of being alive, here and now. For having his dreams come true. "I don't know how I ever deserved you."

"Same here, Benny," Harlan said. "You're a gift, and you always have been. Every day I'm with you is a miracle." Two men in love: miracle upon miracle, that they had found each other, that their love had endured so long, that their union was now the equal of anyone's, that love like this could change the world.

THE END

A Brief Timeline of Censorship

While censorship is often viewed as only applicable to sexual content, censorship laws have been used to restrict a wide range of materials, from abolitionist and antiwar pamphlets during the US civil war through contraception and sex education in the late 19th century to the Parents Music Resource Center in the 1980s and 1990s objecting to the content of rap and metal songs.

Using obscenity as a test for whether a book should be censored invites a host of ideological abuses. What one person considers obscene may be inoffensive to the next person, and until recently US courts often have sided with allowing the broadest range of ideas to be available to the public.

The following are some key events referenced in this book.

1873

The Comstock Act

Named for its chief supporter Anthony Comstock, head of the New York Society for the Suppression of Vice. The act permitted searches of US mail without a warrant under the guise of preventing the transport of obscene material, which has at times included contraceptives and information about birth control.

1957

Roth

Charged with distributing obscene material through the mail, New York bookseller Samuel Roth took his case to the US Supreme court, whose ruling set the standard of obscenity as: "whether to the average person, applying contemporary community standards, the dominant theme of the material, taken as a whole, appeals to the prurient interest" (Roth v. United States 1957, at 489.)

Ten North Frederick

Citing obscenity, Detroit police threatened booksellers with arrest for carrying the critically acclaimed novel *Ten*

North Frederick, not for sexual content but for its honest depiction of divorce. The publisher Random House successfully sued the city and police force, arguing that they did not have the authority to determine whether or not a work was obscene.

City Lights Books

In 1957 a shipment of Allan Ginsberg's epic poem *Howl* was seized, but the Collector of Customs was forced to release the books when federal authorities refused to confirm the charge of obscenity. Local police later raided the to the landmark San Francisco bookstore, arresting the manager Shigeyoshi Murao and later the store owner, poet Lawrence Ferlinghetti, with selling an obscene book. Their trial lead to a precedent-setting verdict stating that any book with "the slightest redeeming social importance" merits First Amendment protection.

1959

Lady Chatterley's Lover

Charles Rembar successfully defended the publisher Grove Press in a case surrounding the importing of DH Lawrence's 1928 novel *Lady Chatterley's Lover*. Rembar employed the argument that the work as a whole was of "redeeming social value" and its sexual content thereby qualified as protected speech. He would go on to use similar arguments in defense of Henry Miller's *Tropic of*

Cancer and the ribald 18th century novel *Fanny Hill*.

2004

Same-sex marriage

Notable not for a victory against censorship, but for being the year that Massachusetts became the first US state to legalize same-sex marriage, following the Supreme Judicial Court's decision in Goodridge v. Department of Public Health.

OTHER HISTORICAL NOTES

CHAPTER 11 – The Algonquin
The Algonquin Circle was a literary social group which met regularly at the Algonquin Hotel in New York. Famous members include the critic Dorothy Parker and the playwright Noël Coward.

EPILOGUE – GMHC
(formerly Gay Men's Health Crisis) a New York based nonprofit AIDS service organization

About the Author

Author, poet, and general nuisance Will Forrest writes unusual – and usually queer – romances with a dash of mischief and mayhem. Will (they/he) grew up on a steady diet of Douglas Adams and classic bodice rippers, and has a diploma of fashion design, a degree in social theory, and a bad habit of changing careers, life goals, and continents. Currently they live in a very warm part of Canada with three lovely humans and a succession of martyred houseplants.

willforrest.com

Join the Readers Club for advance access, free books, and (occasionally) recipes.

willforrest.com/newsletter/

WILL FORREST'S BOOKS

COMING SOON

STARMAN – a '70s High School Love Story
AFTER THE AFFAIR – a collection of Gay Historical
Romance novellas
Join the Readers Club for updates & free books: willforr
est.com/newsletter/